THE TYRANT SKIES

"We are strong," the Red Skull said. "But so is Doom. To underestimate him is fatal. *I* know that. We ruled Latveria once, and we lost it."

It had been worse than a defeat. It had been a humiliation. The Red Skull and the Exiles had conquered Latveria overnight, but in Doom's absence. He had returned, and reclaimed his throne with contemptuous ease, and amused himself not just by hurling the Skull and the Exiles back to the island, but by convincing them of the illusion that they had shrunk to six inches in height.

The Red Skull forgave nothing. But for mockery, he reserved a vengeance of a refined and brutal venom.

"Doom must suffer," the Skull promised. "Exquisitely. He cannot see it yet, but the noose has already closed around his neck."

MARVEL UNTOLD

DOCTOR DOOM IN:
THE TYRANT
SKIES

DAVID ANNANDALE

ACONYTE

FOR MARVEL PUBLISHING

VP Production & Special Projects: Jeff Youngquist
Associate Editor, Special Projects: Sarah Singer
Manager, Licensed Publishing: Jeremy West
VP, Licensed Publishing: Sven Larsen
SVP Print, Sales & Marketing: David Gabriel
Editor in Chief: C B Cebulski

Doctor Doom created by Stan Lee & Jack Kirby

First published by Aconyte Books in 2023

ISBN 978 1 83908 195 8

Ebook ISBN 978 1 83908 196 5

Cover art by Fabio Listrani

Distributed in North America by Simon & Schuster Inc, New York, USA
Printed in the United States of America
9 8 7 6 5 4 3 2 1

ACONYTE BOOKS

An imprint of Asmodee Entertainment Ltd

Mercury House, Shipstones Business Centre

North Gate, Nottingham NG7 7FN, UK

aconytebooks.com // twitter.com/aconytebooks

For Margaux, always, for all our horizons and everything beyond them.

Cruelty has a Human Heart
And Jealousy a Human Face
Terror, the Human Form Divine
And Secrecy, the Human Dress

The Human Dress, is forged Iron
The Human Form, a fiery Forge
The Human Face, a Furnace seal'd
The Human Heart, its hungry Gorge

WILLIAM BLAKE, "A DIVINE IMAGE"

PROLOGUE

Expect poison from the standing water.

WILLIAM BLAKE, "THE MARRIAGE
OF HEAVEN AND HELL"

The storm began in New York City, on a cloudless July afternoon. In Latveria, where the stars glinted bright with perfect indifference, Doom sensed the first stirrings of the hurricane to come.

In his study in Castle Doom, he sat before two screens and watched an inevitability unfold, frustrated that he could not stop it.

The screens had risen from the surface of his gigantic desk. The dais on which the desk sat had rotated to face the north window in the circular chamber. Fifteen feet high and vaulted, with floor-to-ceiling bookcases on either side of it, the window looked out from the study's high tower, giving Doom a view of the castle and Doomstadt below. When he looked up from the screens, though, his attention went to the stars. He had rotated the dais several times in the last hour, each time to gaze at the stars from a different point of the compass. The stars stared back, remote, as indifferent to his concerns as the fools on the right-hand screen, the General Assembly of the United Nations going through the motions of a deliberation with a foregone conclusion.

The door to the study opened. Boris entered, bowing his head in apology for the intrusion. "Is there anything my lord requires?" he asked.

Clever old man, Doom thought. He had timed his arrival for the close of deliberations. He knew Doom well and sensed the monarch would require an audience for his anger. Doom wasn't surprised. Boris had saved him as a child, and had been the sole constant human presence of his life. What might have been presumption in anyone else was the faithful anticipation of need in Boris.

"Come here," said Doom. "Come and see how easily the duped, the greedy, and the ignorant make the world worse."

Boris climbed the steps that spiraled around the dais and stood a respectful step behind his master.

Doom tapped the left-hand screen. It showed satellite surveillance footage of a small island. "Here is Wolkenland in the mid-Atlantic," Doom said. "And here" – he jabbed an accusatory finger to the right, at the General Assembly hall – "are the sheep about to officially recognize the sovereignty of Wolkenland and grant it membership to the United Nations."

"There is no chance the vote will go against Wolkenland?" Boris asked.

"None," said Doom. "Latveria will vote no, and a few other nations will join us, I think, but not enough. We need more than a third of the members to vote our way, and it will not happen. The Security Council has recommended Wolkenland's admission, and has done so unanimously."

Behind his mask, his lips tightened in a grim, contemptuous smile. "How charming to see the great powers of the world agree so congenially to make a grave error."

"What could have swayed them so?"

"Myopic self-interest," said Doom. "As ever. The wealth of Wolkenland carries great influence. So, too, do its new citizens, all of whom maintain powerful ties with the nations of their birth." Doom grunted. "Wolkenland has many ways of ensuring that the other states of this world see only what they wish to see."

"I know my lord will see what they do not," said Boris.

Doom shook his head. "No," he said. "Wolkenland thwarts my gaze." He gestured at the satellite's live streaming of the island. "Tell me what you can see of the nation-to-be."

"I can see its contours," said Boris. "It appears to rise to a higher elevation at its southern end. I see what I think are structures, but it is hard to tell from this distance."

"That is correct," said Doom. "There is very little else beyond dimensions to be noted here." Wolkenland was an elongated oval, narrowing considerably at either end. It was about fifty miles long, and just over twenty at its widest point. "Now see what happens when we approach."

Doom tapped the screen. The Latverian satellite, which he had retasked to a geostationary orbit over Wolkenland, zoomed in on the island. The satellite's lenses were powerful enough to zero in on a single blade of grass. But the screen showed only a gray, formless, pixelated mass.

"Wolkenland has jamming technology the equal of any I have encountered," Doom said. "Its masters do not want to be seen. Yet there is much talk of transparency, and those lies have gone unchallenged by the Security Council. I will say this for Wolkenland, though. It has been very transparent about at least one of its purposes. It is a haven, Boris, a haven for the ultra-rich, where they can be free of all taxation and other vexatious laws."

"Was that transparency sufficient, then, for the Security Council?"

"It evidently was. A misleading honesty, Boris. For if that was the sum total of Wolkenland's purpose, why would it need so formidable a shield against prying eyes? No, there is more at work. I have looked into this Lance Diffring, who presents himself as chief executive officer of the island. He is a puppet, not a leader. He is a buffoon for the cameras, a fiction of convenience. There is someone else behind him who chooses not to be seen. There is a deeper reason why Wolkenland seeks to be recognized by the United Nations. The reason is hidden from me, and Doom does not permit anything to be hidden from him."

He pulled the satellite's perspective back so the entire island became visible and in focus again. Then he returned his attention back to the General Assembly. The deliberations were over. Latveria's ambassador had made her objections known. The voting had begun. Doom watched in silence. Boris, knowing his place, remained perfectly still.

When the results were announced, they were as Doom had predicted. Only a rough dozen nations voted against the island's recognition. The resolution passed, and Wolkenland became the newest member of the United Nations.

The moment the results were announced, the island vanished.

Boris stifled a gasp.

Doom's mood darkened. He stared at the empty ocean where Wolkenland had been. He began a full instrument scan of the area, but already knew he would find nothing.

This is dangerous.

The conviction came to him, certain as night, though he could not divine the nature or the direction of the threat.

The storm had begun.

PART I

I was angry with my friend;
I told my wrath, my wrath did end.
I was angry with my foe;
I told it not, my wrath did grow.

And I waterd it in fears,
Night & morning with my tears:
And I sunned it with smiles,
And with soft deceitful wiles.

And it grew both day and night.
Till it bore an apple bright.
And my foe beheld it shine,
And he knew that it was mine.

And into my garden stole,
When the night had veild the pole;
In the morning glad I see;
My foe outstretched beneath the tree.

WILLIAM BLAKE, "A POISON TREE"

ONE

Maybe he shouldn't be wearing a tie.

It was time to go. The media from around the globe had gathered on the tarmac of the heliport. The reporters had been kept waiting long enough to sharpen their appetites for answers even more, and it had them stirring and restless. He should be on his way now to address them and, through them, the world. The moment was crucial, for him and for Wolkenland.

But the tie could ruin things.

"A tie, yay or nay?" he called out.

"You'll sort it out," Addyson, his wife, answered from down the hall.

Lance Diffring ducked back into the en suite bathroom. He looked again at the tie he had just spent fifteen minutes picking out, and at the image he was about to present.

Diffring had years of experience with public appearances, selling projects, or even just concepts of projects. His company, Fusionomics, nominally specialized in tech developments in fields ranging from clean energy sources to disposable rocket engines.

In practice, only a handful of its projects had ever actually come into being. That didn't matter. What Fusionomics did well was provide flashy-sounding investment opportunities that the right people got into, and then out of, early and fast, leaving the endlessly renewable ocean of the gullible to arrive too late and be left holding shares of vaporware.

Diffring was the face of Fusionomics. He had perfected the persona of the approachable billionaire, the man to imagine (but *only* imagine) having a beer with. The social media poster, but not the socially concerned citizen, not the troll. He was the good side of money, the reason why *really, let's be honest, can I be frank?* there should be no such concept as *obscene* wealth.

The reality, yes. He lived it. Just the concept of obscenity. Do away with that.

Eyes wide and caring, face lightly freckled with innocence, light brown hair kept short so he could make a show of not paying attention to it. He still had, in his forties, the excited glow of youth. He was his own best product.

Today, though, he would be selling more than himself, more than Fusionomics. For the first time that he could remember, he would be answerable to a higher authority.

And so the question of the tie. He had opted for the more formal look, a change in visual tone in keeping with his new role.

A mistake. That would send the wrong signals. That look could be read as if he were moving away from Fusionomics, or, worse, that the informal Diffring had been a lie all along.

No. He'd been trying to fix what hadn't been broken. He

was letting his awe of Wolkenland, and the adventure he had become part of, get in the way of his skills.

He knew what he was doing. He had the billions to prove that. All he had to do was let the Lance Diffring magic shine.

He went back to the bedroom and sauntered into a walk-in closet twenty feet deep, pulling off the tie. He kept the slacks but took off the dress shirt and replaced it with a polo shirt, one without a monogram.

There. That was better. He felt more like himself.

In the bedroom again, he paused to look out the window. *This is what I'm working for.* His mansion rested midway up the terraced hill that ran the length of the starboard side of the island.

Starboard, he told himself. He had to remember that. Wouldn't look good to get his directions wrong when he spoke. He had become used to thinking of his hillside as being on the east side, which it had been when he had first moved to Wolkenland. But the island was no longer in the mid-Atlantic. It was in the Mediterranean, and its orientation had turned ninety degrees from what it had been.

Bow and stern, port and starboard. Think of Wolkenland as a ship. He could do that.

Another terraced hill faced his on the port side, a twin slope of greenery and mansions. Between the hills was the promenade, twenty-five miles of formal gardens, parkland, fountains, and statues. Diffring looked at the statues now, marble colossi a hundred feet tall, representations of muscular perfection and achievement.

He smiled. The statues were not aspirational for the residents of Wolkenland. They were mirrors.

In the center of the promenade, surrounded by fountains, stood the neo-classical council hall, modeled on the Parthenon. Its name was a formality, at least in practice. It existed to give the residents of Wolkenland an outlet for their egos, a place for them to meet in splendor and play at governance, even though they might as well host Snakes and Ladders tournaments for all the impact their deliberations would have. To date, there had only been three gatherings there, all of them ceremonial rituals of self-congratulation to mark various milestones as Wolkenland achieved completion and became fully operational.

Diffring didn't know much about how Wolkenland had been constructed. He didn't have to. Not his concern. In one of their meetings, though, the Skull had raved triumphantly about weaving the seamless from the patchwork. Whatever that meant, whatever the patchwork components were, Diffring had to hand it to the Skull. Wolkenland was a magnificent whole, a product rather than a sum of its parts.

He stepped into the personal elevator next to the bedroom door. It took him to the mansion's rooftop landing pad and the waiting hovercar. The pilot, clad in the black uniform of Wolkenland's security forces, nodded respectfully as Diffring settled into the passenger seat. The canopy settled smoothly down over him, and the hovercar's near-silent antigrav engines lifted them into the air.

The sleek, stubby-winged car rose to the height of the jagged peaks that lined the entire perimeter of Wolkenland. Before the car crossed their line and began its descent, Diffring looked sternward, to the harsh, treeless plateau and the castle. Dark, hard, unforgiving, the castle was a brooding mass, a skull porcupined with turrets and spires. The contrast between the castle and the verdant paradise of the mansions made Diffring's stomach clench. He guessed that effect was deliberate. He should be used to it by now. All the same, he tended to keep the blinds drawn over his mansion's stern-facing windows.

Then the hovercar dropped below the peaks, and the castle passed out of sight. Diffring looked down toward the starboard heliport, and his assembled audience.

He grinned. A big crowd. *This was going to be good.*

Five minutes later, he mounted the podium that had been erected on the tarmac. It put him ten feet above the scrum. He appreciated the utilitarian look of the podium. Nothing fancy, nothing grand. The goal today was to reassure, not intimidate. Diffring congratulated himself on his final choice of attire. He and the podium were a good fit.

He waved at the reporters, the cell phones, and the television cameras. "Hi everyone," he said. "My name's Lance Diffring–" like anyone watching wouldn't know, but a touch of the humble never hurt "–and I'm here to welcome you to Wolkenland. And maybe answer a few questions while I'm at it." He grinned. "Because I'm guessing you might have a few."

They did, and they all started asking them at once. Diffring laughed, let the cacophony go on for a few moments, then raised his hands to ask for quiet.

"Please," he said, "please." When the surf roar of shouts receded, he said, "Let me try to cover some main points for you first." He smiled again at an expectant world. "Let's start with this: what is Wolkenland, and how did it get here? In a nutshell, Wolkenland is an island, but it's also a ship. As solid as the land feels under your feet, we are, in fact, floating. Pretty impressive, right? How does it all work? That, I have to admit, is beyond me. Some geniuses put this all together, and that's good enough for me."

"But Wolkenland moved here undetected," someone called out before he could go on.

Diffring didn't mind. The question gave him the segue he wanted to his next point. "Yes, it did," he said. "That's pretty impressive, too, isn't it?" He paused half a beat, long enough for the reporters to think of their questions, but not long enough for them to start asking them. "But why bother? Why should Wolkenland shield itself from view? Because this is more than a mobile island. It's a home. It's a sanctuary. It isn't news to anyone that we now live in a world where privacy is a vanishing resource. On Wolkenland, privacy matters again, and thrives again, because we have the technology to ensure that very thing."

"Privacy for whom?" came the question.

Diffring answered with a self-deprecating grimace. He'd practiced the look for hours before the mirror the night before. The press conference had reached the first of its crucial moments. Diffring had to get all of them right.

"Well, for me, for one. And for the people like me."

"For billionaires."

"OK. Yes. Yes, that's who we are. Don't get me wrong, now. I'm not looking for sympathy. We're a pretty fortunate bunch. But I think everyone can understand the need to not live in a fishbowl, if only for a little while."

"Isn't that a nice way of saying you're trying to avoid scrutiny?"

Diffring looked in the approximate direction of the question. This was a tougher crowd than he was used to, and he didn't recognize any of the faces. He'd come to know many of the reporters on the tech and finance beats, and liked to use their names when he answered. But this was the foreign bureaus crowd, the reporters used to traveling far for a story, and from many different countries. Still, he'd expected this, and prepared for it.

"What you call scrutiny," he said, "I think the fair-minded might also call persecution. Look, I know the score. It's easy for people to hate us. I mean, yes, we're rich. Really rich. Over-the-top rich. And? The world economy depends on us, like it or not. We're the wealth-creators. Some of us are even super heroes."

"On Wolkenland?"

"No, not here as such. That was just an example, you know, of why you have to be careful of overly wide brush strokes." Work the self-deprecation again. Hunch up a bit, raise the hands in a *don't look at me* shrug. "I mean, I'd *love* to be a super hero, but…" Flex the bicep, show it lacking. "Yeah, I don't think that's me."

Wait for the laugh.

It wasn't as big as he had hoped. Good enough, though.

"Kidding aside, though, we're doing good here. Wolkenland is actively doing good." He made a little production of looking at his watch. "Yeah, looks like it's time. Time for me to stop yammering at you and show you something instead." He stepped down from the podium and started walking toward the fore end of the heliport. "Hope you're wearing your hiking shoes," he called out. "Follow me! Follow, follow!"

He led the reporters off the tarmac to a path carved into the foreboding cliff face that surrounded Wolkenland. There were only a couple of spots that provided any kind of access to the island. One was the heliport, which was a platform that projected out from the cliffs. The other, a mile further along, was the port. Here the cliffs turned inward, forming a deep harbor, one wide enough to permit entry to even the largest cargo ships. A long bank of elevators was there to take passengers up the cliffs, while cranes hung over the peaks, the largest and strongest Diffring had ever seen. They could lift huge pallets of cargo the thousand-foot height up over the peaks and onto the island proper.

A passenger ship was just pulling in when Diffring and the reporters arrived.

"Is this part of Wolkenland's fleet?" a man asked.

"No," said Diffring. "Wolkenland doesn't have any seagoing ships. We don't need them."

"Is there no transport off and on the island?" a woman wanted to know.

"We find travel by air works fine for our needs," said Diffring.

"There's enough for your whole population?" the journalist pursued. "And what if the island sinks?"

"We have preparations for every contingency. Believe me, I wouldn't be here if I wasn't completely convinced it was safe. And we do charter ships as needed." He gestured at the liner. People filled its decks. "This being a case in point."

"More of the one percent?" another reporter asked.

"On the contrary," said Diffring. "Refugees."

"From where?"

"From everywhere. From anywhere they have fled,

whether driven out by war, famine, persecution, or any other reason. You see, Wolkenland really is a haven. It isn't just for the rich. It's for anyone who has lost their home or doesn't feel at home. We're a small nation, but we'll take in as many as we can."

"What system of government is welcoming them?" the woman who had been pressing him asked.

Diffring laughed. "Do we talk about the government of a cruise ship?" The answer was disingenuous, and he knew it.

"Then who is your captain?"

"Who's to say that we have one?" This was one of the important lies to sell. "We're all the captains of our destiny."

The ship's gangways unfolded and touched the pier. Crowds began to move down them.

"Shall we head back to the heliport?" Diffring said. "I think these people deserve their privacy, too. Don't you?"

Castle Wolkenland's panopticon occupied a windowless chamber near the top of the main body of the structure. Screens covered the walls and the slight dome of the ceiling. In the center of the room, a throne sat on a piston that rose and descended on command, just as the throne rotated and tilted, providing the best angle for viewing at a moment's notice. Controls in the arms of the throne changed the views of any of the screens, flipping to any of Wolkenland's thousands of surveillance cameras.

From his throne, the Red Skull saw everything that he had made, and behold, it was very good.

True, he had not constructed Wolkenland with his bare hands. He had not designed its power sources. He had not found the way to fuse its disparate parts together into a functioning whole. None of its technological miracles were his creations. He did not necessarily understand how any given facet of the island worked.

None of this mattered. He had gathered the people who did understand these things, and who had the skill to make his vision a reality. He had willed Wolkenland into being. Thus, it was his creation.

Just as he was his own creation. Many decades ago, there might have been someone named Johann Schmidt born into this body. But the Skull had not thought of himself as that person in a long time. Johann Schmidt had been a weak construction, a rough draft of an identity that had simply provided the raw material for the Red Skull. And if Hitler had shaped Schmidt into the Red Skull, then the creation had so long and so greatly surpassed his father that the credit for what he now was belonged to him and him alone.

Raw material. The true genius was the one who knew how to command it to take its true form.

The Skull thought a lot about what really constituted genius. More than he would like. Wolkenland should serve, he believed, as a balm for such bitter musings. It manifested his reasoning in the world, because the so-called geniuses who had labored to create it, labored for *him*. They answered to *him*. They made what *he* commanded. His, then, was the supreme genius.

Any intellect that did not serve him would be destroyed. Wolkenland would see to that, too. Through it, he would see one particular intellect brought low before annihilation.

Nowhere did he feel the rush of ownership, pride, and

control more than in the panopticon. This was his favorite place in the castle, and on the entire island.

Here, he held Wolkenland in his grasp. He saw everything. He saw the landscape from the perspective of the castle, the interiors of the mansions, the approaches from all sides, and more. He knew every secret, and he could govern every action. This was where his ownership of his creation was at its purest, most concentrated, and most absolute.

At the moment, he was dividing his attention between Lance Diffring's press conference and scanning through the operational and propulsion centers of the island. Diffring seemed to be handling his assignment satisfactorily. He had chosen Diffring for his selfishness, as pure and absolute as a flawless diamond. It had led Diffring to a blissfully untroubled embrace of fascism long before he had joined the Skull's ranks. It also gifted him with a facile plausibility before an audience. He concealed what passed for his true self whenever necessary. He was, the Skull had judged, perfect as the public face of Wolkenland. And Diffring had proven him right. While he spoke, facial recognition software scanned the faces of the reporters, cataloguing who was present, recording every question for the Skull to make notes later of who was hostile, and would be punished in due course.

More important, and more gratifying, were the reports he was seeing on the aftermath of Wolkenland's maiden voyage.

If those reporters only knew, he thought, and grinned tightly behind his crimson mask. If they only knew that Wolkenland had not sailed from the Atlantic to the Mediterranean. It had flown.

The patchwork creation, the assemblage of so many pieces,

his vision, had flown. The years of work and struggle had been rewarded. Wolkenland was a whole, and it flew.

The idea had come to him on Exile Island, and the largest part of Wolkenland had been excavated from his frequent home. The largest part, but also the most mundane. The crucial elements of Wolkenland had come from Lemuria and Atlantis. To the technology of the sunken cities had been added fragments of the Power Cosmic. There was even, to his immense pride, some recovered essence of a dead Celestial. That one element had required three years of planning, preparation, and gathering of resources to acquire.

The other great resource he had harvested was brainpower. He needed the scientists, the engineers, the eccentrics, and the dreamers who would turn his will into reality. Some of those he sought embraced his vision readily, falling over themselves in their eagerness to serve. Others had to be forced to fulfill their destiny. Kidnapping, blackmail, torture, enslavement…

The tried-and-true methods never failed to persuade.

The other thing he had needed to create Wolkenland was money. A great deal of money. That had been the easiest of all the resources to gather. A population of the ideologues and the willfully ignorant had rushed to become part of the nascent microstate.

Still, the effort to create Wolkenland in secret had been great, and the years longer. The Red Skull was not a patient man. Obsession and hate gave him the strength to see the project through to completion.

And Wolkenland was almost complete. There was one more piece to be added to it, and that would be arriving before too many more days had passed.

On the screens, the press conference ended. The reporters filed into the various crafts that had brought them here, and departed.

Good.

When the last of the journalists had gone, the Skull rose from his throne and left the panopticon. He made his way to the central rooftop of the castle, to his private heliport. An armored hovercar waited to take him to the harbor. It was time to greet Wolkenland's newest residents.

The elevators, each capable of transporting fifty people at a time, carried refugees to a warehouse-sized chamber inside the perimeter peaks. Corridors led from it to other destinations on the island, always inside the hills or underground. The entire transfer of refugees took place without any of Wolkenland's elite residents having to witness it.

Unless they wished to. Audience galleries on the port and starboard sides of the chamber looked down on the floor. A few dozen spectators had gathered today. The Skull's reviewing platform jutted out of the fore wall, above the main exit from the chamber, opposite the elevator banks. The refugees would pass beneath them on their way to their fates.

The Red Skull made a point of coming here on days that the big ships arrived, bringing hundreds of new arrivals to the island. He came to enjoy the double shock that hit the refugees. The first came as they spilled out of the elevators and saw the Red Skull. People stumbled in surprise. Some cried out in horror. Others began to weep. All of them started to realize the depth of the deception that had been worked on them, and to feel the violent death of all their hope.

The second shock came moments after, reinforcing the first with action. Officers of Wolkenland's black-clad security forces surrounded the refugees as they moved into the chamber, and slapped manacles on them, attaching them to a chain that threaded between their legs.

Fifty people in each elevator, a hundred to each chain. The arithmetic of oppression, for the satisfaction of the Skull.

He stood with a wide stance, arms clasped behind his back. He remained silent and motionless until all the passengers had arrived and been shackled. Then he spoke, hidden receivers picking up his voice and amplifying it across the space.

"Insects," he said. "That is what you are. Maggots squirming in the flesh of society. You have no place. That is why you are here. You are the rejected, and the ejected. You have no value, and you had the arrogance to come to Wolkenland expecting the welcome and the handout. You will receive our justice instead. The world has no use for you. But we do."

He let the last sentence hang in the air, a threatening spur to their imaginations. Then the guards led them away, out of the chamber and to the dark places of Wolkenland.

In the galleries, the audience applauded.

Six weeks later, the final piece arrived. Retrieving this piece had been the first part of the project that the Red Skull initiated, but it had taken the longest to complete. After five years, the probe he had sent to low orbit over Jupiter returned.

On the roof of the castle, beyond the Skull's heliport, was another flat, circular area, a wider one. An hour after sunset, the Skull walked to its edge and looked up. A bright glow in the clouds became the flare of retro-rockets as the probe descended, the thunder of its engines rolling across the sea. The reinforced steel of the landing zone, ten feet thick, split into four wedges. With a heavy grind, they pulled back, and the probe, not much larger than the fuselage of a small, private plane, descended into the castle. The landing hatch closed again, and the Skull hurried back inside, descending to the launch and recovery bay.

The team had already removed the cargo and transferred it to a stasis tank. At the base of the probe, the project's leader, Greta Thorne, watched as her subordinates rolled the tank away.

"Well?" the Skull asked. "Is it viable?"

"It is," said Thorne.

"And it will respond to the procedure?"

"It should. The results of the preliminary scans are what we expected. Of course, we won't know definitively unless we go ahead with the procedure."

"Don't," said the Skull. "Not unless I give the order." He would not risk any ambiguity on this matter.

"Of course." Thorne gave a brisk nod but looked disappointed. She wasn't just willing to cross lines. She lived for the thrill of transgressing them. That made her valuable to the Skull, but it also meant he had to keep her on a short rein. There were contingency measures he did not want deployed unless he had no other choice.

"What about the exoskeleton?" Thorne's other project had begun as a thought experiment by the Skull. Its use wasn't something he planned on, either. It would defeat the purpose of everything else on Wolkenland. But he wanted all possibilities explored.

Thorne frowned at a transgression that had eluded her grasp. "None of the results satisfy me," she said. "Too much instability. That isn't unexpected, given what we're working with, but the problems remain intractable. We will continue to press forward if you wish, of course."

"But you are not optimistic."

"Given enough time, everything is possible."

The Skull nodded. Every task for Thorne became an obsession. If it involved something terrible, it also became a passion. The exoskeleton could wait, though. The Skull had less faith in its success than Thorne. What the probe had brought back was much better. He looked at the stasis tank. "This is your first priority."

"If you need it, the specimen will be ready."

"Good," said the Skull. "Then we are ready." He tapped the communicator on his wrist, opening a channel to the control centers of Wolkenland.

"Security, all shields and cloaking systems active," he commanded. "Engine room, signal lift-off.

"Navigation, set course for Latveria."

TWO

Wolkenland had disappeared from the Mediterranean in September. It was now October, and Doom had been unable to find any trace of the island.

The failure frustrated him, as all failures did. They ate at the back of his mind during the day, and eroded his sleep. Failure, large or small, should be foreign to him in a well-ordered universe. But failure, in one form or another, endlessly dogged his steps. Even on this day, which celebrated a triumph, though the victory disguised another failure.

He had tried to push thoughts of Wolkenland away a week ago. No evidence pointed to the island being a threat to Latveria specifically. He had watched the press conference, unimpressed with Lance Diffring's lies, and especially mistrustful of the show of humanitarianism.

He had also learned nothing useful. The care with which the conference had been stage-managed, showing the world's cameras nothing of the island, while delivering all the right, reassuring phrases, was all the proof he needed that Wolkenland had much to hide. But did that make it a threat to Latveria specifically? No reason to think so.

No reason to think about Wolkenland at all, except as another source of frustration.

Doom strode across the moat bridge of Castle Doom. An honor guard lined both sides, standing to rigid attention. Ahead, on top of the main gate, a reviewing stand awaited his presence. He could hear the sound of the parade that had reached the bottom of Vandorf Street and would be making its way up toward the gate.

He had declared another Doomsday, this one to mark the one-year anniversary of the victory over the urvullak. The plague of soul-eaters had swept over Latveria and had come close to destroying the country. The source of the plague had been the Devourer, the vortex that consumed all souls and held all memory. Doom had destroyed the Devourer and ended the plague. Urvullak still existed in Latveria, and always would, part of the dark shadows that defined the nation and its history. But they were few, and no longer posed an existential threat to Doom's domain.

A great victory. One the people longed to celebrate.

Doom gave them leave to revel in the day, and to show him their thanks for their salvation. He ascended the gate's stairway on the inner side of the wall and mounted the platform. The crowds lining the castle ring road and Vandorf Street roared, shouting his name, proclaiming their obedience.

A great victory.

Except for the failure beneath it.

Doom had sought the power of the Devourer for his own.

In seeking it out, he had freed it. In destroying it, he had lost what he sought, the key to omniscience.

More frustration to gnaw at him, displacing for now the irritating puzzle of Wolkenland.

Drums beat in a martial rhythm, brass sounded triumphant fanfares. The parade moved up Vandorf Street, drawing near the intersection with the ring road. People filled the windows of every house, waving and cheering. Doomstadt's Old Town erupted with the clamor of celebration.

At the head of the parade marched the palace guard, who had been the front line against the urvullak in Doomstadt. And at their lead were symbols of the heroic struggle, captain of the guard Kariana Verlak, and Doctor Elsa Orloff. Verlak, the commander who had almost given her life in the fight. Orloff, her wife, the neurosurgeon whose abilities and inventions had turned her into the hunter and the urvullak into her prey.

As they reached the top of Vandorf Street, Verlak and Orloff looked up at Doom and saluted, as did all those who followed.

Doom nodded to them. In Verlak and Orloff, at least, he saw no reminders of frustration. Verlak served him with a skill and loyalty as ferocious as they were beyond question. And he had guided Orloff into becoming a force more useful to him than a neurosurgeon.

The parade moved east down the ring road, and Doom took in the salutes and the praise. They were his due, and the balm of Doomsday began to ease the sting of failure for the moment.

"This is your moment," Kariana said as they passed by Doom and felt his approving gaze. "And it won't be the only one."

The eyes behind the mask were so powerful that even though Orloff could not see them from this distance, they blotted out her awareness of the cheers and the drums and the horns. For a few moments, she felt herself become the focus of the Lord of Latveria, and the sense of immense will and power in that focus was something that did not diminish through exposure.

Orloff and Kariana moved on, and Doom's gaze left them. The sounds of the parade, and of the more mundane world returned, and Orloff was able to think about what Kariana had said.

This is your moment.

Certainly, it was one that meant a lot. She had not fought the urvullak for the glory. She had hunted and destroyed them for Latveria, and for Kariana. The sight of her wife, grasped by one of the urvullak, fighting to keep her soul and her life, had left her with a memory scar that would follow Orloff for the rest of her life. She had gone after the undead with a fury she had never known existed within her. And she was glad for the celebration now, for the joy that it had been a full year since the end of the plague.

She had remained a hunter and had tracked down more remnants of the urvullak during the last twelve months. She had left her former life in Doomstadt Hospital far behind. But the war had been won, and though she remained vigilant, she could also rest in the peace that had come. And after the rest? She wasn't sure. The hunter Doom had awakened in her would not be content with idleness. That much she knew. She guessed that Doom would not let it remain idle for long either.

But for now, she would enjoy the peace. The parade recognized that peace. Kariana was right. She should accept that as much as the parade was designed to honor the monarch, her place at the head of the march was an honor, too. With a pang of melancholy, she wished that her parents were alive to share the moment with her. Could they have imagined a day like this for their trans daughter? Not during the reign of King Vladimir, and not during their years of exile. They had lived to see her a neurosurgeon, and they had been proud then. But if they could see her today...

They couldn't. Let it be enough that she knew how they would have felt.

"*The Hawk and the Blade!*" the people shouted, waving at Orloff and Kariana as they went by. "*The Hawk and the Blade!*"

So the nicknames that had originated with Kariana's troops had spread to the general population. Orloff smiled. She had been a little wary when Kariana had first told her about them. Kariana as the Hawk was easy to understand. The captain had the perfect, coiled bearing of a bird of prey, her eyes and features as sharp as her discipline was unwavering, and her pursuit of Latveria's enemies, no matter who they might be, merciless.

Orloff had at first connected herself as the Blade being a reference, perhaps mistrustful, to her surgery, and then wondered, self-consciously, if it were about her face, which she thought of as long. Kariana had reassured her on both counts, that they simply saw her as piercing. The calls she heard today showed her that the meaning of the name had evolved as it had spread.

"*Orloff the Blade!*" she heard. "*Bane of the urvullak!*"

"You deserve it," Kariana said. She didn't break the discipline of posture and stern countenance as she marched, but Orloff heard the loving grin in her tone.

"Deserve is a big word," said Orloff. She took advantage of her status as a civilian to look back once at Doom, his cloak stirring majestically in the wind. The means to do what she had done, to find a way of detecting the neurological signals of the undead, and the way to turn that detection into a weapon, had all come from Doom.

"Yes," said Kariana. "Doom commands, and Doom rewards."

"Service is its own reward," Orloff found herself saying. She realized just how much better she now understood Kariana's commitment to her duty.

"And that's true, too," said Kariana.

Orloff looked back again, and she saw the first flash as the bombs detonated.

Verlak whirled at the sound of the blasts. They came in quick succession, seconds apart, the next concussion coming just as the echoes of the previous began to fade. A half-dozen altogether, two blowing windows and masonry across the ring road, the source of the others out of sight on Vandorf Street, but their dust and smoke rising above the rooftops. The drums and horns of the march ceased, and the celebratory shouts of the crowd turned into screams of fear and pain.

Verlak ran toward the blasts. She tapped her earpiece, opening a channel to her troops. "Hold the gates," she ordered. "Watch for attackers from Vandorf."

Before Verlak had even reached the gates, the palace guard

had swung fully into action. Loudspeakers on every street corner commanded calm, and the guards imposed crowd control, clamping down on panic before it had the chance to gather momentum. The people had long since had obedience drilled into them, and especially with the proximity of their monarch, that instinct prevailed. They revered and feared Doom more than the bombs. Doom had left the review stand, and he hovered, suspended by his jet packs, above Vandorf Street, a figure of silent but immense wrath.

Verlak knew his rage, because her own mirrored it. Only the need to perform her duty quickly and decisively kept the red haze from consuming her vision. She took in her first sight of the damage with a forced dispassion.

Storefronts had blown out on the ring road and down the uphill third of Vandorf, all the blasts within a few hundred yards of the castle gate. Shattered masonry and timbers blocked the road, and glass shards lay everywhere. Verlak saw at least a dozen dead, and twice as many injured. Smoke poured out of the gaping holes in the buildings, the worst of it blown away by the wind.

Ambulance sirens sounded in the distance, and Elsa already knelt among the bodies, doing what she could to keep the most badly hurt alive until help arrived from the hospital. Verlak registered that this was happening, and filed it away. Her concern could not be to provide succor. Her duty was to keep order, and to punish the perpetrators.

Before she could punish them, she had to find them, and she knew that in the security center of the castle, the search was on. Standing by the gate, at the intersection of the chaos, Verlak contacted the center. "What do you have for me?" she asked, letting them know that she was alive and in command and wanted results *now*.

"*We're just completing the first scan wave, captain,*" said Isa Kruger, who had day command of the center.

The scan wave would have begun within seconds of the blasts. The feeds from the ever-present drone flights and fixed surveillance cameras would have been subjected to a deep and lightning-fast artificial intelligence examination, starting from the moment of the explosions and working both backward and forward in time. The search functions looked for any kind of anomalous behavior, specifically for people whose facial orientation and expressions indicated their attention was not on the parade. Movement, especially rapid, away from the crowds and against the general flow of pedestrian traffic.

Seconds ticked by, then Kruger said, "*I have them. Six men with anomalous focus, in proximity to the blast sites.*"

"Send them out," said Verlak.

Moments later, holographic projectors around the city displayed enhanced, three-dimensional representations of the six. In the blink of an eye, they became the most wanted fugitives in Latveria. Three sharp klaxon blasts from Doomstadt's warning systems announced the projections. An automated female voice spoke from the loudspeakers.

"*Citizens of Latveria. These men are wanted in connection with the Vandorf Street bombings. Look for them. Find them. Find them.*"

The faces turned slowly, visible to every citizen from every angle. The command from the loudspeakers repeated five times, then fell silent. It would start again every half-hour until Verlak or Doom gave the order to end it.

When Verlak saw the faces, she knew that Kruger and the

rest of the security center team had done their job well. There was a commonality to the faces that disturbed her. The men were young, white, and appeared to be in their early twenties. They all had their hair cropped very short and shaped into widow's peaks. The style was not one typical of Latveria. If the men had all been gathered together, they would have been noticed. Though they wore a variety of clothing, there was something about the group of faces that made Verlak think of uniforms, and of uniform hate.

Ten minutes later, the holographs winked out after the loudspeakers broadcast the announcement that the men had been found. All of them. The ambulance sirens still wailed, the wounded were still being loaded onto stretchers, and the bombers had been located. They had fled down Vandorf, and at the bottom of the hill, scattered into the narrow alleys. And that was as far as they had gone. They were all dead.

Doom stood by, arms folded, his silence a thunderhead of contained anger, as Verlak examined the body of the terrorist who had fallen closest to Vandorf Street. The crowded gables of the Old Town houses blocked almost all sunlight, plunging the alley into deep shadow. Still, there was enough light for Verlak to have seen blood, if there had been any. A cursory examination showed no wounds on the body, though the facial features had frozen in sudden agony.

Verlak rose from her crouch. "He wasn't brought down by the guard," she said. "But why would they have been fleeing if this was a suicide mission?"

"Their deaths had another cause," said Doom. "And we must find it. But they were killed. That is clear. As is the fact that Latveria is under attack."

"But from whom?"

Doom did not answer.

He doesn't know, Verlak realized, and felt the day grow colder and darker.

THREE

The dinner presented Lance Diffring with a challenge an order of magnitude greater than the press conference. Then, he had been dealing with people whose knowledge of Wolkenland amounted to a blank slate. He had been able to control the narrative from the start. This time, he had to manage people who knew what Wolkenland was, and who knew, even if often within the parameters of plausible deniability, who governed it.

On the one hand, the shaping of the narrative could be done more effectively, if less diplomatically, by the Red Skull himself. He would declare what must happen, and it would. No one could say anything. But Wolkenland would function much more smoothly if its residents didn't have to look directly at the mask of its ruler. Diffring liked things to run smoothly. He imagined the Skull did, too. So Diffring, one of the few who had one-on-one dealings with the Skull, had been handed the task of being the figurehead of Wolkenland and its policies. The Skull spoke through him, and the citizens looked at his acceptable face instead of the Skull's. Diffring thought of himself as the conduit of plausible deniability. He intended to be a very good conduit.

So he started the gathering in Wolkenland's council hall with a dinner, just to set the right tone, get people full and happy and pampered. Receptive. At long tables in the Great Chamber, the billionaires of the island feasted on courses of delicacies that were rare and elaborate even by their standards. Their setting complemented the feast, reminding the attendees of their grandeur. Tapestries twenty feet high hung on the walls, medieval reproductions of hunting parties and conquerors, the likenesses of the high and mighty present exquisitely captured in the faces of the knights and ladies, monarchs and champions. Tall columns held a ceiling whose fresco depicted the island floating high in the clouds to the wonder of the gods below it.

With dinner finished, dishes cleared away, cognac served, and servants banished, Diffring called the meeting to order. He spoke at a raised lectern at one end of the hall, underneath the coat of arms of Wolkenland, a crossed sword and rifle beneath a stylized skull. Diffring kept the tone informal, calling for attention by tapping a spoon against his snifter. He winked at his wife.

From her seat, Addyson, all shellacked glamor, gave him her knowing nod.

"I'm here with good news," he said, once he had his audience's attention. "As you know, one of the few outstanding issues to face our island has been Latveria's refusal to recognize Wolkenland's diplomatic status. That wouldn't matter if the refusal was coming from, oh, I don't know, say Lichtenstein."

He paused for the polite laughter. "But Latveria is, when we get right down to it, a superpower. And we don't want a superpower hostile to us, especially one ruled by Doctor Doom." He pulled an "oh I'm so scared" grimace. More laughter, a bit more raucous. "Not nice sleeping with one eye open, wondering what that madman will do, right? Am I right?"

Thunderous pounding of approval on tables.

Diffring grinned. "So, the good news, then, is that the steps are being taken to remove the Latveria problem." Now came the tricky bit. He plunged straight in. "What do you do when you know someone's going to come after you, sooner or later? You clean their clock first."

Pindrop silence.

"What do you mean?" someone called.

"As some of you probably know, we're over Latveria now. And the attacks have begun."

"Is the… Is *he* crazy?" Most of the residents never mentioned the Red Skull by name. They felt more comfortable pretending they didn't believe what they did. Plenty of others embraced the naked displays of the island's ideology, and were proud, at least in private, of their alliance with the Skull. But no one would dare refer to him directly when questioning his judgment.

"Not at all," Diffring said, working the reassuring tone in his voice. He crossed his arms and leaned on the lectern, ostentatiously relaxed. "Look, we've all known that this had to come. This way, it's on our terms. It's all been thought through. No risk to anyone. And just think of the leverage we'll have when Latveria is a province of Wolkenland. My mind's boggling at the idea of just how many things will be on our terms from here on in."

General murmurs of agreement and enthusiasm as that prospect sank in. Diffring smiled, pleased with himself. This had gone even more smoothly than he'd thought. He'd been in fine form. Maybe the fact that for once he really believed what he said had added extra zing to his performance.

It was done. The billionaires were at war, and they seemed pretty damn happy about it.

In the evening after the bombing, rescue teams digging through the wreckage of a ruined news stand on the ring road found a corpse with the same close-cut hair as the six bombers. They summoned the nearest guard, who relayed the news to Verlak, and she ordered all work to cease until she had had a chance to look at the scene. Monitoring the communications of the investigation, Doom heard the report, and decided to examine the scene for himself.

He arrived without expecting much, but this death stood out from the others. If there was a reason why this terrorist had been killed in the blast, and that reason could be found, then it might lead somewhere.

Maybe, might, perhaps. Who knew? He was grasping at straws, but he could not afford to pass up even the most unlikely source of a lead. Hours had passed since Latveria had been attacked, and he did not know who had dared this insult. The situation could not be borne. Yet it had to be. He had nowhere to strike. He had to contain his wrath in order to find the path forward to vengeance.

Doom arrived at the same time as Verlak. She did not look

surprised to see him, clearly recognizing that he had come for the same reasons she had. "My lord," she said, lowering her head, waiting for his cue.

Doom nodded to her and entered the gutted store through the gap where the windows and door had been. Verlak followed close behind.

The rescue team had been sent away, and a trio of guards stood watch, leaving the area clear around the corpse.

Doom walked around the body. It lay facing up, and there was nothing mysterious about the cause of death here. The trauma inflicted by the blast was severe. The dead man's face, though, was largely unharmed. His sightless eyes stared up at the broken roof with a stilled, cold hate.

"Something went wrong?" Verlak suggested. "The bomb went off prematurely?"

"I would be more convinced of that if the others had survived the explosions by more than a few minutes," said Doom. The deaths of the bombers were part of the plan, that much was certain. Though the means of their execution was still a mystery, Doom could see the possible motives for it easily enough. Whoever was behind the attack did not want to risk any of their servants being caught and made to talk. But why was this one different? Maybe Verlak was right, although the explanation didn't feel right to him. It was too pat, and he could tell by the look on her face that she didn't believe it either. She had given voice to the theory because it had to be considered, not because she thought it was correct.

"It would help if we knew what kind of explosives had been used," Verlak said. "What kind of detonator. If the bombs were on a timer or if a signal set them off."

Doom looked at the communicator on his gauntlet. He had set its screen to show him the most recent reports of the investigation as they came in. He tapped the screen until he found the preliminary conclusions about the blast sights. He grunted. "No residue detected of the usual explosive compounds. No residue of any kind. No trace of any mechanism either. The device itself appears to have vaporized."

Verlak frowned. "Nothing left at all?" she said. Her frown deepened, now with concern instead of puzzlement. "An energy weapon?" she said.

"I begin to think so," said Doom. His anger had not lessened, but his concern grew sharper. A foe that could do this could also do much worse.

Verlak wandered back to the gap in the outer wall. She ran her hand over the ragged edge of the hole. "We're lucky the damage isn't much worse," she said.

Lucky…

Doom whirled around. He stared at the corpse, at those undamaged eyes, the corpse that had been waiting to be found, the corpse that was interesting enough to draw him here.

"Leave!" he ordered the guards. He lunged at the body, reaching for the intact skull, the most logical place for the trap to be.

The dead eyes saw him, the mind behind the trap mocked him, and the hidden bomb exploded in a flash of apocalyptic energy.

Pure silver devoured the world. A giant's invisible hand slammed into him. His armor's force field repelled the force of the energy blast, and he remained standing in the heart of the explosion.

When the concussion faded and his eyes cleared, he was in the open air. The store and most of the evacuated block ahead of him had vanished, disintegrated by the blast. He had been facing east when the bomb went off, and his force field had whipped out to create a wall eight feet on either side of him. It had sent the greatest concentration of the energy forward, reducing some of the damage behind him, and left a swath directly to the west unscathed. The guards had barely begun to react to his command when the energy weapon caught them. They were gone without trace, erased utterly.

Verlak stirred. Good luck had placed her behind the force field. The wave of displaced air had sent her flying into the street. She rose unsteadily, shaking her head to clear it, and walked back to Doom, her eyes wide as she took in the devastation. She recovered as he would have demanded, though. Before she reached him, she had tapped her earpiece, and Doom heard her giving orders that the bodies of the other terrorists be placed in stasis fields and scanned for weapons.

"Could this be the work of Fortunov?" Verlak asked.

Rudolfo Fortunov, son of the deposed and executed King Vladimir, was a natural suspect. He had already demonstrated a willingness to inflict massive damage on Latveria in the effort to reclaim the kingdom, and Doom's enemies from outside had showed a willingness to supply Fortunov with advanced weaponry. He had done worse than this during his last coup attempt. "It is possible," said Doom. "I do not think so, however. There is a sophistication to this attack that is unlike him."

"Sophistication?" said Verlak. She kept cocking her head as if straining to hear Doom. His mask had protected his hearing and eyesight. Verlak was forcing herself to function clearly despite being dazzled and half-deafened. Her dedication to duty did her credit. She would seek aid only when that duty was discharged, and Doom knew he could trust her judgment. If her wounds impaired her ability to act, she would tell him. That, too, he valued. Subordinates of her caliber were rare.

"If whoever is behind this thought this kind of bomb would kill you, Lord Doom, they are not very clever," Verlak said.

"Precisely," said Doom. "Fortunov would certainly know that, and he would strike to kill. What would the bombing of this day accomplish for him, other than alerting me to his return from exile, and ensuring that I will hunt him down? I do believe, though, that our enemy knew this would not be fatal. Who could have access to such technology and now know of its limits against Doom? Especially since this weapon was not on a timer."

"It wasn't?"

"That would leave too much to chance. Our enemy saw me through the eyes of the corpse and detonated remotely."

Verlak looked past Doom to the empty space where the store had been. "And took away our means of learning how that was done," she said. "Unless the other bodies have bombs in them, too."

"Quite," said Doom. He strode back toward the castle gate. The moat's wall had suffered some damage a few hundred yards to the east, and already crews were at work repairing it. No scar was permitted to mar any aspect of Castle Doom for long.

Verlak kept pace. "If this was not an assassination attempt," she said, "then what was its purpose?"

"To humiliate," said Doom. "To destabilize." He wouldn't rule out Fortunov's involvement completely. The man was a fool, but one that it was still dangerous to underestimate. Doom had learned that to his cost. But he stood by what he had said to Verlak. This was not Fortunov's style. This was the opening gambit by someone much more dangerous.

Doom cursed the veil that shrouded his foe.

In the early morning, Elsa Orloff arrived at Castle Doom, anger coursing through her veins. Yesterday made it twice. Twice in one year she had almost lost Kariana. She had always been conscious of the risks that came with Kariana's position. And there had been near misses in the past. Orloff had been angry then, too, and terrified at the prospect of her wife's death. Her rage felt different this time. Before, she had been helpless to do anything about those, human or otherwise, who tried to take Kari from her. Things were different now. *She* was different now. She knew how to hunt, and how to destroy enemies.

That was what she wanted to do now. That was what she hoped Doom had summoned her to do. Yesterday, she had seen to the wounded. Today, she wanted to make the guilty pay.

When she arrived at the main entrance, the guard on duty told her to report to her laboratory. Orloff raised an eyebrow in surprise but did as instructed.

The lab was deep in the bowels of the castle, a huge space whose walls of interlocking metallic blocks could alter its dimensions to suit Doom's desire. Flexible, robotic arms hung from the ceiling grid, awaiting her commands. It was here that she had scanned the brains of the dead, and where she had developed the weapon with which she tracked and killed the urvullak.

When she saw the six bodies laid out on slabs, waiting for her attention, she felt a dizzying déjà vu. Doom towered over the dead, watching her.

"Are these … ?" she began.

"No," said Doom. "They are not urvullak. Your skills are required for a different task. I am aware, doctor, that you wish to be on the hunt, and hunt you shall. But first we need the scent of the prey."

She gave a solemn nod of obedience. "What can I do?" she asked. She eyed the bodies warily, thinking of Kariana's narrow escape.

Doom caught the meaning of her look. "I have had the wretches scanned thoroughly. They contain no explosive devices. They are simply dead. I want my best neurosurgeon to tell me why." He pointed to the workstation in the center of the lab. "We have the initial autopsy results. They do not satisfy me."

Orloff moved to the console and brought up the reports on the screen. She read through the first postmortem, then went quickly through the others. She turned back to Doom, feeling suspicious herself now.

"Death due to massive cerebral hemorrhage?" she said. "For all six?"

"Simultaneously, it would appear," Doom added.

"That's not a believable coincidence," said Orloff. "The strokes had to be induced artificially."

"Agreed," said Doom.

Orloff walked slowly around the nearest corpse. "How did you die?" she asked it. "An implant of some kind?"

"That would be the most likely explanation," said Doom.

"The reports didn't say anything about any such implants, though."

"None were found. That does not mean all trace is gone, especially to your eyes."

Already, she was thinking about modifying some of the tests she had used on other corpses, deploying Doom's machine that melded science with something far older and more mysterious. The machine that had detected the signs of memories in empty skulls.

"I'll get to work, then," Orloff said. She had been given a new prey to hunt. The fire of purpose burned through her veins.

"There is something else," said Doom. "I believe a signal was used to detonate the bomb in the seventh terrorist. That may well have been the case here as well, with the theorized implants."

"I don't know what trace, if any, a signal might leave."

"Search, and perhaps you will find. I am pursuing other avenues, Doctor Orloff. If a signal is being transmitted, however, it is well-hidden. As well-hidden as our enemy. Search well, doctor. Find the scent. Then we will hunt."

The chains came off at night. When they did, the freedom of movement felt more like a taunt than a relief. There was nowhere to go. During the days, the shackles held the slaves at their assigned positions in the mines. At night, there was almost an invitation to wander through dark tunnels without purpose or hope, and die the same way.

There was no way out, no sign of an exit.

At least, there hadn't been. Tonight, Valeria knew where she needed to go.

The hope, tiny and perhaps illusory, had come toward the end of the day. Another day, as uniform and brutal as all the other days in the mines of Wolkenland, wielding pick and shovel under the eyes of guards who watched for any excuse to strike with their whips and cattle prods. Deep underground, with no way to tell time, the days were endless agony. The nights were declared by the guards, who then herded the slaves into larger caves where they were given a nauseating gruel and left to sleep for a few hours on bare stone.

During the long day, Valeria and her fellow slaves filled carts with stone and kept digging. As far as she could tell, that was all they were accomplishing. There was no coal here, no sign of anything, at least to her untrained eye, that resembled a mineral resource. There were no seams to dig, nothing they were told to seek. Only tunnels to lengthen. The initial surreal feeling of digging in something she knew to be a form of ship faded after the first few days. Wolkenland's foundations went deep. Valeria only had nightmares of unleashing a flood of seawater for the first two nights.

Some of the slaves had the task of installing reinforcing timber in the tunnels, but the supply of wood seemed grudging, as if the idea of preventing a collapse were an afterthought.

The inevitable happened close to what turned out to be the end of Valeria's shift. The ceiling of another tunnel cracked and came down. The crash of stone shook the ground beneath her feet, and she looked up in fearful expectation of seeing tons of rock falling on her. The tunnel settled, though the air became dusty. The guards coughed as they ordered her and her fellow slaves back to work. There were cries of distress in the distance, but none of pain. Valeria could only imagine that there were no injured where the cave-in happened. Only the dead.

The thought weighed on her soul like a stone, heavy and cold. The piercing grief of being witness to sudden death had been numbed by frequent, repeated blows. But the blows still hurt. They still damaged.

When night was declared, she trudged back, shackled to the chain that left only six feet between her and the prisoners ahead and behind. They went by the collapsed tunnel. Valeria saw blood seeping out from the rubble onto the floor, and when she looked away, sickened, she saw the promise of hope. Where the rubble ended, there was a cleft in the ceiling, a few feet wide. As she went past it, Valeria was sure she caught a glimpse of natural light, and a faint hint of a breeze.

A way out.

There was no certainty. She couldn't know if the crack could be climbed, or that it didn't narrow to inches before it reached the surface. She couldn't even be sure that it *did* go all the way to the top. She had to act as if the hope were real, though. She had to believe there was a way out. She couldn't ignore this chance.

The chains came off when the slaves passed through the doorway to the caves, the holding pens, where they would spend the night. There were fifty other slaves in Valeria's sleeping chamber. She didn't say anything about what she had seen. Guards might hear. And there was very little conversation of any kind. Bodies were too exhausted, souls too broken.

Valeria sat with her back against the wall, fighting off the need to lie down. When the cave was full of the sounds of sleep, and the night guard had passed on patrol, she got up. She had counted the seconds between guards going by the entrance, and knew she had about fifteen minutes before another showed up.

She padded to the entrance.

"What are you doing?" a voice whispered.

Valeria froze. She looked down. One of the women who worked the same tunnel as her knelt a few feet away. Valeria could barely see her in the dim light from the passageway. She was a ragged shape, worn and gray, just like Valeria. Dust-coated, filthy, malnourished, maltreated, the slaves were merging into a homogeneous collective of misery.

"There might be a way out," Valeria said.

"Don't be foolish. Think what they'll do if they catch you."

"I have to try. And if I can get out, maybe I can call for help."

"You won't make it."

"I know," she admitted. "I have to try," she said again. And that was true, too. She had to do what she could for the prisoners of Wolkenland, do what she could to end the lies of this terrible place.

She had to try, because of why she had come to Wolkenland in the first place.

She was no longer a refugee, not in the strict sense. She had fled Latveria more than a decade ago. She had been living in the States, and though memories of Latveria and the regrets that came with them had never left her, she had made herself a home. She lived quietly, wary of being seen, or found. Survival habits, once learned, did not go away. She had few acquaintances and fewer friends. Trust came with difficulty, if it came at all. She owned an antique shop in a small town. It kept a roof over her head, and that satisfied her.

But she never forgot what it felt like to lose a home. She knew the pains of exile. She did what she could to help others going through the same thing. She donated time and money to Amnesty International and the Red Cross. And she watched the broadcast from Wolkenland with interest. She liked the words that Lance Diffring spoke. She liked to think he meant what he said, and that here was a true refuge for those who needed it.

She had to be sure.

And so she had boarded a flight to Rome, and from there made her way to the island. She arrived without the help of an official body. She did not pretend to be something she was not, because Wolkenland had claimed to be open to all who needed to come, regardless of the reason. So she came, with hope her only shield.

She found out the truth all right.

The guards took her phone, her clothes, and her freedom away.

Once more, the human capacity for cruelty battered her hope for a better world.

The hope had taken so many beatings over the years. But it had sustained her during the reign of King Vladimir in Latveria. It had sustained her when she finally admitted to herself what Doom had become, and left Latveria forever. And it sustained her now, pushing her to try to escape, because she would not betray herself with surrender.

She started down the hall, listening intently for the sound of bootsteps. Bare incandescent bulbs hung from power cords at twenty-foot intervals, the hum of generators a distant white noise. Valeria peered cautiously around each intersection before crossing. For the first time since her arrival on Wolkenland, her luck held. Her way forward was clear.

She reached the cave-in and looked up at the cleft. It was night on the surface, and she couldn't see the top, but she felt the touch of cool, fresh air again.

The cleft began above the slump of rubble. She climbed up the pile of rock and felt inside the split in the roof. She found handholds.

You can do this. You must.

The hope gave her the strength, and she began to pull herself up.

FOUR

The reviewing hall of Wolkenland Castle shouted the truth of the island, the truth that could not yet be shown to the world. Twenty-foot banners of black and red hung down from the ceiling. Iron eagles, their wings spanning the walls, ruled over the space. Soldiers stood to attention in a long line, presenting themselves to the Red Skull and Jurgen Hauptmann.

The Skull wondered if Iron-Hand Hauptmann truly realized what Wolkenland had done for him. In the past, Hauptmann had led troops into battle. He had been Iron-Hand since not long after he had assumed his first command, his war wound turned into a bionic instrument of strength. But he had been an Exile for almost as long, he and his comrades despised and discarded by a world that rejected the Order they would bring to it. Decades spent wandering, or hiding in the desolation of Exile Island. Sometimes willingly, sometimes not, the Exiles had swallowed their pride and followed the lead of the Red Skull. The Skull knew they did not trust him, but they did share his beliefs.

Now, the Skull had shown that they were right to follow him. Men like Iron-Hand had the chance to bask in his reflected glory. He hoped Hauptmann appreciated the honor. It was in Hauptmann's best interest that he do so.

Legs apart, eyes staring ahead at nothing with unblinking rigor, the troops gave the impression of total homogeneity even though they were not in uniform. As their mission dictated, they were dressed as Latverian peasants and workers. The Skull nodded, satisfied. They would not be noticed until it was too late.

The inspection complete, the Skull addressed the men, Hauptmann one careful step behind him. Hauptmann might not like being visibly a subordinate, but that was the price of being part of the triumph of Wolkenland, and he had accepted that cost. If he ever showed signs of forgetting that fact, the Skull would not hesitate to remind him. Forcefully.

"Your brothers dealt the first blow against Latveria," he said. "Now it falls to you to let this nation of scum know that it is at war. You will teach Latveria fear. You will shake its foundations to their core. Go now, and let this craven population know that Wolkenland has come."

The men saluted, stiff armed. The Red Skull returned the salute, and the troops turned and marched smartly from the hall. The Skull watched them go, indifferent to the fact that he would never see them again, contemptuous of their weakness, even though it served him. They were all young and recently radicalized, ready to believe in anything, including their own survival. They had been told that, once they completed their mission, their lives depended on reaching the extraction point by the deadline, and not a second later. They would never reach the point. That they believed they would was all that mattered.

"How much longer can we afford to throw troops away?" Hauptmann asked.

The Skull turned a withering stare on Hauptmann. The mercenary's iron right hand twitched in instinctive reaction to a threat, but he kept his arm at his side. He tried to return the stare, his left eye blinking behind a monocle. He looked away almost at once.

The Skull shouldn't be surprised Hauptmann understood so little. It was his lack of vision and comprehension that had led to him hiding out on Exile Island in the first place.

"We will use as many as we need until our ends are achieved," said the Skull.

"But won't they start to realize they are being sent on suicide missions if none of their predecessors ever come back?"

The Skull sighed impatiently. "All of the men from this pool share the same flaw. Each thinks he is superior to the others. Failure to return is therefore a failure of skill, to be expected of the inferior soldier. You fail to see the specific utility of useful idiots, Hauptmann. They are useful precisely because they are idiots. If they were not idiots, they would not be what we need at this juncture."

He strode toward the exit, still speaking, forcing Hauptmann to follow. "We have more than enough recruits, committed volunteers all, for our present needs, Iron-Hand."

"But how long will our needs be these?" Hauptmann asked. "We are strong. Why float over Latveria all this time like…" He stopped himself.

Like cowards? Were those the words Hauptmann had been going to speak? He was lucky he chose not to.

"Why float over Latveria all this time?" Hauptmann repeated, as if he had never intended to say more.

"We are strong," the Red Skull agreed. "But so is Doom. To underestimate him is fatal. *I* know that. So should you. We ruled Latveria once, and we lost it. Would you risk a second defeat?"

It had been worse than a defeat. It had been a humiliation. The Red Skull and the Exiles had conquered Latveria overnight, but in Doom's absence. He had returned, and though the Skull had managed to incapacitate him with his own weaponry, Doom had not been helpless long. He had reclaimed his throne with contemptuous ease, and amused himself not just by hurling the Skull and the Exiles back to the island, but by convincing them of the illusion that they had shrunk to six inches in height.

The Red Skull forgave nothing. But for mockery, he reserved a vengeance of a refined and brutal venom.

Hauptmann's face darkened. He had not forgotten or forgiven either. "No," he said. "I will not risk defeat. Doom must suffer."

"He will," the Skull promised. "Exquisitely. He cannot see it yet, but the noose has already closed around his neck."

Orloff met Elizabeth Boehm at Weimer's, a cafe a block down from Doomstadt Hospital. The director of the hospital stood up when Orloff entered the cafe. Short, broad, white-haired, and looking out at the world through thick glasses, Boehm had always been perfectly pleasant whenever Orloff had dealt with her while head of neurology. This greeting, though, was different. Respectful in a way that suggested an awareness of a profound difference in power. Even a touch of awe.

The last time they had spoken, Boehm had delivered the news that Orloff had been summoned to Castle Doom. Now Orloff was the monarch's protege, and a heroine of the war against the urvullak. Orloff had never thought that an aura surrounded her, but Boehm's manner suggested otherwise.

Orloff smiled as they sat down, trying to put the other doctor at ease. A waiter appeared at their table, and Orloff ordered an espresso. The cafe, dark in a comforting way, was busy this close to the noon hour, the tables filled with surgeons and hospital department heads. Orloff felt some curious and deferential looks come her way. No one approached the table, though. She and Boehm would be left to their privacy.

Were they afraid of her? she wondered. No, she decided. Afraid of the sun she now orbited so closely, and that could burn them all so easily.

"Thank you for meeting me," Boehm said. "I'm sure your new duties keep you very busy."

"No need for thanks," said Orloff, still smiling. "If something is happening that concerns you, that's good enough for me." And what Boehm had to say might well have a link to the Doomsday attacks. She had taken to heart Doom's injunction to distrust coincidences.

Chance is the enemy's camouflage, Doctor Orloff. Look behind the random, and you will find the foe.

"I'm grateful all the same," said Boehm.

The relief in the director's face told Orloff another story. Boehm felt she had information that Doom should know, but much preferred to relay it by speaking with Orloff rather than going through the terror of seeking an audience with Doom himself.

The waiter returned with the coffees, and Boehm waited until he was gone before she spoke again.

"There's been a noticeable spike recently of patients, admitted to a number of different departments, but a lot being referred to neurology, whose symptoms are resisting diagnosis."

"What kind of symptoms?" Orloff asked.

"Dizziness, delayed reflexes, a range of inner ear problems, things like that."

Orloff didn't understand. Those were hardly mysterious ailments. And she knew that Boehm did not need her to point that out. "Go on," she said quietly.

"None of the usual underlying causes are present," Boehm said. "We can't find any cause at all."

"That's worrying."

"It gets worse. One of the patients, a farmer, mentioned something that the admitting nurse thought she should flag. I'm glad she did. It was passed up to me. The farmer said that some of his cattle are acting strange. Like they're dizzy."

"And like their reflexes are slow," Orloff finished, worry twisting in her gut.

"Exactly."

"I'm going to guess his case isn't an isolated one."

"You'd be right. I reached out to the veterinary college. They're getting so many reports of this they're beginning to refer to the phenomenon as a plague, even though it doesn't fit that definition."

"A virus?" Orloff wondered, beginning to speculate about a genetically engineered horror leaping across species.

"If it is, we can't find any sign of it," said Boehm.

Orloff wasn't willing to let the idea go quite yet. Bovine spongiform encephalopathy could only be detected through postmortem examination of the victim's brain. "Have any of the affected cattle gone to market?" she asked, fearing the worst. The thought that such a thing could be another terrorist attack chilled her blood. She wondered if this could be an effect of the signal Doom had tasked her to track down. No, she decided, though cautious in her conclusion. The symptoms sounded too widespread, too random.

"None have been sold as far as I can tell," said Boehm, "and we had tests done on one that would have been, which showed the symptoms. Nothing. No sign of any abnormality at all."

"Would you feel safe eating a steak from that animal?"

"I would," Boehm said, definitively. "No BSE or anything similar. And the evidence I have is that the symptoms started appearing in humans and livestock simultaneously. If there's a transmission, it isn't through tainted meat." Boehm shook her head in frustration. "To be honest, I don't think we're dealing with anything transmitted at all. The cases are both very scattered and very widespread. We've had patients from Doomstadt and the smallest villages."

"The whole country, then?"

"No. Unless there are reports we haven't received yet. The cases seem to be concentrated in Doomstadt and the surrounding region. Exposure doesn't seem to be a factor. One person in a household becomes chronically dizzy, while the others aren't affected at all. And I have to emphasize that there haven't been any fatalities, or even hospitalizations. The symptoms are persistent, but mild enough that I'm convinced there are a lot more cases than we've heard, but most people are just carrying on, sure what they're feeling isn't serious. It's only in the last few days that I've been able to put things together and decide that there really is something going on."

"Do the symptoms intensify?" If they did, *could* that be the effect of some kind of broadcast?

"They're persistent, but they don't seem to get worse. But the cases are multiplying." Boehm took a breath. "I almost fell getting out of bed this morning," she said quietly. She sat with both hands flat on the table, frame rigid with the effort the confession had taken.

Orloff put her cup down. She placed her hand on Boehm's. "The dizziness, then. And your reflexes?"

"Fine. So I'm like many. Dealing with an irritant. But something *is* happening."

"Agreed. I'm glad you got in touch." *This really doesn't feel natural. This is an attack. It has to be.* She kept her thoughts to herself.

"One other thing," said Boehm. "And I didn't know about this until today. There has been a spike, too, of people suffering from seasonal affective disorder."

"Really?" It had been a warm, sunny fall.

"Odd, isn't it?" said Boehm. "From the reports I read, it's as if the sufferers haven't had direct sunlight in quite some time." She paused, then plunged on with forced lightness. "My granddaughter keeps complaining that she can't tan."

Orloff looked out the cafe window at the bright day. It suddenly seemed as false as a painted backdrop.

In his study, Doom listened carefully to Orloff. When she was done, he told her that he agreed this was enemy action.

He spoke calmly, in spite of his anger at the news of a new, ongoing outrage against Latveria. And when he sent Orloff back to work on the corpses of the terrorists, he kept his calm by telling himself that at least he had more data. He had something he could, perhaps, follow. Since the bombing, all of his scans had produced nothing. The enemy was completely invisible. Doom could not strike back any more than he could punch air.

He had punched walls instead, deep in his quarters where no one but Boris would know of his frustration. Boris had said nothing, and then seen to repairing the masonry.

He would smash nothing here. He would use what Orloff had brought him. He tapped his desk, and multiple screens rose from its surface. He called up the hospital records. On a map of Latveria, the homes of all the patients appeared. Doom looked carefully at the geographic distribution. Doomstadt was the *precise* center of the phenomenon.

He turned to satellite imaging of the region. He looked for any kind of aberration, starting with radiation blooms. It took him another hour before he finally found something.

There were gravitational anomalies in and around Doomstadt. The readings were faint, inconsistent, easy to miss.

He distrusted the results. They looked masked, as if something were concealing the truth even from the eyes of his satellites.

Doom steepled his fingers. Gravitational fluctuations would account for the symptoms Orloff had described. But the anomalies were themselves a symptom.

What is the cause?

No. *Who* was the cause? The real question he had to answer.

Who would dare?

Who wanted to die that badly?

FIVE

The shaft narrowed and widened as Valeria climbed. Twice, it pressed in so tightly that she became stuck. The second time was the worst. Rock squeezed her, she couldn't move, and she could barely breathe. Her chest hitched in incipient panic. She bit back the choking whine. *Stay calm. Stay calm or you'll die here.* Her arms stretched above her head, and her hands scrabbled for a grip hard enough to pull herself free. Her toes pushed against tiny ledges below her. Finally, she expelled all the air from her lungs, and that let her squirm just enough to start moving forward again.

There were more times when she started to slip, when the shaft was so vertical, and the holds so few and small, she was sure she would not be able to climb any further. The thought of what would happen to her and everyone else if she failed kept her trying. Each time she despaired, fear and horror came to her aid, and she tried again, and then again, and at last her groping fingers found a ledge they could grip, and she kept on going, higher and higher through the pitch dark, reaching for the promise of that breath of fresh air.

When, at last, she reached the top, she gasped with exhaustion and gratitude. She pulled the clean air into her lungs with huge gulps. She rolled away from the mouth of the shaft and lay, panting, on the rocky ground. She looked up at the stars and the full moon, and wept to see them.

She only allowed herself a few minutes before she forced herself to start moving again. It would be too easy to fall asleep here, and she was in a flat, open area, easy to spot. She had to keep moving. If she couldn't find a way of getting off the island or calling for help before dawn, at the very least she needed somewhere to hide during the day.

She had a few hours, she guessed. It was still full dark, the moon high. The guards never did head counts during the night. Valeria wasn't even sure they did during the day. They seemed to be that confident escape was impossible.

And why wouldn't they be? Only compounding improbabilities of chance had given her the means of even getting this far.

Valeria turned around slowly, trying for some sort of sense of where she was. The only things she knew about Wolkenland's geography were its size, and that a ring of peaks surrounded it. The moon shone down on the land, bleaching it of mercy. The earth here was a wasteland of jumbled boulders, hills of mined debris, and pits. To her right, the perimeter chain rose, hulking shapes of gray and darkness.

She started for the hills. In the absence of a clear plan, they gave her a direction. She had a vague idea of finding the harbor and stowing away on a departing ship. She didn't ask herself how realistic that might be. She needed hope, and she needed to keep going. If one goal became impossible, she would turn to the next, and then the next, until she told the world the lie of Wolkenland. She refused to imagine being recaptured.

She had to walk slowly, placing her feet carefully so she didn't break an ankle. After a few minutes, she was in more broken territory, hidden by jagged heaps of stone. She moved without sound, braced for the sound of running boots. But the island seemed as silent as she was. As she drew closer to the hills, she heard a low hum in the air, and ducked down between two boulders. A drone went by overhead.

She waited, motionless, to see if it returned. When it didn't, she wrestled with the instinct to stay where she was, invisible in the night, or move as far and as fast as she could from this spot in case the drone had spotted her and relayed her position. She chose the more frightening choice. She felt vulnerable when she moved, but if she tried to hide, she might never find the courage to break cover.

Valeria reached the hills at dawn. The slopes here were rugged, but she felt she could risk them at night. There was little vegetation, but there were deep clefts, offering her shelter for the day. She found one with a stream trickling down it. She tasted it, and it was fresh. She drank eagerly.

Valeria kept as still as she could during the day, allowing herself only a bare minimum of stretching and stirring. She managed to sleep for a few hours, and woke feeling chilled. Her exertions during the night had kept her warm. She was surprised by how cold the day felt, even with the sky cloudless. Had Wolkenland left the Mediterranean? Was it back in the Atlantic? She tried not to speculate. It would be too easy to lose hope.

Night fell. Hungry, sore, weak, exhausted, she got to her

feet and began the climb up the slope. It was a steep hike, and a slow one, but she didn't have to do any actual climbing except for brief stretches. The peaks came into sight, limned by silver moonlight, and she prayed to whoever might hear that she was on the same side and the same end of the island as the harbor. Fate had thrown her luck this far. A bit more couldn't be too much to ask. She was fighting to save every slave on Wolkenland, not just herself.

Mindful of how vertical the cliffs were on the outer side of the ring, Valeria got down on her hands and knees. She crossed to the edge of the peak and looked down.

Then, dizzy, she grabbed hold of the stone beneath her fingers, clutching hard.

At first, she didn't understand what she was seeing. She had expected to see moonlight reflected on the ocean. Instead, she seemed to be looking down at the sky, at clustered constellations of stars. Gradually, she understood, but the realization only increased the vertigo and dragged a sob of despair from her chest.

The lights weren't stars. She was seeing a distant town at night.

Wolkenland was flying.

Valeria lost track of time for a bit. She stared at the distant lights while the impossibility of true escape settled on her soul, heavy as lead. She had been able to imagine stowing away on a ship. She couldn't sustain a similar fantasy around an aircraft, even assuming there were flights that departed the island.

Finally, she closed her eyes tight against the sight of hopelessness. When she trusted herself not to give in to despair, she opened them again and crawled backward, away from the cliff edge, away from the dizzying sight.

No way to get off Wolkenland. All right, now she knew. That had always been the faintest of chances. Her way forward was clear, and the real purpose of her escape from the mines hadn't changed. She had to pierce Wolkenland's shield of lies. Do that, and bring help to the island.

But how?

The people Wolkenland catered to. They would want to communicate with their interests off the island. Their homes would have computers, links, ways to talk to the outside world.

So Valeria hoped.

It took her an hour to reach the base of the hill once more. The moon was still high, and she had most of the night ahead of her. Plenty of time to try something else before she had to hide again.

She stayed close to the hillside and walked away from the mines. Looking up at the stars, she worked out that she must be heading south. After a while, she left the torn, rugged landscape behind. The terrain became gentle, rolling grasslands dotted with copses. She could move faster now, her footing surer, but as Wolkenland became more beautiful and inviting, Valeria became even more cautious, watching for drones and land-based patrols. She saw neither, though she kept her guard up.

Not long before dawn, she saw the first mansions. The fields and woods gave way to terraces scattered with gigantic homes.

There were lights on in some, and she couldn't go there. Others were dark.

Valeria paused at the foot of the lowest terrace. The house

above her slept in an embrace of cypress trees. With its pillars and verandas, it dreamed grandly of a past of plantations and suffering.

No way to tell from the outside if it was occupied or not. The only way to find out was to take the risk.

Valeria willed herself to face the truth. No matter what she did, she would be caught. Her freedom from the mines would be over in a matter of hours at most, more likely in minutes.

They'll kill you.

Maybe they would. Or maybe a live, miserable slave provided more amusement than a dead one. Either way, if she did nothing, and just tried to hide, all she would accomplish would be a delay of the inevitable. She would probably pass out from hunger before the end of the coming day.

So go to the house. Try something. Maybe luck would bless her just a little bit longer and give her the chance to call for help.

She moved through the trees, staying in the full darkness as much as she could, and went around to the side of the mansion. She found a window at chest-height. It was closed, of course, and locked, but she went through the motions of trying to raise it anyway. Then she took the stone she had been carrying for this purpose since she had left the region of the mines, and smashed it against the window. She worried the glass would turn out to be bulletproof, but after three solid hits, it broke, and she climbed inside.

She heard no alarms, but she had to believe she had triggered them somewhere. Now the time of her freedom would be measured in minutes, or perhaps seconds. No point in being stealthy. Speed was what mattered.

The room she had entered was large and empty. No furniture, no decor. A good sign. The house might well be untenanted.

On the other hand, if there was nothing at all in here, then she had broken in and given her position away pointlessly.

She left the room and found herself in the main hall. It reacted to her presence by activating night lights at floor level in the direction that she moved. No furnishings here either, just a sense of empty luxury awaiting the touch of its owners.

Valeria hurried through the house, through empty room after empty room, her footsteps slapping hollowly on marble. On the second floor, on the east side of the house, she found a room whose features marked it out as the study-to-be. A digital world map dominated the wall opposite the windows. It showed a real-time display of Wolkenland's location.

Valeria stared, time suspended by shock.

Latveria. They were floating over Latveria. Wolkenland had centered itself over Doomstadt.

She reeled, legs going weak. Trap upon trap, potential and real, psychological and soul-deep, seemed to snap shut around her. She had come back to the place that held everything she had ever loved, and everything she had ever fled. Latveria, the home of her dreams and nightmares, passions and griefs, hopes and terrors. She had escaped Latveria physically, vowing never to return. She had never escaped it emotionally.

Looking at the map, she felt as if Wolkenland had brought her to a black hole's event horizon, and here, in this room, she was about to step over the lethal boundary.

She turned away from the map and saw the means of crossing the horizon. Built into the wall to the right of the windows, ready for the new owners, was a communications system. Valeria walked over to it. Touchscreens offered the full range of options to whatever the house's master of the universe desired. Much of the system was dormant, awaiting an owner and passwords. But there was *every* possibility here, including shortwave, and she needed no password for that. She knew how to operate it, too, having learned during the years of resistance to King Vladimir's regime.

Back in the time when Latveria groaned in pain, but Victor was the man she had thought he'd always be.

She had no time, but she hesitated. The one person who was near enough to help, the one who could and would fight the Red Skull, was the one she had fled, the man she had loved who had turned into the monster she feared.

But if she called to him, he would come. That was a truth more certain than sunrise.

And so she started to broadcast, on a wavelength the underground of Latveria had once used. She took a deep shaking breath, and she said, "Victor."

Before she could say anything else, bullets smashed the screens and the room filled with guards.

SIX

The bombs went off within seconds of each other across Latveria. The explosions came in the morning, and rocked busy markets in Doomstadt, and Doomsburg, and Doomwood. Attacks hit the main platform of Doomstadt Rail Station, as well as the northern line, derailing a passenger train fifty miles outside of the capital. Bombs went off at the porticos of the Latverian Academy of the Sciences and the Werner Academy in Doomstadt. And explosions shook what Verlak thought had to be randomly chosen streets in three small villages.

The purpose of the coordinated attack was clear. The enemy meant to terrorize and to shatter the stability of Latveria by making it clear that nowhere was safe, that anything and anyone could be a target.

Verlak raged in the security center, hands twitching with the need to wrap fingers around the throats of the terrorists, one by one by one. But they foiled that need, as efficiently as they spread fear. Once they detonated their devices, they made little attempt to hide. Instead, they ran, and the surveillance cameras zeroed in on their movements, always anomalous in their contexts, within seconds of the explosions.

As before, the bombers dropped dead before they could be caught. Verlak watched them die, their images dominating the huge curving wall of screens in the security center. All ten men died at precisely the same time.

"Did we catch anything?" Verlak demanded of the room at large. "Did we catch the signal?" Some kind of transmission had to be responsible for the deaths.

Technicians looked at Verlak and then turned away in shame. No, they had found nothing.

She forced herself not to scream in frustration.

By noon, the bodies had been brought to Castle Doom, and delivered to Elsa's laboratory. Verlak accompanied the deliveries. She had one small bit of further information to pass on, and seeing Elsa, if only for a few minutes, would give her the strength not to punch her fist through a wall for the rest of the day.

"More gifts for you," Verlak said, staring at the bodies with hate as the guards loaded them onto the examination tables. Verlak noticed a new element that had been added to the lab since the first corpses had been delivered. It was the smooth, black obelisk that had played a crucial role in Elsa's examination of the urvullak. It was one of Doom's creations, a fusion of science and sorcery that went beyond the bounds of either.

"You're so sweet and generous," Elsa said, the cynical levity not hiding the fact that she felt the same anger as her wife.

Verlak gestured at the obelisk. "Going down an occult route again, I see."

Elsa nodded. "Needs must. I haven't been able to find any usable trace to explain their deaths through…" She paused, shrugged. "Let's say *conventional* methods."

"You don't think these men are undead, though?"

"No, definitely not."

"Well, that's a mercy. And not a small one." Verlak embraced the needed bit of good news. Her chest felt a little less tight. "I don't know if this will help at all," she continued, "but we plotted out possible directions the terrorists were heading, based on their headings when they died, and assuming the vectors of their flights weren't random."

"And did you find anything?" Elsa pushed one of the tables next to the machine and began connecting the corpse.

"Hard to say. It does look like they were all heading for the same point."

"What's there?"

"Nothing. A spot in a forest twenty miles northeast from here. I sent a squad there immediately." She raised her hands helplessly. "Just woods. Not even a clearing. It's possible our extrapolation was wrong, of course. They weren't on the run that long before they died. Not a lot of data to go on."

Finished with the connections, Elsa stepped back and examined the dead man's face. "I wonder…" she said.

"You wonder what?"

"When we spoke earlier, you said they didn't try to hide."

"No, they just took off at a sprint as soon as their bombs detonated."

"So they made the effort of staying undercover, and then threw that effort away."

Verlak grimaced. "I wouldn't say they made much of an

effort. When we rolled the security footage back to track their previous movements, it looks like they only arrived in the target cities and villages today."

"From where?"

"Yes, well, that's the question. We don't have an answer yet. But since they didn't travel as a group, they didn't really stand out until they ran." The ease with which the killers moved about infuriated her. All they had to do was stroll up to wherever they planned to leave their bombs.

"Untrained and unskilled, would you say?"

"Yes. And given their reactions, not very bright."

Elsa stroked her chin thoughtfully. "They're all young," she said. "Early twenties at most."

"What are you thinking?"

"Radicalized volunteers," she said. "Not professional mercenaries."

"Right," said Verlak. "The enemy's disposable wind-up toys." She sniffed in disgust. War called for sacrifices. Verlak knew that. She had no fear of hard choices. But the troops under her command were human beings. She would never throw their lives away, and they knew she wouldn't.

Verlak thought about the middle-of-nowhere convergence of the enemy soldiers' paths. "Except they didn't believe they were disposable," she said, following Elsa's speculation.

"We know this look, don't we?" said Elsa, pointing at the severe haircuts, the same for all the dead men. "If they weren't trying to blend in, they'd be wearing brown shirts and jackboots."

Verlak came up behind Elsa. She put her arm around her wife's shoulder. Yes, that aesthetic of hate and imagined superiority was hard to miss. "Not the suicide bomber type," Verlak agreed. "This sort thinks they're special."

"They thought they were going to live," said Elsa. "That's why they were running."

"Making for their extraction point."

"Does that make sense?"

"The location doesn't," said Verlak. "Too many trees, too close together. Hard for any craft to land there. But if the enemy never intended to get them out, and just gave them a random set of GPS coordinates, then why not? All that mattered is that these men believed in the extraction."

"So they were always going to die."

"Yes," Verlak said quietly. She shed no tears for these murders, but the concept of the unknowing suicide bomber horrified her. "Does this help you?" she asked Elsa.

"It might." Elsa turned to the obelisk. "It makes me think I was right to bring this in. Death is the answer, Kari. I need to look at its kingdom."

After she and Kariana had kissed goodbye, and the captain of the guard left to continue her side of the hunt, Orloff turned to the corpse she had connected to the obelisk. "You have things to tell me," she told it. "And I'm going to make you talk."

Orloff activated the obelisk. The room began to hum, the sound low, almost inaudible, but resonating at a profound level, jangling the nerves at the intersection of anticipation and terror. Faint signals appeared on the obelisk's monitors. Even after the destruction of the Devourer, the semi-sentient being that consumed and preserved all memories and created a link with the dead, the traces of memory – not consciousness but the ethereal trace of individual history – were still there for the machine to register.

From a table beside the obelisk, Orloff picked up her helmet. She put it on, and her vision changed. She saw the world in its liminal state, matter becoming translucent, its ephemerality made manifest. At will, she could see through walls and buildings in this world turned into gray, washed by the swirling winds of death. Only the things that hovered in the contradictions and uncertainties between life and death presented a true substance to her vision.

Using the helmet had become second nature for Orloff since the war against the urvullak and the Devourer. She still hunted the undead, tracking down isolated nests in the wilds of Latveria. She also spent hours in the lab and elsewhere exploring what she could see and do in the liminal. Doom encouraged her to keep pushing further.

Knowledge gathers at the extremes.

Doom's words, his mantra of exploration.

Now Orloff looked at the corpses, in particular the one connected to Doom's machine. The postmortems, even the most precise, had found no reason for the fatal strokes. In this state, Orloff saw faint sparks deep in the skulls, and a brighter one in the linked-up body. She looked at the spark, blocking out all other visual input. Her concentration revealed the spot of unnatural light not to be a single spot at all, but a cluster of fragments, the embers of a vanished fire. The longer she looked at it, the closer her awareness came to it, and she perceived the jagged quality to the shards of light. They were the remnants of violence, the trace of the minute explosion that had killed the man.

All right, progress. Confirmation that a cause existed. And the fact that Orloff could see it in this way pointed her toward its nature.

Orloff did not practice sorcery. She had no direct knowledge of its workings. But ever since she had been summoned away from her post at Doomstadt Hospital, and begun working under Doom's close supervision, she had come into continual, and often prolonged, contact with energies and forces that before she became a hunter she would have called unnatural. She had a better understanding of them now, or at least an ability to recognize them and to divine some aspects of their being.

So she learned all she could of the sparks before she went to report to Doom.

"A signal broadcast to the terrorist minds through sorcerous means," Doom said when Orloff had finished summarizing her findings.

"Or at least using a technology that goes beyond what I would consider normal human means," said Orloff.

She stood before his desk in his study and waited for his response. He seemed to be musing again, but now on what she had said. When she had first arrived, though the titanium mask had faced her, she had sensed that his eyes had been looking past her, his gaze on an internal horizon. But she had his full attention now. He had stirred when she had suggested sorcery as the means of broadcasting a signal undetectable by Latveria's surveillance apparatus, and she felt a growing intensity in the room, like the formation of a powerful storm.

"Yes," Doom said at last, his voice hard with an ominous calm. "You are correct in your second surmise. Not sorcery, but inhuman technology. Though the one using it is very much human."

"You know who is behind this, my lord?" Orloff asked.

"The perpetrators of the most recent attacks, in their clear ideological conformity with the first of the terrorists, gave me a clear suspicion. You have confirmed matters for me. Latveria and I have only one enemy who espouses this vileness, and has, in the past at least, had access to this kind of power. The Red Skull."

Orloff felt the blood drain from her face.

"I believe you had not yet returned to Latveria, doctor, when the Skull took advantage of my absence to seize control of Latveria."

Orloff had to clear her throat before she could speak. "That's right," she said.

"No doubt Captain Verlak has told you of that short period."

"She has." It had happened the year before Kariana had begun her training for the guard. The few weeks during which fascism in its purest state had clamped down on the country lived in Kari's memory like a wound that would never close. It fueled the fire that burned in her, the ferocious commitment to the defense of Latveria.

Orloff needed no prompting to imagine what the Red Skull would do, given the chance. "I stand ready to fight, my lord," she said.

"I do not doubt it," said Doom. His attention seemed to be drifting away from her again. "You will have your orders in due course. Leave me now."

Orloff obeyed, thoughts consumed with fear of the enemy, and the need to fight, and fight hard.

Victor...

Doom raised the screens on his desk, but he did not look at them. He leaned on his elbows, fingers entwined, and brooded.

Victor...

Just the one word, his name.

The transmission was so brief, so devoid of content, it might never have been forwarded to him. But the burst had occurred on a shortwave frequency little used in Latveria since the fall of King Vladimir. That had raised flags, and the transmission had been sent up the line until it had reached Doom.

Victor...

He recognized Valeria at once. The sound of her voice had never left him, even long after she had. Valeria had never accepted his vision for Latveria. Never accepted his conception of himself. She had tried to call him back to what he had been, or what she believed he had been, before his exile, before his experiences in America, before his scars.

Before he had gone from being merely Victor, to truly becoming Doom.

He had lost her, years ago. But now he heard her voice again, and the past, the wounded, bleeding, merciless past, fell on him. He could barely concentrate. He kept hearing her voice, that one word, his name, over and over and over again.

She was calling to him. Calling out to him.

He would have dismissed the voice as impossible, as his unconscious torturing his waking mind, if the transmission had not been sent to him by his servants. He could even see the wave form of the recording. It was real.

She was real.

Somehow, Valeria was reaching out to him at the precise moment that the Red Skull had launched a new campaign to take Latveria.

There are no coincidences. Not one like this.

Hope and dread and wrath warred in his chest. The screens waited for him to do something, to take the first steps.

He knew his enemy. He was sure he faced the Skull. There were no other fascists who could find this kind of power, and who would want Latveria this badly.

Now his anger had a target, and with the target came hatred. Hatred for the Skull, for what he represented, for what he had done to Doom's country in the past, and what he was doing to it now.

The screens waited.

The Skull has Valeria.

What else could her presence mean? What else could make her call out to him?

The screens waited.

Just as the Skull did. Waiting for Doom to strike out in unthinking rage and bring catastrophe down on himself and all that he cared about.

That's what the Skull wants me to do.

His fists clenched, and he hesitated, frozen in this moment by the enormity of the trap before him.

SEVEN

For more than an hour, the thought of Valeria's presence prevented Doom from concentrating on anything else. He played her transmission over and over, trying to convince himself that it was indeed real, but the repetition only made her voice seem more and more like the product of a dream.

Not just a dream from his past, but from a part of his past that itself no longer seemed real, even if the pain it produced was real enough. Though Valeria had been present in his life for the beginning of his reign, the truth was that, by then, he had already lost her. The memories of joy, the ones that caused the greatest pain, were from the time before his becoming. That was the time of anger and what seemed like fruitless struggle against the grip of Vladimir, the time of Latveria's agony. It was also a time of summer breezes against his face, of the touch of Valeria's lips on his.

Nothing was real from then. All that had been had turned to scars and ash, to half-formed pieces of agony during restless nights.

Now a memory spoke his name, and he had to make her real.

That need, to *do* something about the voice, restored his focus. Only by finding her would he make her real.

So he got to work. The screens before him became active as he searched for the source of the transmission. The security center had not been able to do so, but the technicians there did not have the tools he did. Doom provided his servants with the technology they needed to perform their tasks, and no more. There was much he reserved for himself alone.

The recording was so short that it gave him only the slightest traces for his electronic forensics to work on. Even so, he found a direction, and worked back through a path of aetheric breadcrumbs to the source.

Or what his machines told him was the source.

Doom frowned. The results pointed to a position more than five thousand feet in the air. Had Valeria been broadcasting from a plane? On shortwave? He could believe a plane had evaded his detection systems. The terrorists were coming from *somewhere* after all. But trying to place Valeria on board with that kind of broadcasting access seemed absurd.

Yet the results were emphatic. Doom went through the process again, and the results were the same.

He stared at the screens for a long while, cursing their bland refusal to make sense.

Then he thought about the gravitational anomalies, and the other inexplicable symptoms that Orloff had brought to his attention, including the ones that suggested, against all visible evidence, the absence of direct sunlight.

"First principle," he muttered to himself. "Assume there is something there."

Let there be an object at the position from which Valeria transmitted. Work backward from that. What mass must it have to create the recorded anomalies? Since the readings of those were inconsistent, now assume they were being disguised in some way. Take the strongest, treat it as the bare minimum indicator mass.

Look at the spread of cases. Treat all of them as results of the same phenomenon.

A picture began to form. A suggestion of mass. A more definite idea of area, and with it a shape.

Doom recognized the shape.

"Wolkenland," he snarled. He should have known. He should have guessed from the facile lies spouted by that plastic puppet Diffring, should have guessed where Wolkenland had gone when it had disappeared. And he *had* known, not consciously, but at a primal level. Why else would he have been so obsessed with the island and its nature? He cursed himself for not having seen the truth sooner, and he cursed the Skull for what he had dared, and what he had thus far succeeded in doing.

The implications of Wolkenland's position arrived in an avalanche. Doom let them come. He let them bury his rage with their mass. Calm again, he took the time to examine them one by one, and learn, at last, the battlefield of the war.

An hour later, he knew what he had to do.

The briefing room attached to the security center was soundproof and protected by a Faraday cage. Nothing said within its walls would be heard beyond them. The chamber was a hemisphere of dark stone, half of the wall surface taken up by a curved display that could be one screen or many, depending on Doom's command. Chairs surrounded a circular table that could itself become another illuminated display.

Doom stood in front of the wall display. Facing him were Verlak, Orloff, and Boris. To them he would entrust much of what he knew and planned, but still only what they needed to know. He trusted them to act as he commanded. He trusted Verlak, too, to pass on to her subordinates in the guard what they needed to know, and no more.

Doom tapped his wrist control, and the wall became two screens, each showing a schematic of Wolkenland hovering over Latveria. The display on the right showed the geographic perspective from above, the outline of the island a deadly footprint with Doomstadt at its center. The left-hand display was a side view, showing the estimated altitude of the threat. The rendering of Wolkenland in both cases was only an outline. Next to it were the known area of the island, and its estimated mass, a threat translated into numbers.

"This is our war," said Doom. "The enemy is the Red Skull, and he has turned his newly created homeland into a weapon against us."

"How long has it been there?" Verlak asked, aghast.

"Based on the symptoms Latverians have been showing, ever since it disappeared from the Mediterranean in September," said Doom. "We have been subject to the Skull's attacks for some time without knowing it."

"And we can't shoot it down," Verlak said bitterly.

She had seized the salient points of the problems, as Doom expected of her.

"Quite," said Doom. "We know nothing of the island except its size. Everything else is extrapolation. Its shields against being seen are formidable. We can only presume that its defenses against attack are as strong." Perhaps even strong enough to protect it from the Damocles satellite's antimatter cannon. Perhaps not, but Doom could not fire. If Wolkenland fell, it would devastate Latveria.

And then there was Wolkenland's population. Not its masters. The refugees who had been tricked by its laws. Now that Doom knew who reigned on the island, he knew the fate of the refugees. Not in detail, no, but in nature. He knew, and his Romani blood burned with rage, the same blood that had been spilled by the Red Skull and his spiritual fellows across the bleak pages of history. He would not add to the Skull's crimes by condemning them to share the same annihilation as their captor.

And there was Valeria. He said nothing about her. Knowledge of her presence was for him alone.

"So an aerial attack is out of the question," said Verlak.

"It is," said Doom. "With no intelligence on Wolkenland's defenses and weapons, and no way of even seeing targets, I will not throw away my air force on a mission that can only end in its destruction. We also face the matter of international relations. The UN has recognized Wolkenland. At this moment, its standing with the other great powers is higher than ours."

Latveria was feared, as it should be, around the globe. It was not popular, and Doom despised the petty games of politics. A nation should be strong, and with strength came respect. It should not be *liked*. But Wolkenland *had* played that game, and that gave it another advantage in the war. "Latveria cannot be seen to be striking the first blow."

"But we haven't," Orloff protested. "The attacks…"

Doom interrupted, "The attacks are easily deniable, the evidence dismissible as fabricated."

Orloff tried again. "But if the world knew that the Red Skull ruled Wolkenland, wouldn't that make a difference?"

"The world does not know," Boris said gently. "And we have no proof."

Doom nodded. "Our enemy's strategy is excellent. It is why he must never be underestimated. As long as Wolkenland hides behind its shields, it is protected from our view, and it is protected from us by the view of others." He disdained the mewling hypocrisies of the world's other superpowers, but he would not subject Latveria to a pointless war with them, one which would play directly into the Red Skull's hands.

"We have no way of attacking what we cannot find from the ground. Especially not with the danger it poses to Doomstadt. Its descent must not be uncontrolled. However, Wolkenland cannot hide or protect itself from Doom," he continued. "I shall go myself. I will pierce its defenses and strip away its shields. The Skull will reap the full measure of my wrath. Until I have accomplished my ends, it is likely that you will not hear from me. Look for Wolkenland to appear in the skies. Then you will hear my commands once more."

He looked at Boris. "Until that time, my presence here is uninterrupted."

Boris nodded in understanding. The Doombots would be visible, maintaining the illusion that Doom had not left the seat of his power. To Verlak, Doom said, "Watch for the enemy forces. We know where they come from now. The attacks will, I am sure, intensify in number and severity."

"We know the profile to watch for now," said Verlak.

"Expect the Red Skull to have anticipated that, and to change tactics." Doom looked at Orloff. "But one thing he will never do is relinquish his power of life and death over his underlings."

"I know what to look for," Orloff confirmed. "It won't be long before I can spot the trigger in a living brain."

"Then a new hunt lies before you, doctor."

She lowered her head in understanding and unspoken vow.

"Protect Latveria," Doom said, addressing all of them now. "I shall throw down the enemy and tear the heart from his creation."

EIGHT

Doom spent the rest of the day preparing. Night had fallen before he was ready. He had to make a special effort of will not to depart for the invisible island in the sky the moment he left Verlak and the others. Valeria's call for help had been intercepted in the early hours of the morning. Almost twelve hours had passed between her transmission and the briefing. The sense of sand slipping down a terrible hourglass tormented Doom. But he could not let his imagination dictate his decisions. He had no way of knowing when the sands would run out, or if they already had. Valeria's call might have ended because the Skull's minions had killed her.

The Skull might already have plunged a dagger into his heart, and he didn't know it yet.

Doom rejected the thought. He would not begin this war wounded by that uncertainty.

He could not rush into battle against the Red Skull without preparing as fully as possible. His adversary had once used his own technology against him and made him a prisoner in his castle. The Red Skull was no sorcerer, but if he had a flying island at his disposal, then he must have access to the Power Cosmic, and very possibly other forms of energy just as fearsome. Doom had to be ready for the unimaginable.

As he chose his weapons and equipment, he thought about his objectives. He went through one option and possibility after another, weighing chances against probabilities, the hopes of victory against the costs of disaster, the things that he *wished* to accomplish against the things that he *must*. In the end, when at last the time came to bring the war to Wolkenland, he had his plan set firmly in his mind.

His first priority would be to disable the island's camouflage. With Wolkenland's attack on Latveria visible to the world, he would have a free hand in his response. The next task would be, if possible, to seize control of Wolkenland's navigation system, and get the island away from Latveria.

Neutralizing the Red Skull would be the quickest way to achieve those ends. Doom did not indulge in the hope that he would be able to finish off his enemy so easily. The Skull would have protected himself. He would not be leading the battle from the front.

And Valeria…

Doom could not search for her and fight the Skull. His victory would have to pave the way to finding her. He had no choice. To do anything else would seal her fate with certainty.

"You know I'm coming." Doom spoke to the Red Skull as he mounted the stairs to the top of a lonely spire on the southeast corner of the castle. He ran a final diagnostic check on his armor while he climbed. "You underestimated me once, too. Neither of us will make that error again. You would not be here if you were not sure of yourself. You must have known that I would find Wolkenland eventually. Therefore, my discovery is part of your plan. It is not just that you know I am coming. You want me there."

Doom reached the top of the stairs. He stepped out onto a small, circular parapet, and looked up into the night.

"Whatever I choose to do," he said, "I must believe that you have expected it. And I believe something else, too. I believe you are afraid, even if you do not admit it to yourself. You are afraid because you know the same things I do as we confront each other on this battlefield. What I expect of you, you expect of me. You are afraid, wretch, though you come to my land with dreams of conquest and blood. You are afraid, but not nearly as much as you should be.

"You should be terrified, because there is nothing you can plan, and nothing you can do, that will save you."

Doom launched himself into the air. His jet packs shot him into the clear October night. The stars looked down on him, indifferent to the imagined land floating between them and Doom.

The spread of gravitational anomalies and physio-psychological symptoms in the human population told Doom the likely orientation of Wolkenland. The southern end of the island was somewhat wider than the northern one. In the absence of other evidence, it made sense as a potential location of the island's power source. Doom angled his flight to the south, gambling on speculation becoming reality.

A bit less than a mile up, a proximity warning sounded in his ears. He slowed down. The sensors in his armor had detected the nearby presence not of a physical object, but of an energy field. Even its presence was shielded. He had to come within a hundred feet for his scans to pick it up at all. The closer he came, the more distinct the field became, its wavelengths and strengths becoming known to him. He slowed down more, until he hovered at the edge of the field.

This close, Doom could study the energy and pry its secrets free. It was, as he had expected, far too powerful for him to try to overload and shut down. However, it could be fooled. It would repel him if he tried to break through, and that impact would no doubt alert the Red Skull to his presence. He would be like a fly crashing into a web. But like a web, the field let air through. The Skull would not want his island hermetically sealed.

Doom completed his scans, then extended his right hand, the gauntlet glowing with shifting spectrums of energy, the aura's vibration shifting to synchronize itself with the field. Doom made contact. The Wolkenland force field hummed to itself, and did not react. It treated his armor's force field as part of itself.

Doom passed through the barrier.

Wolkenland appeared above him.

The stars vanished behind the immense platform of floating rock. The night turned sullen red, lit by the energy plumes from mile-wide exhaust pipes. They emerged from the rock at even intervals around the periphery of the island, but there were two closer together at the wider, southern end.

The stern, Doom thought. His guess looked like it might have been correct.

He had to adjust his armor's sensors now, turning off the signal amplification he had been using. There was so much energy surrounding him now that the readings displayed by his mask's eye shutters resembled images of the sun. Now he had to filter out the exhaust and the shield, whose power he had yet more respect for, since it prevented even the furnaces of Wolkenland's engines from being perceived from the outside.

Doom stayed where he was, just inside the embrace of the force field, applying one filter after another until he had a read on a massive core of power, held inside the island toward the stern.

Would the means to control that power be anywhere near its location? He had to start looking somewhere. This gave him a good target.

Doom flew upward again, closing with the underside of Wolkenland. He traveled past the rock, staying just fifty feet away, looking for any kind of access point. He saw none. Perhaps the Red Skull had been worried about his threat, too. Perhaps he had tried to protect the underbelly of his monster. A wise and sound strategy.

Also, a futile one.

Doom arrived at a point almost directly below what would be the center of the great energy source, an unknown distance straight up. If no door would be granted him, he would create his own.

Right arm out, as if in a gesture of command, he activated the sonic drill built into the gauntlet. A beam of energy struck the rock. In absolute silence, it bored a tunnel ten feet across through the stone. Doom rose up through the slowly lengthening passage, the conqueror worm burrowing through the Red Skull's clay.

Once inside the island, he made all his scans passive. He must not announce his presence prematurely. He knew where he was heading, and the mapping he had been able to do of the interior of the island, rough though it was, would do to get him to his goal.

Progress was slow. The sonic drill was stealthy, and its stealth in part depended on its almost gentle reshaping of the material being of the island. No dust or other fragments fell away from the island to be detected by sensors. The rock struck by the beam simply ceased to be, and the tunnel appeared as if it had always been a geologic feature at this spot. Doom made himself patient with the thought that slow as the ascent was, every moment of escaping detection would add that much more power to his first real blow when he came to strike.

After half a mile of ascent, Doom encountered his first conduit. The side of the pipe showed at the edge of the tunnel, the metal sliced by the drill, but not ruptured. Doom would not be a secret much longer, then. Soon now, very soon, he would cause some damage, and somewhere an alarm would sound, and the Red Skull would know he had unwelcome company.

Doom's passive scans relied on sounds, heat, vibrations, and variations in electro-magnetic radiation to map the way ahead. Enough readings were coming in now to give him a schematic of the vicinity. After another several yards, he closed in on an access tunnel. Rather than cut into it before he had to, he altered the direction of his dig and moved parallel to the passageway. He was walking now, no longer on a steep climb. He had penetrated deep into the foundations of Wolkenland. The more difficult part of the search was beginning. Close now to the core of Wolkenland's power, he had to find the command-and-control centers.

He traveled another hundred yards, tracking the path of the tunnel. It registered as a large one, a good fifteen feet wide, and ran straight for a long distance. A major route, Doom surmised, for the servants of the Red Skull who saw to the proper running of the island. Traveling sternward, he might be fortunate in the tunnel's destination.

Then, a few yards later, it came to an end at a T-junction, and Doom's sensors read two other such intersections only a bit further on to port and starboard. At the same moment, alarms began to wail. Their cries reverberated in the stone, a warning that rang throughout the depths of Wolkenland.

He is here! Doom could almost hear words in the electronic screams. He could almost hear the fear that lurked behind the need to install the alarms, and the fear they now spread. He smiled tightly. Time at last for the people of Wolkenland to awake from their dream of conquest and cry out at the enormity of their mistake.

He is here! Here is here!

Doom is here.

Every single member of the Red Skull's attacking force would have known this moment was inevitable. They had struck at Latveria, and his retaliation was certain as death. They must have known, and trembled, even in the deluding embrace of their beliefs. They had known but they had not, Doom was certain, understood. If they had, they would not be here. Even the Red Skull, for all his hate and ambition and pride, could not truly understand.

He is here! He is here!

Did the wretches, as they scurried to react to the danger, begin to understand? Did their bravado begin to fail as they realized they were in danger in their fortress, that their concealment had failed and now, a mile above the ground, they were on the defensive?

Yes, those things must be true. They could not be human and not feel terror at his coming.

Because he was Doom, and not even Hell was safe from him.

He swung to his right, and the sonic drill blasted through the stone that separated his tunnel from the passage. Rock vanished, and with it ended the prologue of the war.

Doom stepped out into a corridor of rock walls and metal floor. The alarms screamed in terror. To his left, from the stern, where the corridor turned sharply after fifty feet, came the sound of running boots.

Doom turned to face his foes, and to teach them, in their final moments, how little they knew before now of terror.

NINE

The Red Skull's troops charged around the corner. They carried automatic rifles, and they opened fire the moment they saw Doom.

The bullets bounced off his armor, ricocheting around the hall. He hit back with concussive blasts from his gauntlets. The energy bolts slammed through the troops with torpedo impact, flattening them. Doom never slowed. He took the turn quickly and blasted another twenty troops down in the next leg of the hall. Thirty yards on, a junction waited. The direction Doom needed would be to the left, still heading to stern. But he also needed to leave the main pathways.

These first responses from the enemy were negligible, barely worth his time. But once the Skull and his servants had a strong fix on his position, the attacks would become much more powerful. The Skull was here because he believed he could defeat Doom. The power that made Wolkenland fly and kept it hidden could also provide the energy for formidable weapons. Doom did not have the luxury of pitting his strength against theirs. If he failed, then Wolkenland would conquer Latveria.

The troops had come at him with little organization or discipline. They were off-balance, trying to adapt to the sudden threat of his presence. He had the advantage for the moment, and must push forward as hard and fast as possible to maintain it.

No alternate routes off this corridor. The sound of a larger concentration of troops approaching the junction. A risk to take that route, then, but one he chose, favoring speed this time. If there were no alternatives, he would have to forge his own route again.

At the last second before he reached the junction, a moment of caution made him turn on his force field instead of rounding the intersection with a pair of concussive blasts. So, when the energy beam hit him with the power to take out a tank regiment, the explosion threw him into the wall behind, but did not incinerate him inside his armor. The blast filled the corridor with a violence of crimson and silver, a thunder clash of warring light. The bolt left the corridor wider, the walls sheared symmetrically, severed conduits jetting steam into the passage.

Doom lunged out of the cratered wall. The blow had been so powerful, his force field needed to recharge for a few seconds before it could protect him from another such hit. At the end of the hall, the Skull's soldiers readied the cannon to fire again. The weapon had a huge, squat barrel, more than four feet wide. More than its size, what Doom registered in the suspended moment before either he or the enemy could attack was the cannon's age, and the inhuman designs that twined around it.

Lemurian, he thought, and learned that much more about the Skull's resources. Wolkenland itself showed the Skull had access to inhuman sources of power. Now Doom knew at least some of that power came from an ancient civilization that had believed it had the strength to challenge gods, and wasn't far wrong. Doom filed the knowledge away, found his bearings, decided on his strategy, and took action, all before the troops had finished drawing a breath after the weapon's first bolt.

Doom hit back using sorcery, giving his armor the chance to rebuild its energy. He launched a mystical blast straight into the mouth of the cannon. For the space of the troops' quiver of fear, nothing seemed to happen. Then, in their foolishness and terror they activated the cannon. The damaged weapon exploded, its energy unleashed and uncontrolled. The eye-searing explosion destroyed that end of the corridor, and Doom's force field had already recharged enough to protect him from the undirected energy of the blast. Molten rock flowed down from the ceiling and in from the walls, hissing as it covered the wreckage and carbonized bodies.

The enemy had mobilized heavy weapons more quickly than Doom had expected. He had to remember that the Skull would have trained them for exactly this scenario. Wolkenland had been constructed for this purpose above all others. The Skull wanted Latveria beneath his heel first, above all other nations. It was more than a matter of strategy, a matter of wanting Latveria and its technological storehouses. It was a matter of pride, of a humiliation avenged.

A personal war.

For Doom, too.

He turned the sonic drill on the wall to his right, punched

through the remaining stone, and came out into a smaller, parallel corridor. A few yards up, on the port side, he found a utility door. He wrenched it from its hinges, and found himself in a narrow access passage, cramped beside huge clusters of pipes.

Perfect.

He hurried down the passage, still heading to stern, and went deep into the maze of conduits and shafts that fed energy, water, and air to the foundations of Wolkenland. Now, briefly, he would hide as the island had over Latveria, an invisible destroyer.

He would also give the Red Skull and his soldiers things to chase and fear.

He removed a small metallic case from his belt. He set it on the floor and touched a button that was the only feature on its black, matte face. One side slid open, and the contents emerged. The case combined the technology of his molecular projector and the Doombots. Released from the containment field of the case, a dozen miniature Doombots, each about eight inches high, appeared to materialize out of thin air. They did not have all the capabilities of their full-sized models, but they would serve his needs. Their AI had enough autonomy for them to carry out their missions.

The Red Skull's troops were about to learn that they were fighting a war on multiple fronts.

The miniature Doombots raced off into the maze of Wolkenland's nervous system, traveling paths Doom could not, entering regions beyond his reach. Their optic sensors relayed what they saw to him, and he split his attention between his surroundings and those of his avatars. As the bots traveled, their scans updated Doom's maps, and his knowledge of Wolkenland deepened moment by moment.

Minutes after he released the miniatures, they began to spread fear through the tunnels. Doom moved carefully, letting the Doombots be the exposed blades of his attack, keeping himself invisible for as long as he could.

The Doombots relayed gratifying scenes of mayhem and panic. A soldier looked up just in time to see a Doombot drop out of an overhead ventilation grill. He recoiled, colliding with his comrades. They stared, confused, for a precious, fatal moment, and the Doombot hit them with concussive blasts. They all went down but one, the soldier who had first seen the Doombot. Terrified, he broke and ran a fraction of a second before the blasts felled the other soldiers. Doom let the man go to become a useful vector of panic and disorder. The soldier sprinted, screaming, back down the hall. He vanished from the Doombot's perspective.

Doom saw him again a minute later, when he ran into two equally terrified survivors of another encounter, these ones still pursued by the miniature as it followed its purpose of causing maximum disruption. The men screamed, realizing the attacks came from multiple directions. A concussive blast took another down, and the remaining two took off, running back to the nearest intersection and then splitting off down different tunnels, their howls spreading the news of the invader who was everywhere.

Doom laughed. He had had precious little reason to of late. But the panic he beheld gave him the satisfaction he had been denied since the first bombing.

Another Doombot burst out of a conduit into a secondary

control chamber. It took out the technicians in a matter of seconds, then plugged itself into the port of one of the consoles. Data about the heating and water of this sector of Wolkenland flowed from the consoles to Doom. He scanned the information, saw the possibilities, and sent a command back to the Doombot.

The lights went out across the sector, and valves opened, spewing steam into the corridors. A squad of soldiers stormed into the control room a few moments later, heavily armed now with energy weapons. They came in firing, and their combined attack destroyed the Doombot. It also turned all the workstations to melted slag, and the room filled with the smoke of burning electricals, the last data sent by the Doombot before its sensors cut out.

Doom didn't need any further data from that quarter. He had seen, and he had commanded, and the virus the Doombot had injected into the network now circulated beyond the systems of the demolished chamber, havoc spreading in widening ripples.

Soldiers destroyed another Doombot, and when its feed cut out, Doom moved faster. He had a clearer sense of where he was, and where he had to go. Strategy dictated that he get there before the diversionary attacks all ended. He no longer had to focus as much attention on the data streams of the bots.

He found the passages large enough to accommodate him without difficulty. He moved through the veins of Wolkenland as if it were his own creation, readying his blow that would kill the beast.

•••

In the panopticon, the Red Skull watched the storm of chaos gather in strength, and move closer to Wolkenland's power hall. He shivered from the clash of waves of anger, of triumph, of eagerness, and of fear. Doom had come, as the Skull had wanted, as he had planned. But Doom had come on his own terms, and the Skull knew too well what happened to plans that came into contact with Doom.

But not this plan, though, not this time. After today, he would never know fear because of Doom again.

A miniature Doombot appeared at a junction. It looked up at the surveillance lenses, and then the screen went dark. The Skull squeezed a fist tight in fury, more at the sight of the Doombot than at the loss of vision in that spot. It was the size of the Doombots that enraged him. He had seen the same sick anger on Hauptmann's face when the first of the tiny figures had appeared. He had sent the Exile from the panopticon then. He didn't want to see a mirror of his own emotions. He would see this crucial moment through alone.

He ground his teeth. Doom had deployed those weapons as a calculated insult. He had so many devices at his disposal, so many ways he could wage war, but he had chosen these. Their perfectly human movements gave them an uncanny quality that unnerved his troops. But their diminutive stature was the blow that struck home. They were a reminder of how the Skull and the Exiles had left Latveria. Doom had sent them back to Exile Island, defeated and hypnotized into believing he had shrunk them into tiny dolls.

I will do this to you again.

Doom's message. His threat. His vow to make the superior humans feel small. The Red Skull saw the ideological tactic behind the insult. He saw the psychological purpose. And it didn't matter. The simple reminder of what had been done reopened the wound. The Skull felt the humiliation again, and if Doom subjected him to the same hypnotic gas as before, he would experience the ego-smashing blow just as acutely as before. His rational mind would abandon the knowledge that his senses lied, and plunge him into the trauma of the illusion.

Doom could do these things and worse. When he had been on the ground, miles away from Skull, it had been easy to revel in the expectation of vengeance. Now the day had come, and exultation was within reach. Doom *would* fall. Wolkenland would destroy him.

But for now, Doom traveled freely. He had the initiative.

And he had a target.

"You know where you must go," the Skull muttered. "And you know that I am expecting you."

The Skull had had enough of expectations.

"Let us end this, Doom."

He ordered even more reinforcements than he had already sent to the doors of the power hall. The appointed stage for their conflict.

"Let us end this," he said again. Then he made his promise. "I will end you."

The Red Skull's forces had destroyed the last of the miniature Doombots by the time Doom reached the main ventilation shaft that ran over the wide antechamber to the power hall. He had climbed up from the foundations of the island into the center of the castle. The space below was a wide, high-ceilinged circle. Three tunnels led into it at right angles to each other. In the fourth quadrant, a massive vault door dominated the wall. The power signal Doom had been following came from the other side.

The chamber beyond the door was completely isolated from the network of conduits Doom had been navigating. His passive sensors detected powerful force fields and other kinds of volatile energy shielding his target. He would not get there by burrowing through rock. The only way in was through the doors.

The Red Skull had tried to stop him from getting this far, and had failed. He must have expected that failure, the efforts to kill Doom in the tunnels not much more than wishful thinking. Looking down through the vent, Doom saw more than a hundred soldiers, armed with both conventional assault rifles and beam weapons.

And there are other means to stop me that I cannot see, aren't there? You cannot permit me to pass through that door. You stop me here or not at all.

Not at all.

He looked down at his foes, for the first time having the luxury of examining them properly. And judging them.

Black uniforms, red insignia, the same aesthetics, decade after decade, the malignant signifiers of a cancerous ideology. And the people who wore those uniforms, resentful, bitter fantasists of genocide, their kind had bled Latveria and the Romani, Doom's people, and so many others, in the Second World War, and again under King Vladimir, and again when the Red Skull had seized the country.

They were one of the reasons why the world needed Doom, because only he had the will to stamp them and their poison down once and for all. Without his rule, the world had shown time and again that it could not be trusted, that *never again* was nothing more than a platitude.

Doom would show these maggots what *never again* meant.

He would show them what terror really meant.

Starting now.

TEN

Doom crashed out of the vent. He landed in the center of the chamber and spun, unleashing a salvo of concussive blasts. He cleared the space around him, violently hurling troops against walls and other soldiers. He took out a quarter of the enemy's strength in his first strike. The remaining troops opened fire. His force field effortlessly repelled bullets, shells, and beams. Doom took a moment to stand nearly motionless, as if ignoring the assault, merely turning his head to give his foes a long, withering stare.

The gesture was not an indulgence. It was a calculated psychological attack. It told the troops how meaningless their efforts were, and how helpless they were before him. He gave them his contempt with his gaze, and then with his words. His amplified voice boomed over the din of gunfire. "You stand here because you fear the Red Skull. I am the one you should fear. The Skull knows this. He fears me to the depths of his soul."

They had a moment then, a gift of awe-inspiring magnanimity, when they could have dropped to their knees and begged his forgiveness, or fled in the poor hope of escaping his wrath. The moment was far more than they deserved.

A few ran away. The rest stayed and expended their ammunition onto his force field. Perhaps terror held them in place. Perhaps, deprived of reason, they sought to make the nightmare vanish.

No matter. They had rejected his gift, and so must pay for their error. Doom punished them with more concussive blasts, and this time added sorcery to the attack. Crackling darkness, a squirming lightning, radiated from his person. It swept out and embraced the soldiers, squeezing body and mind with the physical touch of terror.

The gunfire faltered. More of the troops ran off, screaming, the terror sinking its claws even deeper as they careened down the halls and collided with reinforcements.

And now, finally, Doom heard the voice of his enemy. The Red Skull shrieked from hidden speakers, his tones sharp as hatred's whip. "*KILL HIM!*" the Skull commanded his dogs. "*HE GOES NO FURTHER! DESTROY HIM OR FACE EXECUTION! KILL HIM! KILL HIM! KILL HIM!*"

A shrill, maniacal howl of desperate anger. The Skull saw how close he was to losing his newest dream to Doom.

Look upon the end of your works, and despair.

The exhortations and threats had more troops rush forward to join the fray. That was all the Skull accomplished. Doom's force field strained no harder in deflecting the bullets and beams from these weapons either. The Skull could not deploy artillery in this space without risking damage to the power core beyond the door.

Doom fired another salvo of concussive blasts, clearing the

chamber for a moment, and turned to the vault door. He had the measure of his foes here now. They could not stop him.

One thought he could. Doom saw him charge from the corner of his eye. A big man, very strong. No doubt used to those around him bending to his will. Frustration and anger propelled him forward. He wielded a hammer, a huge thing, an echo of centuries past refashioned for modern war. He swung it at Doom's head.

Doom did not even glance his way, amused that the man believed that a physical blow would accomplish what guns had not.

The hammer slammed into the force field. The hammer's energy discharge flashed, and so did the field, its electrical blast hurling the man across the chamber where he fell, broken and burned.

Doom focused on the door. He had barely begun to analyze it when two energy beams, much more powerful than anything the troops' rifles could produce, struck him. The force field held, but only just, and the explosion triggered by the two opposing energies threw him against the door. He managed to keep his feet and spun around.

At the entrance to the tunnel opposite him, the troops had parted to make way for his assailant, an old man in a wheelchair. The gray-haired figure hunched forward, his long face haggard with age and bitterness. Swaddled in violet robes lined with white fur, he was a shrunken knot of hate. The chair resembled a crimson throne, and that was, Doom knew, how Franz Cadavus wished to see himself, as ruler of all who came within the range of the Murder Chair.

A growl of disgust and anger built in Doom's throat.

Cadavus, a man consumed by bitter resentment at a world that refused to obey his will, had taken part in the Red Skull's first attempt to conquer Latveria. Cadavus had had a taste of power, a taste of the tyrant's spoils, and the taste had come at Doom's expense.

Cadavus had hit him with a salvo of the chair's full strength. Doom had not been prepared before. Now he was, sending more energy to the force field's forward sector. He stepped away from the door, still dismissing the pathetic gunfire of the soldiers.

"So, the Skull has brought his old playmates," Doom said to Cadavus. "Have you all come? Are all the Exiles here? The full complement of squalling, fascist infants? Or just you?" He advanced toward the old man. "I extended you mercy once. Your lesson will be a harsh one this time."

Cadavus backed the chair away. Its engine rumbled and its wheels screeched. It was a machine designed to be heard, and in being heard, terrify. But now it retreated.

And Cadavus smiled. Doom reached the center of the hall, and the Exile said, "No. You are the one who will learn."

Doom realized his mistake the moment before the trap was sprung. Too late to correct his actions, he saw what had been done. The incessant gunfire and Cadavus's attack had all been a distraction, the constant storm of energy beams disguising the build-up of a greater power. In the moment that he became aware of the danger, the trap closed.

The hall vanished in a blaze of crimson light. Energy born from machines no human had created struck him and held him in place. His armor turned into a prison, a statue in which he was embedded. The continuous blast burned like the sun, and it consumed. It fed on the power sources of his armor. It fed on the force field. It drained him as its terrible heat reached in to burn him to ash. His armor's systems redlined, overloading and running dry at the same time. Red pain consumed him. His teeth clamped down on the howl of agony.

Fool!

He aimed the curse at himself and at the Red Skull. At himself for falling into this trap, and at the Skull for believing this would stop him.

He had known the Skull had access to this kind of power. He should have been ready for any use of it.

The paralysis of his armor held his limbs immobile, clamped by pain, but behind his mask, he made his lips move. The power that attacked him was ancient, infused with the cosmic, and had to be countered with something just as old. The sorcery he invoked could not, on its own, negate the power that tried to destroy him. But with the one resource in his armor that was still left to him...

While he could still think through the exploding waves of torture, he blended the sorcery with the armor's solar converter. He made the terrible heat of the attack his own. The more the energy tried to burn him, the more he stole of its essence. For long eternities of agony, he created a stalemate, his suffering and strength intensifying together. Then, when his armor began to glow red, and he was moments from burning alive, he unleashed the built-up power. He hit the Skull's energy with a counterblast forged from the same essence, fire fighting fire.

The crimson sun in the well went supernova. Doom shut his eyes against the blinding flare, and the crack of thunder staggered him.

The energies canceled each other out, and after a minute he could see again. The walls and ceiling of the space were scorched black. Chunks of stone had fallen to the floor, but the integrity of the chamber seemed untouched, the vast majority of the trap's strength directed inward. It had still been enough to cremate the Skull's troops who had been in the hall. They had not known their role in the trap had made them sacrifices. Cadavus had vanished, retreating from harm's way at the crucial moment.

Doom breathed heavily. He straightened, shaking off the lingering pain of the burn. His armor's systems stuttered, then reset, ready for the next attack.

If there were more soldiers on the way, there was no sound of their approach. The tunnels had fallen quiet. Doom could give the door his undivided attention.

There was no lock from this side, no numerical keypad, no visible means of entry of any kind. Doom imagined that the Red Skull controlled the door remotely. No one could enter the room without his explicit permission.

Doom glanced up. Did the Skull's cameras and microphones still work? Could he see what was about to happen? Doom hoped so. "A poor barrier," he said for the Skull's benefit. "Did you expect it to keep me out? If so, I'm insulted."

Advanced mechanics and electrical fields held the door closed. The simplest of sorceries commanded it to open. The door obeyed Doom's will. He stepped aside as it swung out with lumbering, silent grace.

Doom entered the power hall. The huge, high-ceilinged chamber hummed with imprisoned energy. Consoles ringed the periphery of the walls. Banks of screens showed the health and functioning of every sector of Wolkenland, along with its orientation, speed, and altitude. Others pulsed with the heavily filtered representation of the island's power core. A control throne sat on the peak of a black, dome-shaped rise in the center of the room.

The hall was deserted. Papers lay scattered on the floor beside overturned chairs. People had left in a hurry through the smaller door on the opposite side from Doom. They had fled his coming.

Very wise.

Outside the control room, the sirens still sounded, calling defenders to the stronghold that had already fallen. The Skull had done his worst to keep Doom out, and he had failed.

"To the conqueror, the spoils," Doom muttered. He had taken the heart of Wolkenland. Now, as he had promised, he would rip it out.

Doom walked up the rise to the throne. Two sets of controls waited at the ends of its armrests. Doom sat. He grasped the lever on the right. At his touch, the dome beneath him vibrated. Black metal became translucent. Above him, the upper half of the chamber's dome pulled back, revealing the lower portion of an immense, inhuman machine, a thing of fused monoliths, pulsating geometric lines, and a dense, dark material Doom was sure had not originated on Earth.

The control room hummed like a somnolent volcano, awaiting his commands. Wolkenland was his to do with as he pleased.

A touch screen embedded in the left-hand arm rest invited Doom's touch. He tapped it.

Adamantine shackles snapped tight around his arms

and chest. A beam lashed down from the great machine, transfixing him with pure, cosmic agony as the real trap of the Red Skull seized him.

ELEVEN

Pain consumed Doom's being. Body, mind, and soul disappeared into the infinite explosion of perfect, eternal suffering. He could not think. He had no conception of the self, no consciousness except of the cancerous sublimity of pain.

Only one other perception crept through, a stabbing, fragmentary one, a sense of speeding, perpetual multiplicity. No understanding accompanied the perception, because understanding did not exist in the realm of pain. The perception broke through because it was itself a piece of the greater agony.

Doom came to realize that later, when he could think again, and when the suffering took on a more refined, targeted form.

Before that happened, the pain eased, jaws parting in preparation to bite down again, even harder. The sense of multiplicity withdrew. He could think again, and see again, and understand what had happened to him.

The throne had vanished, and the shackles that held him

were different, clasping his hands together and suspending him over the open rise where the throne had been. Fierce power ran through him, conducted back and forth between the machine above and the coruscating mass of energy below. Though his body twitched and spasmed as if jolted every few moments by lightning, he had no control over his limbs.

The Red Skull stood at the base of the rise, tapping at the screen of a handheld control unit. He looked up at Doom, cocking his head as if trying to divine his prisoner's thoughts.

"Are you with me?" he asked.

Doom tried to curse the wretch. He could not form words. He managed the threatening growl of a wounded animal.

The Skull nodded, pleased. "Good," he said. "That's quite enough. I can't have you casting any spells. I just want to make certain that you can hear me."

Doom growled again. Even if he could have spoken, the words did not exist to express his hatred for the wretch below him.

The lips of the Skull's mask parted, revealing teeth. The man was grinning.

"I should kill you," said the Skull. "There is nothing to stop me." He held up the control. "All I have to do is increase the strength of the Power Cosmic that holds you until it disintegrates you. As simple as that. Some of the Exiles think that is exactly what I should do. Part of me agrees with them." He leaned forward, his voice growing rougher with anger. "But your punishment matters. That is why I had this island built. I want you to know that I am your superior. I want you to know what happens because of your failure. *That* is how you must pay for your crimes against my person." Calming down, the Skull began to pace slowly back and forth, his tone becoming contemplative. "Keeping you alive so you can be punished is worth the risk, I think, especially since the risk is minimal. There is no escaping this prison. You must know that."

Doom did. The energy held him at the physical, mental, and mystical levels. But as long as the Skull kept talking, kept indulging in his ranting need for an audience, that gave Doom more moments to gather his thoughts, and try to find a way out. He must not care what the Skull said. He had heard it all before. The Skull had nothing to say, but had entire volumes worth of the nothing to express.

But the clichés coursed with venom, and Doom could not block it from his hearing.

"The risk," the Skull continued, "came before this moment. There was the chance you would perceive the trap, and that you would avoid it." The Skull stopped pacing. He grinned at Doom again. "But you did not, and the reason you did not is that I *am* your superior, your master. Your blood is tainted. Mine is pure."

Doom snarled, hate shaking him like the blasts of the Power Cosmic.

The Skull laughed. "I'm going to tell you how I caught you. I have earned that, and this will be part of your punishment. You will have all the time in the world to ponder it. Oh yes." He tapped the control unit. "I have recalibrated the settings. When I send you back to Hell, you will be fully conscious and able to appreciate the finer details of your sentence." He paused to let his words sink in. "So, this is how I trapped you. I lured you in with the truth. I really did try to stop you from reaching this chamber. If the struggle were not real, you would have known. You are subhuman, but you are dangerous, and I have learned my lessons on that front. My soldiers tried to kill you, and their sacrifice will be remembered." He spread his arms to take in the chamber. "And this, this truly is Wolkenland's control center. You would have recognized a decoy. You faced nothing but the truth, Doom, and so you failed to spot the single lie – the throne."

Doom's rage turned back on himself. His arrogance had veiled the lie. He had believed too strongly in his triumph. He had betrayed himself, as he had so many times before.

The Red Skull paused again. Deep in the sockets of the mask, his eyes glittered with pleasure. "Do you know which part of the trap I am most proud of? Let me tell you its name. Valeria."

No! No, no, NO! He would not permit the Skull the triumph of that trap. He would not allow the Skull to defeat him through the vulnerability of his emotions. He would not permit the new torture of Valeria's death.

Doom howled in anger, and his wrath jerked his body forward, the movement so sharp that it made the Skull take a startled step back. He fumbled with the controls, then lowered the unit, regaining his composure when he saw that Doom could not break free. When he spoke again, his voice shook slightly, first with adrenaline, then with the rage of wounded pride.

Doom took no satisfaction from the petty victory. There was no comfort there, not when he heard what the Skull said next.

"You had to believe in Valeria, and so she had to believe

in what was happening. She had to believe that she chose to come to Wolkenland. That was a subtle game, and very well-played, to see that she heard enough, from one source or another, to want to see for herself. And when we had her, when she began her term in the mines, a term that would not end until her death, she had to believe in her escape attempt. That required explosive charges to be laid in precisely the right way to create the impression of a chance split in the ground, a split that required further engineering to be something that she could, with some effort, climb. There had to be challenge to her escape. Enough for her to believe she acted according to her will, and not mine." The Skull shrugged. "She knows better now, of course. That is part of her punishment. Perhaps you find solace in the thought that her suffering parallels yours in this way?" The question had the sound of an arched eyebrow. "No? I didn't think so."

The Red Skull played with the controls, and cascading waves of agony swept through Doom's being. His sense of self began to slip away again, but then the Skull brought him back.

"Just another foretaste for you, and some practice for me," said the Skull. "Fear not. I will find the right balance. You will remain conscious. You will have a full understanding of what you experience. But there are some things you might not see, except when I choose to bring you out to your current state. So I will tell you now what is going to happen to Latveria. I am going to break it and its people. Now that you are here, the campaign of terror can truly begin. It will never end, even and especially when Latveria is mine, because perpetual terror is the proper state of being for the people." He pronounced the word *people* as if the taste were foul.

"You will witness their plight from time to time, when it suits me, but now it is time to send you back to your punishment. It was not the work of a day to harness the Power Cosmic to achieve this particular end. I want you to appreciate what I have opened up for you, Doom. You will behold the infinite realities of the Multiverse. The infinite realities of your failures."

Doom gasped, the Skull's words conjuring a dagger of memory that stabbed him in the heart. Hell laughed as it granted him a poisoned gift.

He saw himself in the grasp of the Harrower, the device he had created to scrape the depths of Hell and free the soul of his mother, and that had become a demon-fueled being in its own right. At the height of his struggle with the unleashed Harrower, he had seen and learned something, but in the wake of the Harrower's destruction, he had lost the memories of what he had seen. The only trace that remained was the knowledge of their absence, and the sense that the immensity of what he had learned had bordered on omniscience.

Now a sliver, a dagger returned. He had seen failure and defeat, and now would again.

Hell laughed, and laughed, and laughed, and so did the Red Skull at Doom's involuntary gasp.

Then Doom's personal Hell engulfed him.

He plunged into the ocean of pain and visions. Before, the vistas of the Multiverse had gone by too quickly for him to know what they were. Now the Red Skull had, as he had promised, found the balance of the controls, and Doom witnessed, experienced, *lived* the cataract of humiliations and tragedy. All the futures of horror, from all the extant and possible universes, and all the selves that were or might be fell on him, hammered him, seized him, and tore him.

Doom lived the downfalls, and he observed them from a distance at the same time, the wracking agony of his body keeping him anchored into the reality of *this* universe even as all his other selves burned.

Over and over, so often its repetition had to be a joke that was also a foundational condition for the existence of all things, he achieved ultimate, absolute power and the means to accomplish all his goals, only for his own errors and misjudgments to snatch everything away. Again and again, Latveria collapsed in ruin. Again and again, he authored the destruction of his country.

And Valeria…

Her voice had called him here, and now he witnessed her infinite deaths. In some he had no role to play. In too many, he did. And there was one in particular, one special Hell that took him by the throat.

In that universe, she died by his hands. He sought her out in America, won her forgiveness, and then sacrificed her to dark powers: a new, more sorcerous armor from her being encasing him. He killed her, and then *wore her*.

His body could not scream, but his soul did.

The gods of torture, or whatever mechanism shaped his suffering, recognized the sublimity of that universe's horror, and made him relive the crime and its ultimate futility, carried him through more panoramas of ruin, and then again, and again, looped through the murder of Valeria.

Betrayal and atrocity and loss, committed and witnessed eternally.

Doom raged against his prison. It held him fast. He could not move or look away. The pain of the energy coursing through him shattered his concentration. His only focus possible was the howling need to escape.

He bore down on that need with all his will. He had defied Hell with his will. Even here, in the inferno of failure and horror, his will shaped universes. Now his will commanded escape.

Escape.

Nothing else mattered, because everything that mattered depended on that one thing.

Escape at any cost.

Escape.

Escape.

The Red Skull stumbled back from Doom's prison, dazzled and startled by the sudden, roaring flare of energy. His skin prickled in pure terror, and he raised his hands to ward off the vengeful Doom.

Except Doom remained there, his form just visible in the maelstrom pillar of Power Cosmic.

The Skull started breathing again, but his heart still pounded a heavy beat in his ears. He squinted at the jerking, twisting shape of Doom. Was he really there? Could that be an illusion? Was the armor empty?

Or was that what Doom wanted him to think? Get him to shut off the prison to make sure, and then… Oh yes, he could easily see Doom trying such a gambit.

"There are other ways for me to ensure you are still there," the Skull said. He did not expect or want an answer, and was relieved when none came. He tweaked the settings of the torture and was rewarded by an agonized spasm within the pillar. Good. He consulted the readings on the control unit's screen. They showed the Power Cosmic holding a sorcerous essence in check.

He sighed in relief. That was the most important of the shackles. It held, and Doom was still there, trapped where he would be until the Red Skull tired of the game and killed him.

"No freedom for you," the Skull said, glaring at Doom. "Never again."

The Skull left the center. He could gloat again later, when he really was calm again. He had other demands on his time.

He had a nation to bring to heel.

On a barren hillside, Doom woke, a cold wind breathing against his exposed face.

PART II

O cruel! O destroyer! O consumer! O avenger!
WILLIAM BLAKE, "TIRIEL" 6.23

TWELVE

Unless she needed it for specific reasons, Orloff didn't wear her watch when she worked. Down here in the lab, in the subbasements of Castle Doom, there was no sense of the passage of time. Light was constant, focus eternal.

Orloff had begun the current round of tests before Doom had left the castle. At some point, he had gone, and when she walked away from the corpses to stretch her legs and her back after a long period hunched over the screens she had attached to the obelisk and the bodies, she could tell from her physical fatigue that hours had gone by. Realizing that renewed her sense of urgency. If Doom had taken control of Wolkenland, and the danger had passed, she would have been told. She had heard nothing, so the threat remained, and the more that time passed and Doom did not return, the greater the threat became, and the more crucial her role would be.

She needed a breakthrough.

Orloff returned to the bodies. Eight of them now surrounded the obelisk on slabs, connected by so many cables they looked like she was preparing to reanimate them. Instead, she was searching for their cause of death. She knew a signal had been sent. She knew it had triggered some kind of implant. But she had been unable to go any further in identifying the nature of the implant.

"You're going to make me do this, aren't you?" she said to the corpses.

"Doctor?" one of her assistants, Hildegard Fenner, asked. There were four of them, tallying results of the latest scans. They worked quietly at the periphery of the lab, giving her all the quiet and space she needed, ready to help with anything she required.

Orloff smiled at the young woman. "Don't mind me. Just speaking to the dead again." Her assistants were used to that habit by now.

Fenner smiled and nodded, and the dark circles around her eyes registered. Orloff cursed herself. Driving her assistants to exhaustion wouldn't help anyone.

"I have no idea what time it is," she said, "and that no doubt means it's hell o'clock. All of you go get some sleep."

"You should, too, Doctor Orloff," said Fenner.

"I will shortly," she promised, and got knowing looks in return. Everyone knew her definition of "shortly" was very flexible. She didn't insult their intelligence by adding, "Just one more thing I want to try." Instead, she merely smiled at them as they filed out.

She would get some rest, yes, but not yet. The sense of urgency gave her new energy.

When she was alone, she turned to her helmet. She had held off doing what she knew faced her now because she had

no way to judge the risk versus benefit. She had no evidence
the experiment would bear fruit. She only knew she had run
out of other avenues to explore. The time had come for a stab
in the dark. And because it *would* be a stab, it was better that
she attempted this alone. With the helmet on, she was lethal to
the undead. The gambit she had in mind might make her just
as dangerous to the living.

She connected the helmet to the obelisk and began to work
on its settings.

"Is this what you wanted?" she muttered to the corpses.
"You think you're going to like what happens if I can see on an
even wider spectrum than before? I'm doubtful. I think this
might make your boss really unhappy."

Until now, the helmet had shown her the undead and all
their realities. She could see them at a great distance, walls
and other obstacles fading to nothing unless she concentrated
on perceiving the material world, reduced to a shimmering
gray. She could see through the veil of life, to the winds and
currents of the limbo beyond. The essence that she now had
to reverse was seeing the thing in the undead that held them
back from true death. Now she wanted to turn her perception
around. She had to see the death drive in the living.

She finished the adjustments. She looked at the bronze
helmet, and the dark, unbreakable glass of its visor. It seemed
to stare back at her with cold, unreadable judgment. This
was how the undead saw her in the moment before their
destruction. If she succeeded in becoming the new kind of
hunter that Doom required, it would be some of the living
who would see this bronze blankness coming at them.

When she thought about what those people had done

already, and what they planned to do, she found that the idea of their terror did not displease her.

"Hardly bedside manner," she told herself.

No. It wasn't. And she wasn't the same person who had practiced neurosurgery at Doomstadt Hospital. Her work for Doom had changed her. The struggle against the Devourer and the urvullak had changed her. This new war would change her even more.

All necessary.

She thought about Kariana. "I love you," she said. "I'll keep you safe."

She donned the helmet and turned it on.

She screamed.

At dawn, Verlak forced herself to step down from her post in the security center. She had seen the night through, keeping watch over Latveria while its monarch fought the invisible enemy. She had spent the hours hoping to see Wolkenland appear on the screens, its shields torn away, and hoping for any communication, however brief, from Doom. But Wolkenland remained hidden, and Doom sent no word. The silence gnawed at her, and when the night ended, she knew she had to rest, or she would be no use to anyone, and she would fail in her duties.

She turned the watch over to Lieutenant Knef, and left the security center, not sure how she would sleep with the growing dread that filled her chest and dried her throat.

She headed down to Elsa's lab. She would have been working through the night, too, and would need to be made to rest. Verlak counted on the concern each had for the other, forcing both of them to agree to take a few hours before jumping back into the fray. And maybe Elsa had made some progress. Maybe there was some good news.

The laboratory door was closed. Verlak pushed the call button next to it. No answer. She pushed again, longer.

Come on, Elsa, look up from whatever it is you're doing.

Still no response.

Worried now, Verlak swiped her master-key pass in front of the door's sensor. The door slid open.

Bronze helmet on her head, Elsa lay motionless on the floor next to the corpse slabs.

"Ellie!"

Verlak ran inside, heart frozen in fear. She crouched over her wife, checked that she was still breathing, and then ran her hands over the helmet. It hummed with power. Verlak found the controls on the right side and pushed the button Elsa had told her about.

So you know what to do. Just in case.

The faint vibration ceased. Verlak pulled the helmet off. Elsa's features were frozen in a shriek, her eyes wide and glazed and unseeing.

"Ellie," Verlak called to her again. She cupped Elsa's face between her hands. "Oh, Ellie, it's OK, it's OK, I'm here, I'm here, you're safe."

Elsa's eyelids fluttered, the wings of a moth. Her eyes cleared. Her chest heaved with a huge, racking gasp, and then she sat up sudden as a jack-in-the-box. She stared at Verlak for a moment, and then threw her arms around her. She buried her face against Verlak's neck. Tremors shook her frame.

"Shh," said Verlak softly. "Shh. All done now. All done."

She felt Elsa begin to relax, and now she could breathe more easily, too.

When Elsa finally broke the embrace, she put on an approximation of a wry smile, though she was still pale as a shroud. "Sorry," she said. "Did I worry you?"

Verlak gave her a love punch to the shoulder. "You know damn well you did!" Then she kissed Elsa with the fervor of relief.

"What happened?" she asked, helping Elsa to her feet.

Elsa placed the helmet carefully on a worktable. "I changed what I see," she said.

"Did it work?"

"Too well." Elsa took a shuddering breath. "I saw the mortality in everyone, Kari. For miles around. Death, everywhere, the death that means all hopes and dreams and love will end. Like they don't matter."

"But they do." Verlak took her hand and squeezed. She wanted Elsa to know all the important meaning of that touch. *Can you feel this, Ellie? We're alive, and we're together.*

Elsa squeezed back. "I know they matter. I know. But when I was wearing the helmet, and seeing… seeing the world that way, I *didn't* know. Humans like mayflies. That's all I could see." She shook her head. She freed her hand and picked up the helmet. "I have to fix this. I have to rework the vision again."

Verlak took the helmet from her and placed it back on the table. "Yes," she said, "but not now. You need sleep. I need sleep. Latveria needs us to be capable of functioning."

For a moment she thought Elsa was going to object. But then she nodded, grateful, and her smile was stronger, more genuine this time.

They left the laboratory and made their way back up to the castle's ground level. They walked out of the main entrance into the morning light.

And to a chorus of the insistent beat of multiple explosions, and the distant *pop-pop-pop* of gunfire.

Doom lay on his stomach, his left cheek pressed against stone. He tried to move his right hand. It refused his command. His body felt like disconnected lead weights. Several minutes passed before he finally managed to bring his hand to his face, and touch the ruined flesh, and in that gesture, mark the absence of his mask and armor.

He groaned. He had never felt so weak, so incomplete. He had cast himself out of the Red Skull's trap, folding the most minute portion of space and time for the smallest fragment of an instant. When the fold had straightened, he had been split in two. His body and his mind were here. His mystical essence remained inside his armor. Its loss ached like a phantom limb.

All his sorcery, and all his technology, left behind. He was nothing now but will and flesh. And the flesh was weak.

He wanted to stand. He might as well have wanted to lift up the hill on which he lay.

He could not move. How could he fight the Skull if he could not even stand?

He shuddered, not from the cold of the wind, but from the cold of the past as it reached out for him. The despised memories of who he had been, the weakling Victor before the all-powerful Doom, became fresh and real. He was again as he had been, all those years ago, the youth helpless to fight King Vladimir, a mere victim, just as all his people were victims then. He remembered the impotent hate, the constant fear, the ever-present need to hide.

No. He refused to be that vulnerable again.

Except he was. Drained of all strength, motionless as if chained to the hillside. When would the eagle come to feast on his liver?

As if in answer, he heard bootsteps approaching from behind. He waited, unable to turn his head, raging at his weakness.

Bootsteps, another echo from the past, the sound that meant *Hide! Hide! Don't let Vladimir's guards find you!*

The boots stopped near Doom's head. A pebble, disturbed by the footsteps, rolled against the back of his neck.

"Another one?" said a rough male voice. Doom pegged the speaker as middle-aged. "How do they keep getting out?"

"I heard some rumors about that other one." Another male voice, younger than the first. "Heard she was supposed to get out."

They spoke English. The older voice was American. The other accent was different. Dutch, Doom thought.

"Trust the plan," said the older man. "Trust the plan."

"What about this one? Have you heard anything about him? I haven't."

"No. Maybe he got out after the woman, before the crack got sealed. He doesn't look like part of any plan, does he?"

"And where are his clothes?" said the younger man.

"Do I look like I took them? Don't know, don't care. He's not going anywhere. That's what matters."

A boot jabbed Doom in the side. "You're awake," said the older guard. "I know you are. Get up."

Doom's breath turned into a low growl of anger.

"He's not obeying, Jerry."

"Make him face us, Pieter."

The younger guard grabbed Doom's arm, and with a violent yank, turned him onto his back. The guards recoiled at the sight of Doom's face. He glared at them, the spineless cowards covering their mouths in horror, their eyes wide, and helpless as he was, for that moment he had the upper hand.

Jerry, the American, recovered enough to speak first. "Cover his face," he ordered the other guard.

"With *what?*" Pieter demanded, averting his gaze.

"Your shirt."

"My what?"

"Take it off. Wrap it around his face. I'm not staring at that all the way back to the mines."

"Why my shirt? You don't outrank me. Use yours."

"Who said anything about rank?" Jerry turned on his partner and grabbed his arm. He was taller and heavier than Pieter. He had the look of a man who, until he answered the Red Skull's call, made a habit of going to bars with the goal of breaking as many faces as possible. Pieter, leaner, looked more fit, but also inexperienced. He was the sort who found his outlets for violence from within the safety of numbers.

Jerry punched him twice, meaty fist slamming into Pieter's stomach and jaw. Pieter tried to twist out of Jerry's grip but made no effort to fight back. All he wanted to do was run. Jerry hit him again, and Pieter sank to his knees. He fumbled with the buttons on his black jacket, and then with the black shirt underneath. Jerry tore it from him before he fully had his arms out of the sleeves.

Doom watched their struggle with a contempt so pure it sent heat through his limbs. He still couldn't stand, but his body was beginning to feel like a unified whole again.

Jerry tore the shirt, then turned back to Doom. He tossed it onto Doom's chest. "Cover your face, scum," he said.

Doom grunted. He managed to move his hands, but only a few inches.

"I think he really can't move," Pieter croaked, on his knees and gasping for air.

Jerry snorted, disgusted. He grabbed the shirt again, tore it into long strips, then pulled Doom's head up by his hair and wrapped the rags around his face beneath his eyes. When he let go, Doom's head fell back hard against stone.

"That true, then?" said Jerry. "You really can't move?"

Doom gazed at the guard as he would a pinned insect.

Jerry snorted again. "Give me a hand with him," he said to Pieter.

The other guard obeyed. They hoisted Doom up until they had his arms wrapped around their shoulders. They started down the hill, his feet dragging.

"This is going to take forever," Pieter grumbled.

"You want to leave him?" Jerry asked. "Have a report sent to the Skull that we found an escaped prisoner and just ignored him?"

Pieter didn't answer.

Now that he was vertical, Doom could see more of the landscape. He was in a waste of debris that nestled against gray, rocky hills. Downslope, and a mile or two across the valley, mining structures built of iron rose from the rubble.

Bit by bit, strength returned to his body, and by the time the guards had brought him to the valley floor, he could walk on his own again. The guards encouraged him to with kicks and insults.

At the entrance to the mine, prisoners in chains hauled cars out on rails, emptied them of their cargo of rock, and then dragged them back down into the mouth of darkness. Guards lounged outside a large, corrugated metal shack, watching the work. Others, on shift, walked back and forth along the lines of struggling slaves, striking shins and backs with flexible batons as the spirit moved them. The shack's back wall was flush with the hillside of the mine. A watchtower of iron girding stood fifty yards out from the shack. In its wooden superstructure, a guard armed with a long-barreled rifle watched the prisoners. He seemed as bored as the rest. He had the rifle propped up beside him, and lazy smoke rose from his cigarette.

"Found us a stray," Jerry said as they drew near. He gave Doom a hard kick that would have knocked him down a few minutes earlier. Stronger now, he remained standing.

"What's the mask about?" a guard asked.

"You don't want to know," said Jerry. "Subhuman stuff. Revolting."

Pieter went into the shack and emerged a moment later with the gray tunic and trousers that made up the prisoners' uniform. Doom put them on in silence, picturing how best the guards would pay for their crimes.

"You don't suppose there are others out there?" said another guard. He sounded worried at the prospect of their security being found lax.

"Not a sign," said Jerry. "Figure this one somehow got lucky the other night. No one else is getting out that way."

"Hope you're right."

"Let's get him chained and put to work," said Jerry.

A few minutes later, they had Doom shackled, joined to other prisoners pulling a mining cart.

"There you go," said Pieter. "Back where you belong." He gave Doom another kick, still trying to regain the dignity he had lost when Jerry had taken his shirt.

Doom gave the two guards who had found him long, cold looks.

"What?" said Jerry. "You have something to say?"

"Yes," said Doom. He could speak again, his voice rough as broken glass, his throat a desert of pain. "I want to promise you something. Both of you."

"Is that right?" Jerry smirked, but his eyes narrowed with a hint of uncertainty.

"I will repay your kindness," said Doom. "I will see that you are among the first to die."

And though he was in chains, and unarmed, they took a step back, color draining from their cheeks.

THIRTEEN

Adrenaline and rage burned away Verlak's fatigue. She vibrated with the impulse to storm down the castle's moat bridge, gun drawn, transformed into a fury of wind and fire, to destroy the cowards who struck at her country.

But she was human. Anger could not transform her. She was not the wind.

She was not Doom.

She turned to Elsa in agony, about to do the very thing she had dragged her wife away from. No rest, no recovery, straight back into the fray.

Elsa understood. Verlak saw it in her eyes before she spoke. She understood because she was Elsa, and she always did.

Elsa held Verlak by the shoulders. "Go," she said. "Latveria needs you right now, not later."

Verlak glanced toward the castle gate. Beyond it, in the region of Old Town, a column of smoke and dust rose.

Elsa squeezed Verlak's shoulders. "Don't worry," she said. "I'll be safe. I'm not going home."

Verlak gave her wife a sharp look. "Where will you be?"

"In the lab."

"But…"

Elsa touched a finger to her lips, shushing Verlak. "I'll be good. Boris installed a cot for me, so I'm going to use it. Cross my heart. I'm going to rest, and then I'm going to find the solution to tracking these fascist scum."

"You promise?"

"Both things. On my honor."

Verlak smiled, holding on to a shared moment of levity that would warm her in the struggle to come. "On your honor, my lady?" she said.

Elsa grinned back. "On my honor. Now go, brave knight, and smite our foe."

They kissed, and went back into the castle, and parted at the door to the security center. The brief interlude with Elsa had been enough for Verlak to channel her energy away from a pointless charge, and into learning everything that she needed to know.

The center hummed with tension when she entered, but also with the low murmur of disciplined activity. Her guards were as focused on a battlefield of keyboards and readouts and screens as they would be in physical combat.

It took less than a minute for Verlak to get up to speed, and to see the extent of the latest attack. The enemy had come in much greater numbers. As with the last time, the Red Skull's soldiers attacked on multiple fronts, seeking to spread as much chaos and fear as widely as possible. They came not to seize and hold territory, not yet. They came to destabilize, to break down the fabric of Latveria, to shatter its social order.

The Skull wanted Verlak's forces spread thin, attempting to

put out dozens of fires, and to be demoralized by the sense of being unable to make any measurable progress against a foe that could strike anywhere, at any time.

Verlak scanned the illuminated map of Latveria, its face covered with pulsing lights like so many lesions, each glow another attack. She looked at the screens. Surveillance cameras fed the carnage on livestreams to the security center. Here, now, Verlak was everywhere at once. In the field, she could not be. She had to pick her battle, and delegate the rest.

Once she saw everything, the choice was clear. The largest enemy force was advancing down the Avenue of the Scholars toward the Werner Academy. Bombs had already gone off outside the institute's main gates, no doubt planted by an advance team. The gates had fallen, and the courtyard outside the academy's main entrance lay open. It was not, though, undefended. Security forces had taken up positions at the mouth of the courtyard and at the doors. They could not fend off what was heading their way. The enemy had heavy armor this time, transports and tanks that carved a path of carnage down the avenue.

Wounding her city. Killing her people.

And attacking in force.

This isn't just an attack. This is an invasion.

"The tanks came from outside Doomstadt," said one of the surveillance officers. "They landed in a region we don't have eyes on, at least not constantly. The larger enemy formations are all emerging from the countryside."

That made sense, and it was also a small mercy. If the Red Skull had been able to drop major formations into the Doomstadt without warning, then war would be over quickly.

Things were already bad enough. Where was Doom? Why hadn't he been able to stop this? What had gone wrong?

She couldn't let those questions matter. Doom had put the protection of Latveria in her hands. She had her orders, and she saw the shape of her task ahead.

She issued orders of her own, mobilizing troops to twenty different conflict zones. She would lead the biggest detachment to the Avenue of the Scholars.

The Werner Academy was a target of massive symbolic importance. The Skull had set his sights on one of the great centers of Latverian learning, one named for Doom's father. Verlak envisioned what the Skull intended. She saw the academy in ruins, its libraries in flames. She saw humiliation, fear and despair rippling out from the epicenter of that loss.

She saw what she would give her life to prevent.

Verlak let them have the Avenue of the Scholars. She let them have their revolting revel. She let them because she had to. She even had to let them pound the homes and shops that lined the avenue with shells, and rake the windows with machine-gun fire. Two of the tanks, one at the head of the column and one at the rear, fired energy beams instead of shells, and the blasts cut through walls like a scythe through flesh.

The weapons, Verlak thought, as she crouched in an alley a block from the Avenue of the Scholars, were meant to terrify even more than they were meant to destroy. Beams and shells and bullets, a cornucopia of death to haunt the waking nightmares of Latverians. The citizens of Doomstadt knew how to respond to nightmares at least. The civilians had fled the region. Most would be making for the castle, the most secure refuge in all of Latveria. Others would be in the underground shelters Doom had had constructed throughout the city. Latveria had too many enemies for it to forgo that precaution.

And Latveria knew how to fight back. Already, those refugees in the castle able to fight would be being armed. They would not stay at the castle. When the time came, they would join in the struggle.

The tanks and armored cars were more specters from bad dreams. They had no wheels or treads. They floated a few feet off the ground, propelled by silent energy fields. The Red Skull was showing off the technology at his disposal, boasting of his means.

He thinks we're all peasants, helpless without Doom.

Latveria's greatest technology might reside with Doom, and him alone. But the country was not defenseless without him. In the wake of the Skull's brief reign, Doom had made sure no one could walk over Latveria like that again in his absence. The guard that Verlak commanded was proof of that.

Strut and puff your pride. I'm going to show you what Latverians can do.

The enemy column's full length was engaged on the Avenue of the Scholars. Rubble smoldered along the entire length of the road. Guns roared, shells burst, beams sizzled and flashed. The front of the column was less than half a mile from the Werner Academy.

"Now," Verlak radioed her forces.

She had stationed them in side streets and alleys on both sides of the avenue, staggered so they were not facing each other directly, all a block off from the enemy, sheltered from the worst of the mayhem unleashed by the Skull's fascists. The guard surged forward at her command. At the same time, one of the Doombots assigned to the guard streaked up from behind the academy and came down, concussive blasts striking the lead tank.

Infantry charged over and between ruins, beam rifles strafing the flanks of the column, taking out soldiers on foot and those foolish enough to ride in the hatches of the vehicles.

Two tanks made up the heavy armor of Verlak's contingent. They went at the forward and rear thirds of the column. They, too, rode the magnetic fields, and hovered up and over the destroyed buildings, the obstacles irrelevant.

Verlak and nine other guards piloted ground interceptors. Lightly armored, their advantages were speed and agility, and their guns still packed a punch. They were sleek, night-black, with raptor noses and smooth, stubby wings and fins. Designed to fly a standard ten feet off the ground, soaring over any traffic, they could also shoot higher for short distances.

Verlak punched the interceptor's vertical thrust and took the vehicle twenty feet into the air. So did the other pilots.

The guard attacked the enemy from above, from the side, and from either end. No doubt the Red Skull had warned his underlings of the existence of Doombots, but knowing about them and processing the apparent presence of Doom were two different things. The Doombot's attack shattered the tank's turret, and then blew up its power plant before the crew of the one behind recovered from the shock of its arrival to fire back. And though they did manage to score a direct hit and destroy the Doombot, by then a second one was attacking the rear of the column.

Verlak cut back and forth across the column, holding the triggers down for sustained bursts from the particle beam guns. Return fire sought her out, and a few shots scored the armor. One hit the interceptor hard enough to jolt the controls from her hands for a moment, but she recovered quickly and took the interceptor down behind a heap of rubble before turning around and coming at the column a second time.

The enemy's formation disintegrated. The discipline of the Skull's forces was fiction, a tissue created by the hate that bound them to their master. They had training, in that they knew how to use their weapons, but they had no experience, and they did not have the training of the guard. The Skull's troops outnumbered the guard two-to-one. Verlak routed them in a matter of minutes. They did not advance another yard closer to the Werner Academy.

And when the outcome of the battle was clear, and the guard closed in to start taking the first prisoners, the enemy soldiers died, all at once, fallen puppets.

In the aftermath, Verlak walked among the bodies, cursing under her breath.

"Why do they always die?" asked Joachim Arendt, one of the sergeants flanking her. "Why is that necessary? Just so they can say nothing?"

"Not just that," said Verlak. She stopped beside a gutted tank. "It could be punishment for failure. It definitely makes rebellion impossible. I think it's a message to us, too. The Red Skull is telling us that he has so many troops, he can throw them away. He can kill them himself." His willingness to engage in such casual slaughter of his troops repulsed her, and it worried her. *He's telling us our victories mean nothing,* she thought, but did not say. She could not express such an idea in front of her troops, even to dismiss it.

The trouble was, she couldn't dismiss it. She feared the Red Skull was right. If he could throw soldiers away like this, then he could set a thousand fires of war across Latveria, too many for the guard to extinguish them all. At length, the flash burns would create the great conflagration, and Latveria would fall.

Stop it. Stop being defeatist. She couldn't afford to think in such terms.

Where is Doom?

No way not to ask herself the question over and over. And she could not hold off the fatal truth that lurked behind it. If Doom did not return, all was lost. If the Red Skull could defeat Doom, then nothing Verlak did mattered.

He will return. He must.

"I'm going back to the castle," Verlak told Arendt. "Stand by for new deployment instructions. Our work today is not finished."

When she returned to the security center, Verlak saw her darkest expectations fulfilled. New attacks were occurring all the time. Wolkenland rained paratroopers over Latveria, their descent hidden by the island's shielding until they were well on their way to the ground.

Too many assaults, too little warning.

Verlak blocked her fears with the need to plan and fight.

Latveria's days and nights of struggle had begun.

Slavery made days meaningless. Time became an eternal present of suffering with too little variation to mark one period from another. The only distinction was between work and sleep, and Doom realized quickly that he could not look for any regularity there. The shifts varied in length. They were always long, always driving the prisoners to exhaustion and beyond, but an extra layer of misery came from never knowing when a shift might end, even if there were some means of telling time, and never knowing how short the rest period might be.

For what, he later estimated, must have been the first few days, Doom had little awareness of anything or anyone more than a few feet away. The outside world existed only as a violent prompt to the movement of his body. Even the pickaxe he wielded and the carts he pushed barely registered on his consciousness. He was locked inside his head, struggling with the emptiness inside, the terrible hollowness that came from losing half his being. He wrestled with the void in silence, saying nothing either to guards or fellow prisoners, trapped in another prison of weakness and the need to survive moment by moment.

Slowly, Doom's physical strength returned, and with it more awareness of his surroundings. It became easier to think as he no longer had to commit all his will just to keep going. With coherent thought came the rage. The urge to strike out at every guard he saw burned in his chest. His knuckles whitened as he gripped tools and cart handles, and he ground his teeth in the effort to keep himself from lashing out. He was still too weak. The act would be futile.

But he did grow stronger. He had lost nothing of his physical self. The weakness was temporary, the result of the colossal expenditure of energy that had split him and freed him from the Red Skull's trap. Each shift became easier, at least at the level of sheer physical effort. The emotional cost grew the more he saw, and the more he was able to study and analyze his surroundings, and the nature of what was being done to him and to the other prisoners.

He finally broke his silence while pushing a loaded cart through the mine's viewing gallery. The track ran through a large cavern with elevated, tiered seating on either side. What looked like bulletproof glass shielded spectators from unwelcome smells and any stones a foolish slave might decide to throw. Doom's assigned labors took him through the gallery at least twice a day. The seats were never full, but there were always at least a dozen or so of Wolkenland's citizenry there to watch.

In order to move the carts, the guards had prisoners shackled in pairs to the rear to push, and in groups of four or more to pull. The carts were just large enough to make hauling their full load a task that strained human limits. The slaves chained to the same cart as Doom, though, had things a little easier. He was now able to do the lion's share of the effort.

On this passage through the gallery, Doom was at the rear of the cart. As the wheels ground and squealed against the track, the man beside Doom looked up at the spectators. He stared at them through his long, stringy hair, his sunken, tired eyes flaring with an ember of anger.

"Why do they come here?" he murmured. "Why does this place exist?"

"Cruelty," Doom said, his voice rasping from disuse.

The man looked startled to hear Doom speak.

"Cruelty," Doom repeated. "Cruelty is the point." He looked at the audience himself, and saw, as he expected, the same face in every person there, regardless of individual features. The face of eager, self-satisfied pleasure, and a hunger that could never be sated. "Everything about these mines is in the service of cruelty. Why else would we dig pointless tunnels and gather worthless stone? It's all spectacle for the benefit of the Red Skull, his lackeys, and his clients."

"I wonder why there isn't a bigger audience," said the man.

Doom grunted. "It may grow in time. I think it will." *Given the chance I will not grant it.* "Not all the masters of Wolkenland believe themselves to be cruel. Not yet." He pushed harder against the cart, as if that would get them through the gallery faster. But the cave was huge, several hundred yards long. It took the carts minutes to cross the space. Plenty of time for the spectators to gawk and gloat.

"Some no doubt exist in a profound state of willful ignorance," Doom continued. "Perhaps some truly do not know what happens to the refugees who come to Wolkenland, but if they do not, it is because they choose not to look. They choose to accept the surface illusions the Red Skull offers them. They believe what they wish, and will not see what conflicts with that belief. But others..." He looked at those faces, dining on hate and hungry for more. He met their eyes, and the glass could not shield them from his promise. "What others choose to believe is that you are here because you deserve to be."

The man gave Doom a puzzled glance when he said *you* instead of *we*. The pronoun had not been a slip. He stood apart from the other slaves. He was Doom. And now that his body was strong again, and he had the full grasp of his faculties, he felt a renewed purpose. He could do nothing about the void inside. It would take getting back into the Red Skull's sanctum to free the rest of himself and be whole again.

He would do that, and much more.

Yes, he vowed to the spectators, so very much more.

He spoke more to the other prisoners. He observed and analyzed. At the end of the shift, he listened to the whispers and prayers and desperate hopes, storing everything that might be useful. Their hopes had been reduced to the most basic. He understood. He shared the need for the end of chains, and for revenge. He remembered all these painful emotions from the years of Vladimir's reign. Doom understood very well, but he also analyzed from a distance. He would turn those needs into weapons.

He listened, too, as he had since the beginning of his captivity, for the name, or the hint of the name, that would give him hope. He had looked for Valeria since he had arrived. He had not seen her. The possibility of her death became a heavier and heavier weight on his soul.

But during this rest period, this night if there were a distinction between night and day in the mines, he heard about the woman who spoke, to whoever would listen, of the rescuer who would surely come.

FOURTEEN

"He will come."

The whisper, repeated by one prisoner to the next, a refrain of reassurance, a prayer to bring light to the darkness.

Doom rested in a corner of a holding cell, his back against the wall, keeping to himself, watching, listening. He slept little now, during the few hours when he was not swinging a pickaxe or hauling a cart. He didn't need to. Strong again now in both mind and body, he focused on learning what he had to learn so he could strike back.

It seemed to Doom that he heard the words more and more frequently. It might be that this was only his perception, that he heard the refrain because now he was listening for it. But he didn't think so. In the last few days, the frequency and the intensity of the prayer had increased.

Days. Nights. Doom had come to think of the work shifts as days, the rest periods as nights. With the way the lengths of each varied, Doom knew that the days he counted did not match up to the twenty-four-hour cycle that existed above ground. No matter. The division allowed him to mark the passage of time in an approximately meaningful manner. He could track shifts in the psychological atmosphere of the mines. It was important, too, that he not lose all sense of time, urgency disappearing into the limbo of repetitive misery, and so abandon Latveria to the Red Skull's pleasure.

Someone shuffled by him on hands and knees. The man saw that Doom was awake, and he clasped Doom's hands.

"He *will* come," the man said, seeking to reassure both Doom and himself.

"Who will?" Doom asked, not for the first time.

The man paused. He did not let go of Doom's hands, and Doom had to make a conscious effort not to throw the man across the room for his presumption. The prisoner squeezed Doom's fingers as if this would drive home the truth of what he had said.

"I don't know," the man said at last. "She hasn't said."

"She? Have you spoken with her?" Maybe, finally, his question would be met with a *yes*.

Let it be Valeria.

"No," said the man. "But I know who she is."

Doom leaned forward, eager. "What is her name?"

"I don't know that, either, but she's the one who escaped."

As good as being told her name. Valeria. He had his confirmation that she lived, and that she was the one who promised a savior.

"She can tell you who is coming," the man went on. "She's the one who knows. She says he has terrible power, and that he'll crush the Red Skull like an insect." The man gave Doom a quizzical look. "She says he wears a mask." After a long moment of staring at the rags wrapped around Doom's face, the man shook his head. The savior could not be a prisoner, after all. "He will come," he said again, and began to crawl away.

"I would like to speak with her," Doom said.

The man stopped. He looked back, a grimy, emaciated shadow among shadows. "I would, too," he said, with feeling.

Doom cursed silently. He was no further along, not really. He would have to continue his search for Valeria in the way he had begun. At least he knew that it was she he sought.

Valeria lived. Latveria could not have fallen yet. He had not failed. He would save both.

First, he would find Valeria. Now that he knew she lived, his search took on renewed purpose and energy.

At the end of shifts, when the guards removed the shackles and herded the slaves into the holding cells, they did not assign prisoners to particular spaces. They shoved the slaves through the main door to the holding cell complex, and left the people to fend for themselves. So, each night, Doom chose a different cell. The task would have been hopeless, if not for the human habit. The instinct that drove students to return to the same seats in a classroom even though none were assigned, that need to find a spot and declare it home, even in the midst of Hell.

Doom chose a different cell every night. He asked about the woman who made the promise, just as he did to the prisoners near him during the day. Thus far, no one had spoken to her directly, but knowing definitively that the woman was Valeria felt like progress. It felt like drawing closer.

A few days later, while he hacked away at worthless stone

to create a tunnel to nowhere, a prisoner a few yards down collapsed. The man, small and middle-aged, looked like he might have been an accountant before whatever region had been his home descended into chaos and he had the misfortune to seek refuge in Wolkenland. Sunken of chest and thin of limb, he did not have the build or the stamina for hard labor. The tears in the rear of his tunic showed angry red welts. He had fallen and been whipped for it before.

There had been no guards in this section of the tunnel seconds before. Now one appeared, as if a sixth sense summoned him to the exercise of brutality. He strutted toward the fallen man, thick jaw jutting forward, eyes glittering with the special anger that infused every atom of the guard's being. He was not happy to see the prisoner down. He hated the man for his weakness. He would experience pleasure in the punishment he dealt out, but it was pleasure filtered through frustration and hate. He knew no other way of existing.

Doom's pulse beat a deafening rhythm in his ears. He had purged Latveria of the guard's kind twice already. A third time called, and he was in chains.

The wise move, the patient move, would be to do nothing, let the guard have his satisfaction at the older man's expense, no matter how extreme the cost, and add this unimportant fascist to the list of retribution for when the time came and Doom was ready.

That would be the patient decision.

Doom dropped his pickaxe. It hit the ground with a loud clang. The guard, who had just reached the fallen man, turned his head toward the sound.

While working the mines, the prisoners were not chained

to one another. Instead, they wore shackles at wrists and ankles. The chains between were long enough to permit the use of tools, and a labored shuffle. Doom would not approach the guard. That would give his enemy all the time in the world to prepare his defense. He carried a whip in his hand, and an electrified baton on his belt. The trick was to lure the guard to him, keeping the man's ire up and his suspicions down.

Doom stood still. He made his shoulders slump. He lowered his head as if he were staring in uncomprehending fatigue at the pickaxe. In the corner of his eye, he watched the guard.

The guard hesitated between targets. Between him and Doom, another slave redoubled her efforts on the wall, removing herself from the scope of the guard's wrath. The fallen man lay still, his breathing so shallow he resembled a corpse. Doom did not know if he was conscious at all.

Neither, apparently, did the guard. He decided to vent his fury on the target that would actually feel the sting of the lash. He swaggered over to Doom. "You there," he said. "Were you told to stop?"

Doom said nothing. He did not move.

"You answer when you're addressed," the guard said, "and you answer with *sir*." On the last word, he cracked the whip.

It struck Doom on the left shoulder. It tore his sleeve and his flesh. He had known far worse pain. This pitiful attempt did not even qualify as significant. He did not even flinch.

The guard snarled. He closed in, drawing his baton. "My name is Sergeant Baker. I'm going to teach you to remember it, and to say it with *respect*."

He held the baton up for show. He was using it like a prop, an accessory to intimidation, instead of charging in with a weapon.

Fool.

As Baker stepped in, shouting again to make Doom look, damn it, *look* at the weapon and the uniform and be afraid, Doom lunged. He threw the chain between his arms over Baker's head, wrapped it around his neck, and jerked hard. A snap, and the guard dropped without a moan.

Silence in the tunnel. Every pickaxe froze in mid swing. All eyes turned in shock to Doom. Then the work started up, louder and faster than before, for fear that another guard would come to see why the ringing of iron against rock had ceased.

Only the woman between Doom and the fallen prisoner did not resume her work. She stared at Doom, mouth agape. "They'll kill you," she said.

"I think not." He dragged the guard's body to his end of the tunnel. He examined the ceiling, then grabbed his pickaxe and hacked away above his head. There were safe ways of enlarging a tunnel, and there were foolhardy ones. Doom chose the latter, attacking the ceiling with such energy that the sounds of work coming from this section of the mines became deafening, and so fell beneath the notice of other guards. There was no sport to be had here.

It did not take him long to find and attack a weak spot. Cracks spread quickly, rock grumbled a warning, and Doom stepped out of the way of the collapse. The ceiling slumped down with a dull roar, burying the corpse under the cave-in. Dust rushed down the corridor.

Now someone would come. Doom used the time that remained to march over to the fallen man. He grabbed the prisoner by the arm and hauled him roughly to his feet. "Get up," he ordered.

The man was awake, as Doom had thought. He staggered but stayed upright. He began a babbled litany of thanks.

"Be quiet," Doom snapped. He shoved the man's pickaxe into his hands.

The man held the tool in a trembling grip. "I can't…" he faltered.

"You can," said Doom. "Because you must. Work the stone, and you deny the guards their chance for cruelty. Steal their pleasure from them. Look at the rock." He pointed, and pushed the man toward it. "The rock is the enemy. Strike it, and you strike them. Use your anger. It is your strength. You are not a slave. You are a threat that is merely contained for the moment."

The man attacked the wall with renewed vigor. He grunted with each hit, as if the tip of the pickaxe were plunging into the chest of one of the guards.

Doom returned to his position, to work on a different part of the wall next to the cave-in.

"You are he," the woman said. "You must be."

Doom met her gaze.

"She will rejoice that you have come."

"She?" Doom asked, hoping *this time, this time.*

"Valeria," the woman said.

"You have seen her?"

"We sleep in the same cell."

For a long moment, the simple yet sudden realization of his hope stunned him into silence.

The woman's name was Rita Chen. At the end of the shift, Doom accompanied her back to her cell. They were among the last of the prisoners to return to the holding complex. Their shift had gone long, as they had been harangued by guards for failing to prevent a cave-in. Or rather, Doom guessed, for failing to have died under rock.

The guards did not ask anything about Baker. He had not been missed yet. Doom filed that information away as useful. More evidence of how disposable the Red Skull's minions were, not just to him, but to each other. They valued themselves, individually, though that value was determined absolutely by their body-and-soul fealty to the Red Skull and the ideology he embodied. The Skull shaped their loyalty so that it ran exclusively from them to him, turning them into an army of competitors for his favor.

Something to think about, and he would, later. Now, though, he could think of nothing else but Valeria.

Vertigo assailed Doom as he approached the doorway to the cell. He had not seen Valeria in years. And yet, he also *had* seen her, very recently, and killed her over and over. He had not witnessed the murder from a distance, a vision unfolding like a dream. He had committed it. In realities as genuine as this one, he had killed her. Dizzy, disoriented, he felt himself split between his present reality and the ones the Red Skull had forced on him. The split made him hesitate. His lived experience told him that he would find Valeria dead, a burned husk of a skeleton, a smoking pile of ash and bone. To imagine otherwise was a delusion forged from old memories and vanished hopes.

Chen had entered the cell. "I have such news!" she said to someone.

Her joy could not cut through the vertigo, but it gave Doom the impetus he needed. He crossed the threshold.

Exhausted, filthy, worn bodies filled the cell. A few stood, shoulders slumped with weariness. Many had already collapsed and lay in fetal curls or death-like sprawls, plunging into leaden sleep. A gray uniformity covered everyone, the gray of grime, weakness, rags, and misery. Yet Doom saw her at once, and everyone else in the cell vanished from his awareness.

Valeria. Years older, as he was. Haggard, malnourished, eyes sunken and cheekbones pushing at taut, parchment-brittle skin. But Valeria, still instantly recognizable. Those eyes, sharp and green, the eyes that, a lifetime ago, had looked at Victor with love. The eyes that had looked at Doom with fear and judgment.

Valeria alive. He couldn't move, couldn't speak, couldn't breathe, terrified that a blink, a whisper, the twitch of a finger would dispel the illusion, and Valeria would be gone, returned to the death into which he had cast her, and cast her, and cast her.

She didn't move, either. She seemed as stricken as he felt. She had not seen him without his armor and his mask since before Victor had left Latveria to go and study in America. Victor had never returned. Doom had come in his place. But she knew him. He, too, was a creature of gray, his face covered by disgusting rags, yet she knew him.

"Victor?" she said, as if uncertain what being would answer.

When had he last heard that name? Who had last dared to address him like that?

Valeria? The last time he had seen her?

"You called me," Doom said, hoarse.

"And you came." So much in her voice, too much for him

to parse. Gratitude, anxiety, fear, hope, and emotions so large and ill-defined that neither he nor she could give them a name.

She took half a step toward him, then stopped. He stayed where he was, still half-convinced she would disappear, or he would wake, if he moved.

"I was surprised," said Doom. "I did not think I would hear your voice again. You made it clear, the last time we spoke, that I would not."

"The past is not erased." Valeria's tone grew stronger. "I fled for a reason."

Unspoken: *That has not changed.*

"But when you found yourself here, you turned to me," said Doom. The past existed, yes. So did the present. That counted for something, surely.

Valeria nodded. "I know that there are some principles that you held, and still do." She seemed to be speaking from the depths of a profound sorrow, mourning the loss of a loved one and tormented by the trace of his ghost. "I know that the Red Skull is as monstrous for you as he is for me."

"He is." Now Doom did step forward. "I will crush him." Reality became strong around him as he made his vow. "I will crush him, and I will free you."

"You'll do more," said Valeria.

Doom blinked. If anyone else had spoken to him that way, he would have destroyed them. Here, now, with half his self missing, and Valeria before him, he said nothing.

"You'll free all these people," Valeria continued. "Something that I have never denied about you, Victor, is that you are not just a ruler. You are a *leader*. You may be a prisoner like the rest of us, but I believe you. You will crush the Red Skull. I don't know how, but you will. We need your strength. Everyone here needs you."

She did not need to tell him that. Of course they needed him. The world needed him.

He would show her how truly she spoke.

FIFTEEN

And now that Doom had found Valeria, and found her alive, the pieces of his vengeance came together. He spent an hour in silent planning, warding off any interactions with a look. When the other prisoners in the cell had realized that he was the one Valeria had promised would come, they tried to speak to him, to touch him to see that he was solid flesh, and to seek comfort. He had none to give. Valeria had said he would lead them, and she was right. He would give them leadership, and that meant issuing commands he expected to be obeyed.

His first, as he stood in the corner, still as a funerary statue and twice as grim, was that he not be disturbed. Valeria withdrew to a few steps away from him, and she discouraged the more persistent from interrupting his thoughts. He put together all he had observed of the layout of the mines, the dispositions of the guards, and the realities of the people he would lead out of the underworld.

The prisoners vastly outnumbered the guards, but they were weak and unarmed. Doom would get them weapons, once he started taking down the guards, but he was sure that few, if any at all, of the refugees would know how to use them. He had to assume a complete lack of training in the ragged army under his command.

Could they do the bare minimum that must be done? He thought they would. Desperation would drive them. He would drive them. Once they were in motion, the momentum of those numbers could prove telling.

He could not underestimate the guards, though. He could not let them realize that a rebellion had begun. If they counterattacked in force, they would slaughter the prisoners. Create a bottleneck in the tunnels, lay down a steady barrage of fire, and watch the bodies drop. A simple matter. An end of the matter.

The key, then, was to take the guards out without the word spreading. He also had to act quickly, before word of what was going to happen also reached the guards' ears. News of his presence would not reach outside this cell until the next shift, but then it would rush through the tunnels, spread in whispers, a subterranean fire waiting to burst out into the open. If, though, the prisoners knew that this was the day they would escape, then they would be more careful about what they said and when. At least long enough for the escape to begin.

So, the break-out had to be during the next shift. Any later, he risked the guards hearing about the man Valeria had called for, and once they heard, so would the Red Skull. Doom pictured his exultation in knowing that he had Doom doubly enslaved. And he imagined the horrors that would flow from that moment on him and on Latveria.

The next shift, then. Doom was ready. He had no need for delay. He had seen all he required in the days before finding Valeria. He had formed his plan, and he had no doubt as to its success.

He was Doom, and what he willed must be.

During the work in the mines, the opportunity to strike would come. The guards were spread out then, feeling no threat from prisoners in chains. They wandered down the tunnels, looking for weakness to punish. The only concentration of force would be at the entrance to the mines.

In Doom's mind, that barrier had already been breached.

Morning came, or what passed for morning. In the absence of sun, in the perpetual, amber-lit gloom of the mines, the brutal call to labor took the place of dawn. Doom walked past the guards at the doorway from the holding cells, and made them a silent promise that this was the last time they would watch their charges file out, shoulders hunched with fatigue and the weight of the shackles around their wrists and ankles.

Doom eyed the faces of the guards. He saw the same hate and contempt that had always been there. He also saw the boredom that found its occasional release in cruelty. Good. He wanted them bored, not suspicious. If they had noticed that one of them had gone missing, they still did not think it possible that a prisoner had done away with them.

Doom had spoken to the people in his cell before the morning. He had told them what must happen and when, and what they must do. For all but Valeria, they had nothing to do initially except to pass on, as best they could, the announcement that freedom would come today, and for the injunction to be ready. This was the first gamble, but Doom had confidence that the secret would be hidden from the guards long enough for him to act.

A few hours into the shift, the moment arrived. Doom worked beside Valeria. When the guard in their section of the tunnel wandered away to glower at slaves elsewhere, Doom turned to Valeria. He dropped to a crouch and stretched his arms out, wrists on the ground. Valeria hacked at his chains with her pickaxe. The sound of metal against metal blended with the din of so much metal against stone, and no guards came to investigate. As Doom had surmised, they could not imagine the possibility of slaves freeing themselves. After a few strikes, Valeria broke through the link close to his left wrist. Doom wrapped the length of chain around his right arm, then sat so Valeria could tackle the chain between his legs. This one she broke close to both ankles.

Freed, Doom leapt to his feet and grabbed his pickaxe. With a few rapid, ferocious blows, he shattered Valeria's shackles. She then moved on to the next prisoner. While the line of refugees in the tunnel worked to free each other, Doom sprinted down its length. He turned right at the first intersection, following the route he had seen the guard take. At the next junction, he saw the man, baton out, beating a prisoner even older than the one Doom had helped the day before.

Doom charged. He shook his right arm, loosening the coil of the chain. It hung below his wrist, a whip of iron. The guard turned at the sound of running. His eyes widened in alarm, and his mouth gaped in surprise. He froze in uncertainty. Prisoners did not attack guards. The event simply could not happen. If he had had the training to deal with that eventuality, his belief system blocked his reaction. He did not call for help, and his reflexes were much too slow.

Doom snapped the chain out. He slammed it into the left side of the guard's head with the impact of a locomotive. The guard went down, a sack of lead. Doom snatched the guard's earpiece from his right ear and put it in his own, then picked up the baton.

Up and down the tunnel, the prisoners started the process of freeing themselves. They looked at Doom with awe, and that awe spurred them on to do as they had been told to do.

Doom listened to the conversations on the guard network. More boredom, unnecessary chatter and racist jokes cluttering up the channel, interspersed with the phrase *code white* again and again, clearly indicating nothing amiss.

An irritated voice, barking with seniority, broke in, loud. "*Brock, sign in. What's your status?*" The voice was much clearer than the others, and speaking directly to the owner of the earpiece.

Doom tapped the communicator. "Code white," he said.

A grunt from the superior. "*Don't be late next time.*" Then a short burst of static. The officer had broken off communication. No need to answer.

Valeria and the prisoners from the first tunnel had arrived now and were speeding up the freeing of the others.

Doom turned off the communicator's transmitter. "Follow me," he said to the prisoners. "We move through the tunnels until every chain is broken. I will take care of the guards. Take their weapons and earpieces." He explained the code that should be used if they heard a challenge.

He searched the pockets of the fallen man's uniform and found his pass card. He held it up. "Take these, too. We will have cause to use them before this day is done." He handed the card to Valeria. No pockets in the tunics, and he needed both hands free to take down the enemy. "Stay close," he told her.

She nodded, and that simple gesture of agreement thrilled his heart more than logic allowed. He needed her close by for the pragmatic, tactical reasons of the break-out.

Except that he wanted her close for other reasons. Her presence made the years of her absence even more painful. He did not want to return to them.

Stay close, he had said.

And she had nodded. *Yes.*

Then, frothing and rabid, the memory of her murder sank its teeth into his heart.

He shook the memory away. He clamped down on the emotions roiling in his chest. He had no time for them now. They would only hamper him.

Doom picked up the electric baton in favor of the pickaxe and headed back down the tunnel to another intersection.

The chatter of the guards guided him as he hunted. He knew the layout of the mines well. Over the course of his imprisonment, he had committed every passage to memory. The night before, he had planned his route through the mines, and now he adapted it to what he heard through the earpiece. He knew where the guards were, and what they thought.

He became the angel of death, a scythe passing silently through the mines. He took the guards one at a time, and not one stood a chance. Most tried to fight. A few had some knowledge of combat, and that knowledge bought them an extra second before the electric baton stabbed their throat, or the chain whip shattered their skull. None of them had the chance to sound the alarm. Doom made certain of that.

A scythe, and also a wind. Doom moved quickly, ridding the tunnels of the foe so quickly that the commanding officer, no doubt reclining in bored luxury at the entrance to the mine, registered only irritation that the *code white* responses were coming in more slowly and with greater irregularity. In his wake the train of the liberated grew longer and longer. The people carried weapons, but he had not commanded them to fight yet. They would only get in his way. For now, only he was the hand of vengeance in the mines, and he embraced the role.

You do not see what is happening, Red Skull. You do not see what is coming. But it is coming. Perhaps you feel it in your dreams.

Tireless, feeling stronger than he had since he had split himself in two, Doom scoured the mines. In less than two hours, he had freed the prisoners, more than a thousand of them, and had the mines, though the guards at the exit did not know yet, under his control.

The fiction of *code white* relayed back to the headquarters outside still held. It couldn't much longer. Even officers the most dulled by boredom would, sooner or later, pay just that little bit more attention to what they heard on the communications network, notice that things sounded a little different, and grow curious.

Doom had to ensure such curiosity came too late.

They saved the region of the gallery as the last to be liberated. He brought his army of refugees to the inner exit from the gallery and called a halt a dozen yards down the tunnel from where the prisoners and their carts emerged.

"Free them as they reach you," he instructed. "But go no closer. You must not be seen by the spectators." Then he indicated the twenty nearest prisoners, including Valeria. "Come with me," he said. He checked to see that they were all armed.

Doom had not only committed the layout of the tunnels in the mines to memory. He had also noted the locations of access doors used by the guards. There was one in the left-hand wall just outside the gallery exit. Doom brought his group there, then paused while Valeria swiped the panel beneath the handle with the pass card. The door beeped, and Doom wrenched it open.

On the other side, stairs led up. Doom climbed two flights and reached a landing from which a hall stretched in two directions, as he had expected.

"We are going to the spectator bleachers of the gallery," Doom said. "I will go this way. Five of you come with me." He pointed left. "The rest of you go the other way. We will attack simultaneously."

"Attack," someone repeated nervously.

Doom controlled his temper. He had expected this. "I command you to do simply this: prevent anyone from leaving, and from getting a warning out. How you do that is up to you. But if you fail me, you fail everyone."

"We understand," Valeria said. She gave him a look that promised that they did.

Doom nodded. "Then show them your wrath," he said. "And take their pass cards."

The prisoners left him, faces set and grim. Yes, he thought. He did not know how far they would go, but they would, at the very least, do what had to be done.

Doom watched them go, then marched down his own path, Chen and four others hurrying to keep up with his pace. The corridor led to another flight of stairs, and these went up to the staff entry to the gallery. "I will do what is necessary," he said to the small group. "You will bind our prisoners."

"With what?" Chen asked.

Doom's lip curled under his mask of rags. "They will be well-dressed. It does not take much cloth to immobilize someone. Use their clothes if there is nothing else."

Then he burst through the doors, shock baton at the ready. He entered the viewing space in the middle of the rear wall. The first thing he did was jab it into the intercom next to the doorway, shorting out the communications from this side of the gallery to the outside world. The spectators, who had been watching the last of the slaves passing through the gallery, whipped around in surprise, then stilled in shock. There were about twenty of them, and a similar number in the seats on the other side. The audience, Doom thought, had been growing, and becoming more assiduous in attendance.

The door to the other seating area burst open as the spectators there, noticing something amiss among their fellows across the way, had begun to rise to their feet. Satisfied with the timing of the attacks, Doom focused his attention on the people below him.

"You can't be here," a man said, his face turning purple with outrage. The fact that he might be in danger hadn't registered yet. He was someone who had never even been challenged in his life, so perfectly had his wealth shielded him from even the smallest inconvenience. He could not conceive of a threat directed at him, not until the threat became reality.

As was about to happen.

"Yet here I am," said Doom. He strode down the tiers toward the spectators closest to the main exit from the viewing space. The other prisoners waited by the staff doors, blocking that escape.

Not that anyone showed signs of trying to leave yet. The bubble of their privilege still blocked the concept of danger.

"Someone call a guard," another billionaire called out, so used to delegation that it did not even occur to him to take that action himself. That he sat closest to the exit didn't seem to occur to him, either.

Doom reached him and struck him with the baton. The blow and the electrical charge knocked him senseless. He jerked violently, then slumped in his seat.

Now, finally, the rich and mighty understood the safety of their wealth had abandoned them. For a brief moment, some of them looked as if they were thinking of trying to rush Doom. A few more blows of the shock baton convinced all the others of the wisdom of surrender. They backed up against the right-hand wall, on their knees and cowering. They did not fight when Chen and the others took their jackets and began to rip them, turning them into ropes. They protested, though. Their conviction that the universe must not permit their victimization remained strong. They protested. They shouted. They raged against the perversity of events.

"You have no right to do this!"

"And yet I am," said Doom, standing before them, baton at the ready, while they were bound.

"Do you know who we are?"

"Parasites," said Doom.

"We did nothing wrong."

"You observed, and took pleasure," said Doom. "You are the willing accomplices of the Red Skull. You have done much."

"What are you going to do to us?"

"Keep you here, for a start," said Doom. "But I promise you this: your penance has only begun."

When their ankles were tied together, and their wrists behind their backs, and they had been relieved of their pass cards, Doom headed back up to the doors. He checked across the way and saw that the binding there, too, was almost complete. *Good.* Already, the escape from the mines had become tinged with the beginnings of his retaliation. He savored the taste.

Chen hesitated before following him. "Are we leaving them like this?"

"Would you prefer to kill them?" Doom asked.

She shook her head.

Doom took his small group back down to the entrance to the access corridors, the shouts for help muffled behind feet of stone, rapidly becoming inaudible. Valeria and the others arrived soon after, and Doom took them all back to the main body of the prisoners.

"The mines are ours," he announced. "But the way out is not clear yet. That is my task alone." It was one thing for a group of his new followers to overcome an unarmed collection of the rich, who were just as bereft of training but nowhere near as desperate. He did not want any foolish attempts at combat interfering with his own actions. "You will follow me, but at a distance. When I tell you to stop and wait, you will stop and wait."

He did not ask if they had understood. He had been clear enough.

Doom returned once again to the access door and made his way up the stairs again. He had noticed that the corridor that led to the viewing hall kept going past it, in the direction of the exit. He took that route now, the long file of the liberated extending far behind him.

Valeria walked with him. "The watchtowers," she said. "What are you going to do about them? They'll have snipers. They'll shoot anyone who isn't a guard."

"They won't have the chance," said Doom.

The corridor was a long one. When another door at last came into sight, Doom held up a hand. "Wait here," he said.

He moved to the door and pressed an ear against it. He could just make out voices on the other side. A few, not many. The sounds of a conversation. No one shouting in alarm.

Doom threw the door open and rushed into the room beyond.

He had entered the corrugated shack outside the mine's entrance. It was night, arc lights outside the tunnels shining through the windows. Four guards lounged on folding chairs. They reached for their pistols. Doom spun from guard to guard, lashing out in quick succession, a whirlwind, preventing attacks with initial strikes and electrical shocks, breaking hands and triggering convulsions. He picked up a pistol dropped by a nerveless hand, shot out the lights in the shack, and trained the gun on the outside door.

He had taken the building in less than ten seconds.

The door opened. Two guards rushed in. In the light spilling in through the windows, Doom recognized them.

Pieter and Jerry.

They had their guns drawn. They squinted in confusion at the darkness and the twitching bodies.

Doom fired.

"I kept my promise," he said.

He waited another minute. No one else entered the shack. A shot from a beam rifle stabbed through the ceiling. The guard in the watchtower had fired, but he had no target other than the building itself.

Doom's eyes had adjusted to the gloom. He could see well enough to take stock of the shack's inventory. Against the left-hand wall, he found the expected weapons locker. He opened it and took out two of the beam rifles.

He examined the weapons. They were simple things, basic in their construction. It was child's play for him to disable their power packs' safety override. He approached the window and took aim with one of the rifles at the closest leg of the watchtower. He supercharged the rifle and expended its entire energy store in a single shot. The beam struck the leg and melted it away at the base.

The panicked guard had just started climbing down when Doom unloaded the second rifle's shot, melting the second leg. The tower collapsed in a chaos of broken metal and wood. Dust blew past the arc lights, turning the area outside the mine into an amber limbo.

Doom stepped back into the corridor. He summoned the prisoners with a gesture. They used the tools in the shed to remove the manacles and the broken chains. Then Doom led more than a thousand of the Red Skull's victims into the darkness.

"You have been refugees, you have been prisoners, and you have been slaves," Doom told them. "Now you are something new. Now you have become our enemy's nightmare."

SIXTEEN

Alvin Gates was the first to notice the impossible, that something had gone awry on Wolkenland. The idea was so contrary to his experience that not only did it take a while for him to be aware of the glitch, he stared at it for another length of time without understanding what he saw.

Gates was on the graveyard shift of the security detail. He sat on a swivel chair that didn't quite lean back far enough to be good for napping, in a circular room whose curved walls were covered with screens and banks of status lights. A miniature, diluted version of the Red Skull's panopticon, it did not serve to observe everything that happened in Wolkenland. That was the Skull's exclusive purview. The room simply scanned for signs of anything happening that shouldn't be. That had never happened once since Gates had joined the Skull's army. Especially not at 3AM, when nothing happened at all on the island.

Bored, sleepy, Gates passed the hours surfing online, trolling, and frothing in comment sections. Eventually, fatigue made even that boring. He glanced up at the clock, hoping it had moved forward more than he knew it had, and his eye happened to catch a sensor flashing red. He tapped the light as if that would make it behave. He couldn't yet take on the idea of a warning.

The red kept blinking.

Finally, he understood that the blinking meant something. He flipped through the thick binder on the workspace beneath the screens and sensors, and found what this light meant. The guards at the mines had not done their hourly check-in. All they had to do, Gates knew, was flip a switch on their console, and the code white confirmation would be done. Really not too much to ask.

He sighed, and sent them a prompt from his terminal, then went back to his browser tabs. Ten minutes later, the light still blinked, and it was really starting to irritate him. Even when he turned his back to it, he could feel it winking away behind his head.

Muttering under his breath, Gates picked up his phone and called the mines.

No answer.

He let the phone ring and ring. Inconsiderate jerks were asleep. If he had to be awake and miserable, then so did they.

No answer.

When he finally hung up, he felt the first pangs of uncertainty. He'd done what his training had covered. That should have taken care of the problem. The fact that it hadn't left him adrift. His chest tightened. In the Skull's army, there were no more questions. All the answers were there. Gates was confirmed as one of the genetically chosen, and all the right people were blamed as was right. No more questions. But now he didn't have an answer. Now, he was required to do something, for the first time, on Wolkenland.

But what?

There was something. Only he didn't like the idea. He should call his supervisor. Only that would mean waking her up.

The security shifts had become more skeletal since Doom had been captured and the invasion of Latveria had entered a more intensive phase. Wolkenland required boots on the ground below. In the sky, the island floated serene and impregnable now that the great enemy had been defeated. Invisible, it could strike but could not be attacked. The prisoners were helpless, and the paying inhabitants of Wolkenland were unlikely in the extreme to take action against its, and their, interests. Security watches, especially in the dead of night, were not supposed to be much more than a formality. Bottom-rank unfortunates like Gates had to sit in the monitoring station and do nothing for hours. Superiors, like Madeleine Rhodes, were nominally on call, but slept through the night in the expectation of nothing happening. Rhodes had made it perfectly clear to Gates that he better not disturb her without a very good reason.

Did this count? One flashing light?

One flashing light and no communication at all with the mines.

Gates wrestled with the temptation to ignore the light and pretend he had never seen it, or that it only began in the last few minutes of his shift, by which time it would be proper morning. He defeated it with the realization that the punishment he might receive over raising a false alarm would be as nothing compared to what would happen if he ignored a real problem.

So he picked up the phone again and called Rhodes.

"*What?*" she answered, anger muddied by sleep.

"Sorry to wake you, unterwachtmeister," said Gates.

"*Is this an emergency?*" she asked before he could get any further.

"No. At least, I don't think so."

"*Then why am I awake?*" The anger became clear and dangerous.

Gates swallowed hard before finding the courage to tell her.

Madeleine Rhodes arrived at the monitoring station out of breath. She had run all the way from her quarters. She burst through the door, and a terrified Gates leapt out of his chair and retreated to the far side of the room. The red light reached out to her, its blinking sinking into her vision like a claw.

"Still nothing?" she asked Gates, hoping against hope that all had sorted itself in the last few minutes and she could climb down.

"Nothing," Gates confirmed. "I tried calling again."

Rhodes chewed her lip. Procedure called for her to send a flyover of drones, and a unit of guards. The drones weren't a problem. She could dispatch them with a few keystrokes.

Or she should have been able to.

Rhodes frowned. "You haven't sent any surveillance flights there, have you?"

"There was a scheduled flight supposed to go over about an hour ago."

Rhodes checked the monitors. Those were the units she was trying to order. "Where are they?"

"I don't know."

They weren't responding. They had gone as silent as the mines.

Rhodes called up their last transmissions. Their feeds appeared on the screens above the terminal. Empty landscapes went by in the bleached monochrome of night vision. Nothing unusual appeared. Then the images broke up and ended.

"Oh," said Gates. "That's not right, is it?"

Rhodes gave him a glare of contempt that shut him up. Soft man in a hard uniform, thinking he was something. He would never rise in the Red Skull's army. Not like the truly hardened.

Only she didn't feel hardened, not right now, and Gates was right. None of this was normal.

Rhodes called up another flight of drones and rerouted them to the mines. It would be another half-hour before they arrived. Sending actual personnel to the mines presented a problem. The guard unit posted there was the largest number in that region of Wolkenland. Those guards were the ones who would have been sent to deal with problems elsewhere. The mines going dark was not a contingency in the realm of the imaginable.

It had to be something stupid, simple, unimportant.

But meanwhile, the nearest guards would take even longer to reach the mines than the drones.

Rhodes hesitated over her options. She could wait until the new overflight told them something concrete. Or she could push the panic button before they knew anything at all.

She did not want to be seen to be the one who waited too long.

So she kicked the problem higher up the chain.

Caleb Mueller, the Red Skull's major-domo, experienced his own bout of hesitation when the news of the mines' silence landed in his lap. Outside the Skull's bedchamber, he cursed silently that the final decision should be his.

Really, though, there wasn't a decision, was there? He just didn't want to be the decapitated messenger.

Mueller took a breath, straightened, knocked on the door, and opened it.

The Red Skull's chamber occupied a curved protrusion at the top of the castle's keep, the frown of a heavy brow. A shell-proof panoramic window took up the entire exterior wall. It looked forward on the island, giving the master of Wolkenland an unmatched perspective of his domain. The panopticon allowed him to peer into the very grain of the island. Here, he could look at the island as a whole, gaze down upon it as a god.

Conscious of the power of that view, and that it did not belong to him, Mueller carefully kept his gaze averted from the window, even with the Red Skull asleep. He crossed the marble floor to the immense bed. He coughed politely. The Skull did not stir.

"Your pardon, leader," Mueller said. "I'm sorry to wake you, but something has happened."

The Red Skull jerked awake to the words *something has happened*. He shot out of bed, adrenaline coursing through his veins. His body responded to the emergency before his head could clear of sleep. He grabbed the pistol on the side table and, still in his bedclothes, sprinted from the room, Mueller at his heels.

Something has happened.

Mueller was calling out something, but the Skull didn't hear him through the panicked pounding of blood in his ears. Only one thing could have happened to warrant waking him up. The impossible had occurred. Doom had broken loose.

The minute it took the Skull to rush down the halls and take the lift down to the power chamber was an eternity of terror. When he arrived, and saw Doom still caught in the shifting energy streams of the Power Cosmic, he had trouble processing the good news. Properly awake at last, he verified that this was no illusion. As he saw every day, the readings of ethereal agony continued uninterrupted across the screens.

The Red Skull turned to Mueller. The major-domo had turned red in the face, and was panting hard. The Skull pointed at Doom. "What do you see there?"

"Our enemy, my leader."

"He isn't free, is he?"

"No."

"His freedom would have justified waking me. Nothing else."

"I am very sorry, my leader."

"You most certainly are," the Red Skull said, and shot Mueller in the forehead.

The Skull stepped over the corpse and headed back to his chambers. He would have to give some thought to a suitable replacement for the major-domo. Until tonight, Mueller had done his job well. But he had seen the Red Skull vulnerable and afraid. That was unforgivable and why he had to die.

The Skull dressed and took the private hall that led from his quarters to the panopticon. Doom hadn't escaped, but Mueller had been concerned enough to make a grievous error of judgment. Best to look into the problem and deal with it. The Skull wasn't going to get back to sleep now.

In the panopticon, he saw the security alerts, and read through the reports. He frowned. He didn't like silence from the mines. He couldn't imagine anything serious being behind the anomaly, because with Doom in his control, nothing *could* be serious.

Then the drone flights Rhodes had dispatched arrived at the mines. The Skull stared at the images of the fallen watchtower. He grunted in disbelief.

Then more reports came in, of more monitoring cameras and sensors going dark, no longer just at the mines, but in locations where the Skull placed real importance in ensuring that nothing ever went wrong.

The homes of his wealthy clients.

The Skull ordered that Hauptmann be woken. Time for the Exile to earn his keep.

The journey from the mines to the starboard mansions went smoothly, as if the universe were repenting for its rebellion and had begun to refashion itself to conform to Doom's will. A thousand people found the energy to move swiftly over the barren earth around the mines, and then through the woods that separated that region from the residential sector of Wolkenland. They did not encounter any guards. The flying island slept, secure in its arrogance, and did not know that poison moved through its veins.

Doom distributed the first real weapons to his army before beginning the march. There had still been a few beam rifles in the guards' shack. He kept one for himself, and gave the other three to the refugees who stepped forward to say that they had some experience with firearms. A small step, and not enough to take on a concerted attack. Doom would change the balance soon enough if the universe obeyed him.

It did.

The only threat he had to deal with before they came out on the other side of the forest was a drone flight. He had expected something of the sort, and had kept close eyes on the night sky as he led his followers between the hills, sticking to the deeper darkness beside the slopes.

The red lights on the noses of the drones were dim, easy to miss, and Doom would have, if he hadn't been so alert. He caught the dimness because it moved, and it moved in a formation. Three faint hints of red. Three faint targets.

He spotted the drones before they flew over the escapees. He stopped suddenly and brought the line behind him to a halt. He brought the rifle up, tracked the movement, and fired three quick shots. The beams struck. The drones broke apart, bits of scorched fuselage spinning down to the ground.

"More will come, won't they?" said Valeria.

"They will, but they won't find us here," said Doom. "We will be found elsewhere, on my terms. We are not fleeing Wolkenland. We are waging war. And the battle will be joined when we are ready."

The army passed through the forest and came to the terraces and the mansions.

Now chance had a part to play. They had many of the

elite's personal pass keys, but the simple red cards had no indication as to which mansions they would open. The spectators would have flown in their personal craft to the mines, and they could have come from any of Wolkenland's homes. Doom had to gamble on the hope that it would still be the residents who lived closest to the mines who would be the ones to come most regularly. Valeria had been caught in a portside mansion. For no other reason, he decided to try the starboard homes.

With time passing, he needed luck even more. Or no, not luck. The obedience of fate. The silence of the mines would be noticed soon if it hadn't been already. The Red Skull's scrutiny of his island would suddenly grow much sharper, when complacency turned into fear.

Doom commanded absolute silence. The order flowed down the line behind him, ripples through a pond. He entered the manicured grounds of the first mansion on the lowest tier. He, Valeria, and Chen tried the collection of passes on the front door. When none of them worked, he returned to the wooded trail between estates and moved up to the second tier. The properties were wider than they were deep, so they could try houses faster by climbing the terraces.

A bit further up, a mansion's front door unlocked at the touch of the second card Doom tried. He moved through the great house as quickly as he could. It was dark and empty. However many people lived here, they must all have gone to the mines. Doom took in the work terminals and, within minutes, had a good sense of what technology powered the house, and what he could do with it. It took him less than another minute to disable the AI's surveillance functions.

The house, with its dining space and entertainment hall, was large enough to hold half the refugees easily. Doom left them there with instructions on how to start preparing. He would return as soon as he could.

The universe obeyed his commands again when the next house he tried, midway up the terraces, also responded to a key. It was big enough to hold the rest of the army. Doom had what he needed, and he got to work making the mansion's power sources his own.

He didn't need this house to be empty.

When it turned out not to be, and the owner was the public voice of Wolkenland, Doom knew he had seized the reins of fate once more.

"What?" said Lance Diffring, blinking and startled.

No one answered.

He rubbed his eyes and turned on his right side. His arm reached across the empty side of the bed.

Strange. Addyson wasn't back yet. His wife had decided to go to the mines for an evening's view. He had begged off. He liked going. A good way to unwind at the end of the day. Good to see the promise of a new world being fulfilled. But he'd been up late the night before, and hard at it all day, working on the messaging Wolkenland would put out once Latveria had fallen. The conquest was taking a bit longer than he had expected, but it was still a foregone conclusion, and the Red Skull wanted all the talking points in order.

Addyson hadn't returned when Diffring went to bed, but that wasn't unusual. The viewings often went late. Seeing the slaves at end-of-shift, when exhaustion really bit hard, was when the good stuff happened. More people falling down and needing to be punished.

He didn't know what time it was, but he must have been asleep for some hours. She should have been home by now. But her side of the mattress felt cold, so she hadn't just gotten up. She hadn't just asked him something which had woken him up.

Diffring closed his eyes, then snapped them open.

He heard movement downstairs. Before he could tell himself that it was his imagination, he heard more. Lots of movement, growing louder, as if a silent crowd were filling up the rooms on the ground floor.

Mouth dry, heart pounding, skin prickling, Diffring stared into darkness. He didn't know how to react. The domestic staff had keys, and they were all gone for the night. They weren't due until 6AM. They wouldn't be early. Who would be there? A break-in made no sense. Wolkenland didn't have break-ins. The idea was ludicrous.

But there were people below.

Diffring got out of bed. He threw on a robe and cinched it tight. He stepped into his slippers and ran his fingers through his hair. He wished for a weapon, then told himself not to be silly. This couldn't be anything serious. He would read the riot act to whoever was here. That would be that. He squared his shoulders. He hoped he looked authoritative. He couldn't hope for intimidating. That had never been part of his brief as a public face. He also wished he could swallow. He cleared his throat a few times. It wouldn't do to croak when he demanded to know what these people thought they were doing.

Why are there so many?

Is someone coming up the stairs?

Didn't matter. It *couldn't* be serious. It just couldn't.

"House," he said, "lights on." Illuminate everything. That was the ticket. Make him feel better and startle whoever was here.

The mansion's AI ignored him.

"House," he said again, louder. "Lights. On."

Still dark.

What is going on?

Diffring opened the bedroom door and stepped out into the corridor. He fumbled for the switch on the corridor wall. He flicked it. Still nothing.

Butterflies fluttered in his gut.

To the right, midway down the hall, dim light glowed under the closed door to his study. More rustling from inside, and the murmur of low voices. Diffring marched to the door and threw it open.

"Now listen," he began, then trailed off, mind refusing the evidence of his eyes.

Slaves from the mines filled the room. They were moving around his desk and computer. The AI panel had been removed from the wall. Diffring stared at them, at the ragged tunics and trousers that belonged in the squalor of the mines, not surrounded by luxury. He tried to wake up.

The slaves could not be here. Not in his house. Impossible. He was dreaming after all, and he would have a great cocktail story when he woke up, because this was the most bizarre and most convincing dream he had ever had. He could feel the silk of his robe against his wrists, and the comfort of Italian leather around his feet. He didn't think he'd ever had tactile sensations in his dreams before.

A big man, his face hidden by filthy rags, came forward. Diffring started to laugh. His fear dropped away, and he began to enjoy the absurdity of the situation. "And who are you supposed to be?" he asked.

The man hit him, shattering his cheekbone. Diffring screamed in pain. He dropped to his knees, clutching his face, the dream splintering into fragments.

"I am your reckoning," the man said. "I know you. I saw you speak. You are one of the Red Skull's favored useful idiots. Now you are going to be useful to me. Or rather, your house is. Its technology has possibilities."

The reckoning took Diffring by the throat and lifted him up. Terrible eyes burned within the shadows of the filthy mask. "As for you, though, there are no possibilities."

He threw Diffring across the room. The wall came up fast, and the impact sent Diffring into darkness again, where new dreams waited and cackled.

SEVENTEEN

Latveria was cursed by the past, Verlak thought.

She moved through the narrow, smoke-ridden streets of Old Town, leading a squad of armed civilians toward an ambush against a concentration of enemy troops. A Doombot had these foes under surveillance. It relayed coordinates to Verlak while it dealt with another cluster of enemy soldiers, these ones dug into a row of ancient houses half a mile away. It circled the enemy nest, drawing and returning fire.

Verlak made her approach cautiously. The omnipresent smoke gave her and her charges cover. But made a potential counter-ambush of every dark, broken window of the gutted houses on either side of the street.

So much ruin. So many deep scars of every kind as Doomstadt descended into the hell of urban warfare. As it had again and again. Cursed by the past.

Just in the last couple of years, Verlak had seen the past's claws sink into Latveria's flesh and draw blood no less than three times. The Fortunov dynasty refused to let go of its past glories and tyrannies. It tried, in the shape of Rudolfo Fortunov, to drag Latveria back into the swamp from which Doom had lifted it. And for a moment, when Doom had vanished, and Fortunov had led his troops in triumph over the castle moat, it had seemed that the past had indeed come to swallow the country whole.

And when, defeated, the past had been forced to retreat, it came back again, with a nightmare from the deeper recesses of myth and night in the form of the urvullak. They had laid siege to the entire country, and they had almost devoured it.

And now, again, another horror from the past, the undying dream of monsters from the Second World War. The Fortunovs had embraced those beliefs, and with the scope of the siege, it seemed to Verlak that the vicious past had fused its last two attempts to destroy Latveria.

As had happened during the war with the urvullak, Castle Doom had opened its gates to refugees. This time, instead of fleeing the undead, many of whom had once been their loved ones, the fighting destroyed their homes and businesses and drove them, helpless, into the streets. The castle stood strong. The paratroopers that rained down from unseen Wolkenland could not take it. They became visible still high enough for the castle's defenses to take them out.

After two waves had been repulsed, the Red Skull had apparently rethought his strategy. There had been no further direct assaults on the castle. Instead, havoc came to everywhere else, in Doomstadt and in all the major towns of Latveria. Some villages had fallen, and so had Doomwood. As with the urvullak, the siege had a thousand fronts, the enemy attacking everywhere, and out of nowhere.

There were some differences with the struggle against the urvullak, though. There had been no defense against the monsters until Elsa had found the way to cut them off from the consciousness that controlled them. The Red Skull's troops were not undead. They did not infect with a mere touch. They were human. They could be killed. By anyone.

And so the people were frightened, but they were also angry. They wanted to fight, and their time had come. They raged at the monsters from the past and hungered to retaliate, to reject the fear the enemy sought to inflict on them, and return it with interest.

Verlak welcomed their anger and put it to good use.

The Red Skull had come with an army, one that he had clearly gathered for the express purpose of conquering Latveria. It outnumbered the guard. Verlak had had to spread her troops thin in dealing with the attacks. The guard would be at a breaking point, if not for the people's wrath. Verlak ordered the formation of militias. With a single guard commanding each squad, she multiplied Latveria's strength many times over. There was no time for training, but sheer numbers made a difference, and not all of the Skull's troops were elite. He had his share of sheer enthusiasts of hate. Against people fighting for their homeland, that put them at a disadvantage.

So Verlak kept telling herself, as she fought through physical and mental exhaustion. She had to believe the struggle would end. But the paratroopers kept coming down, and the attacks kept multiplying. Only days ago, she had been able to imagine keeping the enemy out of Doomstadt. That dream had died. She had been able to push back hard enough to keep most of the enemy's heavy armor bogged down. The infantry spread across the city like a plague. Any street could see a pitched battle erupt without warning. The city burned. A blanket of smoke blotted out sight of the sky. Wolkenland could have shed its veil, and Verlak would not have been able to see it.

As the militias formed up, Verlak engaged in more raids using the ground interceptor. This dawn, she had left that to other officers, and led her own militia to the ambush position. She needed a more intimate sense of the war. And, if she was honest, she needed to fight back on a more personal level.

So she led her civilians through the quarter that they, and she, called home.

They were butchers, dressmakers, weavers, mechanics, teachers. The youngest had only started his studies at the Werner Institute in the fall. The oldest had retired from her garage a few weeks before. Different ages, different sizes, different abilities, and yet they were the same, too. Like her, they wore the grime of war. And they all had the same look, the same refusal to be frightened, the refusal to let monsters take their country.

The street narrowed ahead, until it was barely wide enough for a single vehicle to pass. The houses leaned in to each other, their gables almost touching. Verlak held up a finger warning for quiet. Her earpiece fed her updated coordinates from the Doombot, and she turned into an open doorway on the right. The house had been divided a century ago into separate apartments. The windows had been shot out in an earlier skirmish, and shell holes pockmarked the façade and the interior walls. Dust coated every surface. Sudden abandonment hung heavy in the air.

Verlak took the narrow, uneven stairs to the upper floor.

She crossed the hall to the bedrooms that looked out over the street that ran down the far side of the house. Her team split into two, each group taking up a position at the windows.

Below, Veidt Street ran by, sloping down to the right. It was slightly wider and straighter than the lane the militia had left behind. It made movement across Old Town easier, faster. An attractive option for people who did not know the maze of the quarter.

The enemy came into sight, coming up from the right. The paratroopers had come down near the market square half a mile up, gathered, and were making their way south, toward the edges of Old Town. A battle had been raging there for the last two days, fighters for Wolkenland and Latveria entrenched on opposite sides of the boulevard, neither force able to dislodge the other. This new group of twenty would be coming up behind the Latverians, trapping them in a pincer attack.

But not if they never made it to the end of Veidt Street.

This block had already seen heavy fighting. The house in which Verlak crouched had been damaged, but not nearly as badly as most of the rest of the buildings on Veidt. They were ruins, looking as if a bomb had been dropped on them. There was nothing left here to fight for, and the Red Skull's troops were moving quickly, not cautiously, treating the area as if it were a shell crater, a past battlefield.

They passed under the bedroom windows. Verlak and the militia opened fire. Latveria beam rifles were light, easily mastered, and their energy blasts packed a punch over a long range. This close, the enemy troops received the full force of the shots, as if Hell itself had opened up above their heads.

Verlak and the civilians cut the enemy squad in half before any of the troops in the street could return fire.

Verlak watched for the soldiers with better training and took aim at them. She fired at the ones who reacted quickly, who dove for the ruins and the sides of the house. Take them out, remove the threats, and let the civilians concentrate on the slow, the panicked, and the confused. Verlak shot three more, and then there were only a handful left.

They had found cover behind fallen stones in the wreckage across the street. Beams and bullets came at her, streaking through the window, scorching the ceiling and raining plaster into the bedroom. The student took a shot in the throat, and fell back, blood splashing wildly. The other civilians in the room cried out in horror and anger, but kept firing.

One of the Skull's soldiers raised his head an inch too high and died.

Good, Verlak thought. Not many left. The ambush had succeeded. Only one casualty in this room. She didn't know the situation in the other bedroom, but she saw a steady hail of beam fire from its windows. Most of the militia were still in the battle. Another few minutes at most, and they would have finished off this squad. And then they could move on to help break the stalemate at the edge of Old Town.

Then the morning went dark.

Verlak looked up, into a storm of paratroopers, so many that their chutes turned the sky black. Thousands of enemy soldiers dropped on Doomstadt, the biggest single assault yet. Someone in the room shouted in terror, and Verlak couldn't blame them. She had seen images like this, in black-and-white footage of the Second World War. Images like this, but not identical. No aircraft cut through the sky, and the paratroopers appeared out of nowhere in the last stages of their descent. Some were not coming in on chutes at all. They rode what looked like hang gliders, but were engine-propelled. They slashed through the air in aggressive descents, leveling off as they approached rooftop level. These troops carried heavier weapons.

She couldn't blame the cry she heard, but she could not permit its despair to catch. She couldn't let it infect her. Though her hope vanished at the sight of the onslaught, she turned herself to stone inside, remaining fierce with her hate for the enemy.

"Stay strong!" she commanded. "So the Red Skull throws his greater strength at us. That shows how hard we have hit back." She kept shooting while she spoke and took out the next-to-last surviving member of the squad. Then, without breaking rhythm, she altered her aim and shot at a paratrooper. The figure went limp. "So there are a lot of them. Do they outnumber the people of Doomstadt? They don't. We'll show them what happens to anyone who seeks to conquer Latveria."

No cries of anguish now, just shouts of determination and anger. The people would not give up. They were Latverians, and they would fight to their last drop of blood against the monstrosity of the Red Skull. While a few kept up their fire at the last of the soldiers below, the others began to shoot at the descending paratroopers.

One of the glider soldiers angled straight at the ambush position. He carried a long tube. He raised it to his shoulder.

Verlak's blood froze. "*Out!*" she yelled, loud enough for all to hear. She hurled herself back as the tube flashed crimson.

A fist of thunder exploded against the house. Verlak flew through a storm of fire and stone. The house became a maelstrom of wreckage. She saw only red, and then only darkness, darkness that was pain thick as bone.

And then oblivion.

She woke to pain, coughing up lungfuls of dust. She lay on jagged bits of masonry. She had been thrown clear of the main fall of wreckage. Her ears rang, and blood soaked her hair and the right side of her face. It took her an eternity to be able to move, and even longer to push through the agony and learn that nothing was broken.

You can't stay here. Get up. Get up. Get up!

She pushed herself up to her knees, and then to her feet. She had lost her rifle, and when she looked around, she could see none of her squad of civilians.

Anger and grief welled up, and she forced them back down. She would have the luxury of mourning in the future, but only if the enemy was defeated. She had to fight, they all had to fight, if that was to happen.

But if Doom does not come back…

No. That thought came from the despair she could not afford.

Verlak looked up at the furious sky, and the invaders were still coming down, in wave after wave.

Move. Move. Move.

She could not afford the indulgence of pain. She had to get under cover. She could not afford to be seen. If the enemy had even the most basic intelligence, the troops would know her for a high-value target.

Verlak moved one leg, then the other, and then she was

stumbling down the pile of rubble, into the street. Her body began to obey her demands more readily, and movement came more easily. She shook the cobwebs from her mind and assessed her position.

Shelter and weapons first. Then get back to the castle.

This was her neighborhood. Her immediate goal became obvious.

Home.

The sound of boots coming down hard behind her. She looked back. Some troops had landed at the top of the street, threading the needle to come down between the leaning houses.

Verlak broke into a run. As she reached the intersection and turned right, she heard a shout.

They knew.

She zig-zagged through the streets. Not the most direct route home, but the one that gave her a fighting chance of making it there. She knew the maze, and she used it, taking every crevice-thin alley, streets that looked like dead ends but in truth made turns too sharp for any vehicle to navigate, and hidden courtyards created by the unplanned, random constructions of centuries past. Old Town pressed around her, embracing her with its wounded buildings, its walls blackened by the grime of ages, the smoke of battle and smoldering ruins becoming her camouflage and shield.

Even so, she couldn't shake the pursuers. She stayed ahead and put more distance between herself and them despite the ache in her body, but they never lost her trail. Scattered shots struck the walls and cobblestones. Energy burned rock, bullets ricocheted, and the whine of instant death stung the air around her. She and the enemy moved too quickly for the shots to be accurate.

Now and then, she heard shots that came from nearby, but were not aimed at her. Brave citizens of Doomstadt, still in their homes, doing what they could for their captain.

Pride and gratitude gave her wings.

She reached Wegener Road. Home waited a hundred yards ahead, uphill. Her lungs burned. Her legs hurt so much she felt detached from them. They were someone else's possessions, things that obeyed her only provisionally. But the sight of the apartment building gave her the energy of determination, and the hope of retaliation.

A round smacked into the doorway, inches from her head, as she shoved through the main entrance. She dragged herself up the stairs. The power had gone out in the building, and she climbed in acrid gloom. At the top, breathing like she had a chest full of broken glass, she fumbled her keys out of her pocket and let herself in.

All the windows were broken. One corner of the living room had been blown open, and the blast had strewn debris and belongings as if a hurricane had raged through her home. Verlak blinked away the shock of the destruction and made for the bedroom. She kept a weapons locker next to the wardrobe. Ash and dust covered every surface of the room. The dresser mirror had been shattered when the building shook and cracked, and its shards crunched under Verlak's boots.

She knelt in front of the locker, counting the seconds before her pursuers entered the building. She held her palm against the lock. It recognized her print and opened. She pulled out a pistol, tucked it into her belt, and grabbed a rifle and shotgun.

They were all energy weapons, all what she wanted and needed for her retaliation.

From below, the crash of a door kicked off its hinges. Boots on the stairs. A shout.

"You can't hide, Verlak! You're going to die, you coward!"

She rushed back to the apartment entrance, pain an irrelevance now, new strength in her soul, new death in her hands. Shotgun at the ready, she stepped out onto the landing and aimed down the stairs.

Heavy tramp of boots, more shouts, the yells of a group sure of its intimidating presence.

The stairs switchbacked once before reaching the upper floor. Verlak waited in the shadows until the soldiers came into sight. She saw them well before they saw her, marching up in a line, rats in a bottleneck.

The shotgun's energy blast roared down the staircase, disintegrating wood and flesh. Verlak lunged out of the shadows to the top of the stairs and fired again, pulling the trigger as fast as she could. In the confined space of the staircase, the shotgun became an artillery cannon. The soldiers vanished, leaving scraps of burned cloth and charred bone.

Verlak stayed where she was for five minutes. No other attackers appeared. Then she staggered back into the apartment, granting herself a few moments to breathe and deal with the pain she had held at bay.

Not long, she reminded herself. She could not stay here. She had to get back to the castle.

She went to the broken window and looked out over Doomstadt. The paratroopers still came down, wave after wave of them, a black rain of plague blanketing the city. A long sound, a sigh and a growl, escaped from Verlak's chest. She forced herself not to think of Doom, and what the scale of the invasion and his absence might mean. She turned her thoughts to Elsa instead.

"We need you, my love," she whispered. "We need our hunter."

Orloff couldn't remember when she had last slept. A real sleep, hours long, the body prone and recharging. There had been catnaps instead, a few minutes at a time snatched when she sat hunched over a terminal, fighting with the helmet, struggling to reshape it to what she needed. It did not resist her. It became what she programmed. It was her commands that were wanting, the gap between their enunciation and her intent frustrating her and condemning her to nightmare after nightmare each time she donned the helmet.

She had grown more skilled at ending the experiment whenever she saw too much. She had ordered the labs evacuated, and she was alone in the subbasements of the castle, as distant from living things as she could be, but still her vision reached far, up through floors and walls, and she saw the death curled in life, the mortality that defined existence rushing into her awareness every time, hammering her to her knees.

She could not fight the enemy like this. The worst fear was that the helmet's weaponization, which she had created to fight the urvullak, would trigger without her conscious desire, unleashing a wave of death up through the castle and beyond.

She was a hunter, not a monster. She would not become death itself.

This time, though. This time. She would make the right weapon.

She had jerked out of another bout of head-nodding with a burning sense of urgency, and the conviction of an answer. As she worked, she did not look at her watch. The time and the date were meaningless. They would tell her nothing of what was happening above, in the streets of Doomstadt. They wouldn't tell her if the war still raged. They wouldn't tell her if Kariana were still alive.

No one had come to announce her widowhood. Doom had not returned. The Red Skull had not walked into her lab. So she still had her duty to perform, and time had not run out yet.

But it would soon. The tension in her shoulders told her that.

She had the key, though. She had the angle of attack. She had to consider the Red Skull as if he were the Devourer, and the signal that he sent as a symptom of the connection that he had created between the death triggers and himself. Just as she had perceived the connection that ran from the Devourer to the urvullak, she had to see the tie that bound the soldiers to Wolkenland.

She couldn't target the center of the connection. The shields of the island seemed to block her death-sight as they did every other means of perception. In the moments when she had subjected herself to the onslaught of death's existence, she had seen nothing above Doomstadt. But she didn't have to. She hadn't attacked the Devourer, or even looked directly at it when she fought the urvullak. She had just severed the link.

She wouldn't become death. She would become one specific version of its messenger.

Orloff worked with feverish precision, driven by inspiration and need. Fatigue dropped away from her mind, and her eyes no longer felt encrusted by sand. She saw the way forward, a crystalline pathway of creation.

When she was done, she donned the helmet without fear, and turned it on, certain of what she would see.

The world shifted into shimmering gray liminality. Objects and walls appeared solid or as transparent phantoms according to her concentration. She kept her gaze down as a precaution, but she did not feel the pressure of thousands of future deaths present in the castle. She looked at the corpses of the Red Skull's soldiers. She saw the remnants of the link, an ethereal trace like the mark of a wound that lingered beyond death. The helmet resonated to the frequency of the trace. Its dark music was hers, too, now.

"You will pay," she whispered to the corpses, anger mixing with growing excitement. "All of you are going to pay."

She took the helmet off and donned the armor that Doom had created for her. It protected her, but it also amplified the power of the helmet, turning the gauntlets into weapons, the agents of destructive potential. Ready for the hunt, she carried the helmet out of the lab and marched to the elevator that would take her to the surface for the first time since she and Kariana had parted.

Orloff stepped out of the castle into a dark morning of smoke and an enemy sky. She rushed to the parapet, wrath building as she took in the vista of spreading fires and descending paratroopers. The very air had been conquered and turned against Doomstadt.

She would take it back.

Orloff placed the helmet over her head and turned it on. The world shifted, and her vision became the sight of the hunter. She saw the enemy troops in the air and in the streets, inside their tanks and in the buildings they had seized. She saw them, and she saw the triggers inside their heads, and she saw their frequency.

"You're mine," she snarled, and she raised her hands, a lethal conductor. She slashed at the air, and her claws reached out, high and far, and it pleased her to know that her targets would feel her grasp close on them, and there would be time for them to have the full knowledge of their fate.

The sky began to scream. Verlak saw bodies twitch and struggle, and then hang limp, dead weight swinging at the end of their chute's cords. The gliding troops went into terminal tailspins. An invisible scythe slashed through the air. Soldiers shrieked in fear and died. The scythe came again, and again, its swath visible in the spasms and sudden stillness. The Red Skull's army descended helplessly into the claws of the hunter.

Verlak laughed. She howled and raised her fists in triumph. "I see you, my love!" she roared, and the sky screamed and screamed and screamed. "*I see you!*"

EIGHTEEN

Jurgen Hauptmann led a column of troops to the forward end of the starboard terraces. As the target came in sight, his jaw set in a grim smile. Finally, some satisfaction. Finally, an outlet for his anger.

As the war progressed, and the fighting intensified, Hauptmann had had to work hard to keep his frustration from showing. He had grown used to clamping down on it when in the Red Skull's presence. He did not like to bow and scrape before the man. He was Iron-Hand. That meant something. And he was a Hauptmann, of a line that traced its worth through centuries of aristocracy. Who was the Red Skull? How did he support his claim of purity of blood?

He didn't support it, at least not through history and identity. He simply claimed it. And he backed up his position with massive power.

As arguments went, Hauptmann conceded that it stood up well to contradiction.

He still resented the Skull's airs of superiority. But he did as the Skull commanded. He knew better than to disobey, and he had to admire what the Skull had accomplished with Wolkenland. The island was a machine of conquest unlike any he had ever seen. He would humble himself before the Skull if it meant he could join in grinding the rest of the world beneath his boot heel.

So he held his anger in when he spoke to the Red Skull, and asked, with each passing day, to be sent down to Latveria to join in the combat. He belonged there. He belonged at the head of the troops, marching unstoppably over the skulls of the defeated. But the Skull said no.

"Why not?" Hauptmann asked the first time.

"Because the moment hasn't come."

The moment. It took Hauptmann several days, and repeated rejections, to understand what the moment had to be. The Red Skull would not permit Hauptmann or anyone else to enter the field if there was any risk that they would be the one to march in victory through the castle gates and into the throne room. Hauptmann would go down only when the Skull did, and keep one step behind the new ruler of Latveria.

Hauptmann understood all right, and understanding only made the frustration worse. It roiled in his guts even more ferociously as he could not let it out, even when alone. The Skull saw everything.

Now, though, he had a way to vent the frustration. He had someone to punish. A massive assault on Doomstadt had begun, and he could not be part of it, but even as the final defeat of Latveria loomed, a rebellion had broken out on Wolkenland.

It should have been utterly impossible. Even a coup

mounted by the more egomaniacal of the island's paid residents was beyond absurd. They could fantasize all they liked about being the new power on Wolkenland, but it could never happen. An insurgency by the slaves? Hauptmann still couldn't come up with any explanation as to *how* this could be occurring. He didn't have to, though. All he had to do was end it, and that would make up for a lot.

The information at hand was sketchy, and that was a bit disturbing. The mines were empty, the guards dead, and two properties, including the one owned by that smirking dilettante Lance Diffring, had been seized by the slaves. Again, the how of all this baffled Hauptmann. He didn't like the fact that the watchtower and a flight of drones had been destroyed, and the two houses had been so completely cut off from Wolkenland's grid that it took visual confirmation to make sure they still existed.

Had some god come down from the heavens to help the slaves? Hauptmann knew better than to think that, but the idea was hardly the most ridiculous explanation.

That *how* could wait. It would all come out in due course. Hauptmann had come to put an end to absurdities.

At the bottom of the terraces, at the entrance to the trail that led up past the mansions, he called a halt, and mentally rehearsed the next move.

"Oberleutnant Manning reports his troops are in position," Unteroffizier Parrish told Hauptmann.

"Good." Manning had charge of a second column, which had closed in along the top terrace, and would descend at Hauptmann's command. The two forces would advance down the main trail, split off to take the narrower paths that ran along the estate walls, and then punch through the walls simultaneously. Hauptmann had asked the Red Skull how much leeway he had with regards to property damage.

The Skull had shrugged. "What was built once can be built again. Anyone who complains will be taught not to. There may be some beneficial lessons for our clients that will emerge from this rebellion. Crush it, Hauptmann, by whatever means necessary. Crush it out of existence."

A lot of Wolkenland's armed forces had been mobilized to Latveria, but Hauptmann still had more than enough troops to do the job. The slave population was just over a thousand? Very well. Hauptmann's columns were a thousand strong each. The value of the overwhelming force came as much from the terror it created as the annihilation it inflicted.

Hauptmann noticed that Parrish kept blinking and rubbing her ear.

"What are you doing?" he snapped.

"I'm sorry, sir." She dropped her hand to her side. "But do you hear it?"

"Hear what?"

"That hum?"

He listened, and now he did hear it, damn her, and he wanted it out of his head. A deep hum, almost inaudible, but strong enough that now he was aware of it, he felt its slow, cyclical throb in his chest. "What is that?" he muttered.

"Could it be the enemy's doing?"

"The houses are off the grid…" He stopped. The mansions had become dark patches on Wolkenland's monitors. That should mean that they had no power. But all that could be said for certain was that they could not be monitored.

He snorted. He mustn't let his imagination run away with him. The kind of scenario he had started to picture could only be accomplished by one person, and Hauptmann had seen him in torment in the castle.

The hum bothered him, but there was nothing to be done about it. It might not even have anything to do with the seized mansions. Whatever the slaves were up to, he would put a stop to it. They had been lucky. Obscenely lucky. But luck could only get them so far, and it would not get them anywhere against the force he had brought to confront them.

"The hum is nothing," he said to Parrish. "Ignore it. And tell Manning to start his advance."

"Yes, sir."

Hauptmann raised his hand, the metal gleaming in the sun, and he gave the signal to march.

The column moved up the trail. As Hauptmann climbed past the terraces, the hum became louder. He felt it in his teeth. His eyes wanted to water, though they stayed dry. He glanced back at his troops and saw discomfort in their faces. The level of morale displeased him. He hadn't heard any murmurs about the level of deployment against Latveria. No one said aloud that the war was taking a much larger toll than anyone had expected. But if the thought had crossed his mind, he knew it had occurred to others. And now an insurrection on Wolkenland, the island that should be immune to such a thing. It made no sense to the soldiers that they should be inconvenienced by people they considered subhuman.

A slaughter would help. A good massacre to reestablish the proper order of the world. Hauptmann would feel better. His troops would, too.

If only that hum would stop.

At the terrace with the column's target estate, the hum seemed to be coming from everywhere, as if the rocks of the ground, the trees along the trail, and the bricks of the estate wall had all become tuning forks. By the time Hauptmann and his troops arrived at the main gate, he could see a faint vibration in his hand. While he waited for breaching charges to be placed on the walls, he had to keep his mouth open so his teeth wouldn't buzz against each other.

"Sir," said Parrish. She looked strained from the hum, her brow pinched, a grimace tugging at the corners of her mouth. Down the row, soldiers winced and rubbed at their ears.

Parrish held out a communicator. "The oberleutnant wishes to speak with you."

Hauptmann took the communicator. He refused to wear an earpiece. Constant chatter was distracting. Juggling communication was the job of a subordinate. "Yes, Manning?" he said.

"*Charges are set, sir. But this hum…*"

"Ignore it," said Hauptmann. "If it is an attack, it's nothing more than an annoyance. Begin the attack in one minute from my count. Starting now."

He clicked off before Manning could answer, taking his obedience as a given, and tossed the communicator back to Parrish. "One minute!" he called.

The edge of the terrace was narrow. The properties took up almost all the available space. Only about fifteen feet lay between the wall and the edge of the terrace, a sheer, thirty-yard drop. Hauptmann had to pull his troops back left and right of the charges to reach a safe distance.

The minute passed, and explosions shook the terrace and the one above, the blasts going off with near-perfect simultaneity. Hauptmann had ordered that more powerful explosives than necessary be used. He wanted the intimidation factor of the thunder and the fireballs. Let the enemy know that the end had come.

The thunder satisfied him with its magnitude, a roar of wrath, and its echoes still rolled as Hauptmann led the charge through the long breach in the wall. A thousand soldiers stormed into the mansion's wooded grounds.

The hum grew worse the closer they came to the mansion. The sound stayed low, but the pulse increased in frequency, like a power source ramping up.

The groomed parkland of the mansion ended at a wide garden of gravel paths and knee-height, manicured hedges. A clear run from here to the mansion's portico and great doors. Hauptmann paused at the edge of the trees and waved the troops forward.

"Open fire!" he ordered. "Kill anything that moves!"

Energy beams and bullets slammed into the mansion's façade, a massive barrage that would suppress any attempt to return fire from within the mansion. For the first few seconds of the attack, Hauptmann grinned at what he perceived as the success of his strategy. If the slaves had any weapons inside, they weren't able to use them.

Then his smile faltered. For all the flashes he saw go off in front of the building, there was no damage. No windows broken, no masonry chipped. The mansion remained untouched.

His mind raced, and the explanation that occurred to him explained the hum, too. A force field?

But how…? The houses were not equipped with force fields. The Skull had permitted no defensive technology in the mansions. The residents had to depend on him for protection, and they would never be able to protect themselves *from* him.

So how…?

No, the *how* still didn't matter, all the *hows* could wait for after the battle.

Hauptmann stayed where he was. He let the charge continue. He would see how strong the force field was, whether it could really stand up to the impact of the massed attack of his soldiers. If they noticed that their fire did nothing, they didn't show it. They shouted as they ran, creating a human thunder to follow the explosions, and they hurled themselves like a tidal wave at the mansion.

And now, after the thunder of the charges, and the thunder of voices, came the lightning. Terrible, unending, a blinding wall of silver, and the hum turned into a scream of energy, a shriek from a maw the size of the mansion. The sound wave lifted Hauptmann up and threw him back into the trees. Trunks splintered and branches flew in the gale of the scream. Hauptmann slammed into a thicker, stronger trunk and slumped to the ground.

He struggled for breath and covered his eyes. His ears rang, and his head felt like he had been trapped inside a struck cathedral bell. The wind of the shriek ended, and the fiercest glare faded, but the lightning continued, a flashing, convulsing wall that obscured the mansion from view and extended the full width of the estate.

Hauptmann staggered forward, cautiously now, to the new, ragged edge of the woods. He stopped there, hiding behind a trunk that had been blown apart a few feet above his head. He stared at the grounds littered with incinerated corpses. From a point a few yards ahead of Hauptmann's position to the energy wall itself, nothing moved. His heart sank, and he couldn't believe what he saw. The initial burst of the wall had devastated the attacking forces. Closer to the woods, a few figures stirred. A few had regained their feet, and were moving back into the tree line, retreating before he had given the command.

Hauptmann slumped against the trunk. He didn't have the strength to call a halt. He would be making his own departure soon. The battle here was over. He didn't know where Parrish was, couldn't communicate with Manning, but he didn't have to. He knew the same thing had happened on the other terrace. Only a fraction of the troops he commanded had survived.

He would have to find Parrish, if she lived, or commandeer the communications system of one of the mansions below. He had to tell the Red Skull what had happened. He feared the response, but even more, he feared the mind that had created the wall of lightning.

It couldn't be Doom. But who else could have done this?

The questions and the impossibilities gathered, terrifying in their implications. Hauptmann tore his mesmerized gaze from the wall and stumbled away from the mansion, pursued by the horror that he might have been seen.

From the rooftop of Lance Diffring's mansion, Doom observed the energy barriers. Nothing came through. They rose high, a hundred feet beyond the roof, and came together in a tight mesh of cat's-cradling flashes. He nodded, pleased by his handiwork.

It had been a simple matter to reroute and reshape the power of the houses to his will. The Red Skull had not commanded the creation of a power source for the houses independent of the one that fueled the island's flight and shields. Why would he when he had an inexhaustible supply of energy? He had not foreseen the possibility that someone in the houses would seek to tap into the power for reasons other than the ones intended.

No. The thought that someone would wish to do that, and would have the skills to make their will a reality, would have been utterly beyond his imagination.

Doom glanced over at the mansion's helipad, and the craft that sat on it. A poor tactician might try to use that in the hopes of a quick flight to the Red Skull's castle. Doom had no interest in such an attempt. The path he had marked out was slower, but certain. From the moment Valeria had broken his chains in the mines, every step of his conquest of Wolkenland had unfolded as he had decreed. Even without his armor, and without his sorcery, he felt himself truly becoming Doom once more. A nation trembled before him, as it should.

A large group of the refugees had gathered on the roof. They kept a respectful distance from him, their awestruck eyes going back and forth from the barrier and him.

Valeria had come up with them, and she stepped forward, stopping when she had crossed half the distance. Acting as the bridge between the people and Doom, she said, "What happens next?"

"Next, we advance," said Doom. He pointed aft, down the corridor created by the two halves of the barrier. "I will make an adjustment, and the power I have harnessed will extend through the estate wall as far as the next mansions on each of the terraces we have taken. I will harness the energy in those houses, and so we will advance, in a tunnel of fire, until we reach the castle. There the battle will be truly met." He looked past Valeria to the others. "Do you understand what that means?"

"We're ready," someone called out, and the others shouted their agreement.

"Better to die in a fight that matters than in the mines," someone else said.

"Then go below and tell your fellows, and contact the other mansion," said Doom. "We leave in ten minutes."

"Who *are* you?" Chen asked. She gazed up at the flashing vault, and then back at Doom. "How can you do these things? *Who are you?*"

No need for secrecy any longer. In the mines, and in the early stages of the liberation, when he was vulnerable, he had had to ensure that there had been no chance of the Skull learning that he was free and active. He had told Valeria this, and she had understood. Now, though, the march toward the heart of the Red Skull's empire had truly begun, and he would realize, sooner or later, the identity of the enemy who faced him. Doom wanted him to realize. He needed the fear and uncertainty that the knowledge would create in the Skull's mind.

"I am Victor von Doom," he said. "Lord of Latveria. And for the Red Skull, I am Nemesis."

Doom. A whisper, and then a murmur among the refugees, the sound of the first stones beginning the rockslide.

"Go now," said Doom. "Make ready, as I have commanded."

They left. Valeria stayed on the roof. When she and Doom

were alone, she crossed the rest of the distance to him. "They will follow you anywhere now," she said.

"Yes," said Doom, unsure why she felt the need to point out the obvious.

"Anywhere," she repeated, and gave him a pointed look.

Ah. So she thought to inspire caution in him. "They must," he said. "If they want to be free of the Skull, they must do as I say. Not all will survive. There is no other way. You could not have expected otherwise."

"No," Valeria admitted. "I know what we're up against. And I know that you have done everything you could to ensure their survival."

Doom said nothing, uncertain how to process this form of praise, unwilling to interrupt its flow.

"When we get there," Valeria said. "When we get to the castle…" She hesitated.

"The Red Skull's defenses will be strongest there. He will be at his most powerful, and his most desperate."

Valeria reached out and touched Doom's arm. His skin burned where her fingers brushed him. "Are you going to fight him as you are?"

There was worry in her voice, but also hope.

"No," he said, and he saw her face fall. "Why? Do you wish to see me fail?"

"No!" she said, visibly shocked. "Of course I don't! I just…" Hesitantly, gently, her touch light as a breeze, she took his hand. "I never thought I'd see you again as you once were."

"I don't know what you mean. That past is gone, along with its face."

"I think you do," she said softly.

Maybe he did. And with her hand in his, he wanted to understand. He wanted the past, some part of it at least, to live on. Memories rushed in. No, stronger than memories, visions of the past, vivid as now and poignant as yesterday. Visions of the days of happiness with Valeria, the happiness stolen from the darkness of Vladimir's reign, the idylls in the midst of struggle. The happiness he had abandoned when he left Latveria, that in truth he had already begun to abandon when he committed himself to the path of anger and vengeance, the path that had saved Latveria, would save it again, and would yet save the world.

She held his hand, and he wanted so very much to believe that he did not have to give up this new memory, this present, that it could continue into the future, that he did not have to let go of her hand.

He would let himself want that, at least a bit longer. He would give himself that hope. But for now, the moment had to end. They had torn it from another darkness, another struggle, and the darkness would only be patient with them for a short time. The war would not wait long.

Wouldn't it wait, though, another few minutes? Wouldn't it wait for him to say words that might do more than prolong the moment? They might turn it into a reparation, a bridge from the past to the present, and a foundation from the present to the future.

No, he could not indulge. He must focus on the war. If he let indulgence have its way, and took his eye off the prosecution of the war, he could still lose. Victory and defeat balanced on a dagger point. If the Skull won, that would sound the death toll for so much.

And Valeria had died because of him in a great many universes.

"I cannot fight the Red Skull as I am," said Doom. "Not if I would be victorious. I am incomplete. The Skull has the greatest part of me imprisoned."

"Not the greatest part," Valeria said.

This was not the time to argue the point. "The most powerful part, then," he said. "I am a fragment of myself, Valeria. The Red Skull holds half my being imprisoned. It must be freed if I am to defeat it."

"How will you free it?"

"I won't," said Doom. "The Skull will."

"Why would he do that?"

"Because of his fear. In the end, that is what governs his actions, and so it will now. Because he fears me, he will free me."

"I don't understand."

"Neither will the Red Skull, until it is too late."

NINETEEN

The Red Skull already knew the bad news when he heard from Hauptmann. On his throne in the panopticon, he saw the readings, and the drone pictures. The mansion had vanished from the grid, then vanished from sight but reappeared on the sensors with a vengeance. An energy firestorm marched with gradual implacability in the direction of the castle.

And the bad news kept coming. What should have been the final conquest of Doomstadt had faltered. The messages from the commanders in the field were panicked, fragmentary, many of them ending in a final scream of terror and pain. Something was killing his paratroopers in midair and targeting his troops on the ground. They were dying without ever being in battle. They died as if the Skull had commanded it, as if a mirror version of himself were engaging in a remote-control rampage, eliminating his own forces out of sheer perversity.

He couldn't understand what was happening. He had Doom, he had absolute control over Wolkenland, and he could attack Latveria anywhere, at any time, with virtually no warning. How then could it be that Wolkenland appeared to be under attack on two fronts? As if the truth of the situation were precisely reversed, and Doom had launched a dual assault on the Red Skull.

The Skull had multiple screens showing him Doom in the portal trap, and the readings of ethereal, multi-dimensional agony. He had to keep looking at Doom to reassure himself of his prisoner's presence. He had already gone to the power chamber twice this morning to confirm with his own eyes that all was well. He couldn't afford that luxury any longer, with the situations spiraling out of control. He glared at the image of Doom, knowing the chaos would please him, grateful at least that he could deny Doom that small grain of comfort.

"Suffer, Doom," the Skull snarled. "Whatever happens, all you know is suffering. And if, somehow, the events of this universe pass before you, then you'll see that it doesn't matter how Latveria defends itself. I haven't done anywhere close to my worst."

Thinking about what he had in reserve made him feel better. He didn't believe he would have to use what the probe had returned from Jupiter's orbit. But knowing he controlled the endgame, no matter what, helped.

Hauptmann's call only added to his frustration, though.

"You had a simple task," the Skull told Hauptmann when he came on the line, cutting him off before he could speak. "You failed to subdue unarmed slaves with a greater number of armed troops. What good are you, exactly?"

"*There was nothing I could do.*"

"You could have done what I ordered."

"*I tried!*"

The Skull said nothing, waiting for Hauptmann to realize how pathetic he sounded.

"*That energy attack wiped out my command,*" the Exile continued, oblivious to shame, pleading for sympathy. Such an embarrassment. The Skull debated shooting Hauptmann when he next saw the man. "*How could I attack without an army?*"

"And you had no warning of the imminence of such an attack?" the Skull asked. He had seen drone footage of the disaster. He had heard, after the fact, the building hum.

This time Hauptmann stayed quiet.

"I see," said the Skull. "And did you attempt to do anything other than march your troops into oblivion?"

Another long silence. Finally, peevish, Hauptmann said, "*That isn't what's important.*"

The audacity stunned the Skull. Iron-Hand would never have dared say that in his presence. "Is that so?" he said, voice tight with menace. *Think carefully about how next you greet me, Hauptmann.* "Then tell me what *is* important."

"*The energy barrier! Its existence! Who did this? It must be Doom.*"

"It is not."

"*It must be! Somehow it must be!*"

Doubt gnawed at the Skull's gut. He looked again at the image of Doom convulsing in the portal. "Doom is before me, helpless and agonizing. He is a threat only to the degree that you believe he is. I tire of your sniveling, Hauptmann. Get back here, and show me you can make yourself useful."

"*But what are we going to do about D– About the slaves?*"

As Hauptmann spoke, the two energy barriers leapt

forward, taking over two more estates. The Red Skull hissed in frustration. A screen showed the perspective of an armed drone as it dove at the top of the barrier. Its beam guns fired, to no visible effect. The Skull tapped a key on his throne, overriding the drone's collision detection, forcing it to keep going. He willed it to pass through the barrier.

The drone hit the lightning. The screen flared white, and the image vanished. Static danced, indifferent to the Skull's curses.

Hauptmann was wrong about Doom. The Exile's dread of the Latverian had distorted his thinking. But the problem of the uprising was real and growing worse.

"*If it isn't Doom behind this, then who is?*" Hauptmann refused to let the idea go. The Skull wondered if Iron-Hand could be of any use at all any longer. His defeat had addled his thinking.

"We'll know who is behind it all when we stop them," the Skull snapped. He tried to think. The competing demands of the situations on Wolkenland and in Doomstadt pulled his attention back and forth, making it hard to see a way clear. He didn't know why things had turned against him on either front. He didn't know what strategy he should use to combat problems that shouldn't be occurring.

He saw two options for the Doomstadt situation: massive reinforcements, or annihilation. If he sent more troops, he would stretch his forces thin, and not be left with enough to deal with the problem on Wolkenland. If he deployed his final sanction, he would lose any chance of the triumph he had envisaged for himself. He deserved to enter the gates of Castle Doom at the head of his army, and to sit on the throne that had been Doom's.

If he kept all the strength he had on Wolkenland, then the disaster in Doomstadt would be complete.

The Skull cursed fate and reality's failure of reason. But in the end, he saw what he had to do. Wolkenland mattered more than Doomstadt. The survival of one meant the inevitable conquest of the other.

He scanned monitors, gauging the overall status of the starboard side of Wolkenland. Panic had taken hold toward the bow, and was spreading faster as the energy barriers extended their reach. The inhabitants of the nearest estates had already fled portside. The ones in the sternward properties had taken to their rooftops, gazing in the direction of the tumult, or had climbed into their hovercars. They flew away from the struggle and cluttered the airspace, gawking at the chaos from a distance.

The high and the mighty, as contemptible in his sight as any rabble. There might be some superior specimens among them, some of the true inheritors of the earth, the ones who truly shared the Red Skull's philosophy, and looked to him for guidance. Too many of them were self-deluded, the winners of the social class birth lottery who imagined their wealth had something to do with their actual worth. They had been useful to the Skull for the creation of Wolkenland, and for its public face. They were much less valuable now. Certainly less so than the preservation of Wolkenland at any cost.

They would obey his commands, or they would die. If they died, they would serve as object lessons to the other residents.

"We clear the starboard side," the Skull said. He spoke more for his own benefit than Hauptmann's. Iron-Hand was not much use to him either, now, though he supposed Hauptmann's presence could still serve to enforce the order.

"*All of it?*" Hauptmann asked.

"All of it."

"*Some will resist. They will insist on their rights.*"

"Their rights," the Skull spat. "They have the right to do as I say." They had surrendered everything else for the privilege of being part of the new order of Wolkenland, whether they knew it or not. Hauptmann was right, though. Those more than a couple of terraces away from the barriers might consider that the battle had nothing to do with them.

Yes, Hauptmann would have his uses after all.

"Execute any who resist," the Skull said. "Do not be subtle about it. I want the lesson learned." At the same time, he didn't want Wolkenland depopulated of its paying residents. He would prefer not to have to wipe out the starboard population. But that was a preference, not a commitment.

"*Those mansions are huge,*" said Hauptmann. "*It will take time to chase after holdouts.*"

"If the cowards hide, leave them to their fate," said the Skull. He had little interest in preserving such stupidity.

"We clear starboard," he went on, "and then we bring out the heavy cannons."

"*I thought they could only target external threats.*"

Four huge beam cannons lined the outer walls of the castle, their barrels aimed at the sky. They did face outward, aiming port, starboard, and off the stern.

"They can see off any eventuality," said the Skull.

The cannons were mounted on rails, and the crane mounts that supported them could have them angling downward as easily as up. The Skull had never expected an insurrection on Wolkenland. He had prepared for one, all the same. The cannons would draw on however much power they needed to punch through the energy barriers. The weapons and the shields might have the same power source, but the mansions still had limitations to their pull. The Skull had taken that precaution, too.

And if, through some evil miracle, cannons and shields encountered a stalemate, he would not hesitate to carve away the entire section of Wolkenland and let it become the falling of the sky on Doomstadt.

Even that would be a mercy compared to what he foresaw doing to the city.

The passing whim, the simple twitch of his finger on his control panel, and Latveria would learn what he had retrieved from Jupiter's orbit.

A sick, delicious tremor ran through his frame. His skin prickled with anticipatory gooseflesh.

No. Only use that in the last extremity.

The Skull ended the communication with Hauptmann. Iron-Hand had his orders. Moments later, so did the technicians in the control rooms, and the officers in the castle and across Wolkenland.

The Skull sat back in his throne to watch the war unfold. He glanced at the image of Doom and smiled. He felt better. He would force the day back to his advantage. And while he waited for the world to right itself, he shivered deliciously as he imagined the consequences that would follow if it proved itself intransigent.

Götterdämmerung.

If it must come, then to be its author would be glorious.

TWENTY

"We've moved quickly," said Valeria.

Doom completed the circuit he had been creating, and the mansion they were in, and the one on the terrace below, shot the lightning corridors forward, across the estate, through the walls, and to the next mansions. The walls of the mansion shook with the unnatural storm's fury.

In the far corner of the office, a man and woman clutched each other in terror. Doom favored them with a contemptuous glance. He knew their faces well. So, too, he knew, did Valeria. So did anyone who had had even the most cursory media awareness at any time in the last thirty years. The press baron and the journalist he had married. The man fancied himself an intellectual and historian, who had determined to shape, through papers and news networks, the ideological streams of the world to fit his judgment. She aspired to be a combination of Oriana Fallaci and Marie Antoinette. In practice, her conception of this fusion meant penning lengthy apologia for dictatorships and encomiums to her own ostentatious excesses.

In more recent years, they had suffered embarrassing legal reversals, though this had done nothing to diminish their self-aggrandizement and voluminous pronouncements implying it was their purview to judge both the quick and the dead. It had amused Doom to see him alternately lionized and condemned by the pair, as if their opinion of him had the slightest importance.

Wolkenland was such a natural habitat for them, he would have been surprised if they had not been present. Their terror now gave him some extra satisfaction. He had seen them before today. More than once they had been in the viewing stands of the gallery in the mines.

Valeria did not seem to mind their discomfort either.

Doom and his army were only three properties now from the end of the residential sector. After that, there were no more mansions. There was an open expanse, and then the castle mount. There would be no links from the last mansion to the fortress gates.

"We have," Doom agreed, satisfied by the progress. Once the advance had begun, he had kept the refugees moving at the pace of a forced march. The only rest periods he had permitted were for the length of time it took him to seize control of each new mansion's power source, link it to the lower terrace property, and send the storm of his anger leaping ahead to the next homes. Beyond the constant blaze of the shields, morning had come again. Morning, but the twilight of the Red Skull's reign.

"Are you anxious?" Doom asked Valeria.

"Of course I am. For me, for you, and for all these people. They have placed their trust in me, and in you. They trust that you are not leading them to the slaughter."

"Do you think I am?"

"No," she said, more readily, and with more certainty, than he would have expected. "I'm still worried about what happens next. You are still…" She broke off, as if ashamed of her own thought.

"Incomplete," said Doom. "Yes. The Skull is not yet frightened enough. His fear is growing, though." Maybe the Skull had heard Doom's name associated with the rebellion by now. If he hadn't, he would soon. And the Skull would wonder how Doom could be in two places at once, or how he could have escaped. Sooner or later, his need to understand what was happening would lead the Skull to his fatal mistake.

Thunder sounded outside, the unnatural thunder of the Skull's forces bombarding the lightning. The attacks had risen in frequency and intensity as Doom took his own forces closer and closer to the castle. The energy barrier neutralized the assaults, conflicting energies erupting in violent flares.

"That is the sound of his fear," Doom said. He turned from the control panel. He strode toward the doorway, Valeria at his side. "His breaking point will come." He paused near the baron and the journalist. He turned his head very slightly toward them, and they shrieked. "And then Wolkenland will fall."

They went downstairs, where the refugees waited for his word to march. Doom stopped in the main hall, where the greatest number had gathered. It had communication panels inset at regular intervals along its marble walls, for the greater convenience of guests at grand balls, events designed to combine revelry, gossip, and the eternal flow of business. The refugees looked at Doom the way all the world should. He nodded to himself, pleased at the proper functioning of the universe. And he would show these people, in due course, that there were rewards for obeying his dictates. Latveria had room for such as they.

Doom touched a screen at the entrance to the hall. His voice resonated throughout both mansions.

"The critical moment approaches," Doom said. "The Red Skull will use his most powerful weapons against us. You will think that the moment of greatest danger has come, and you will be wrong. That is the moment of greatest opportunity. It is when the road to our victory will open. No matter what you see and hear, keep moving. Soon we will be in the last houses before the castle. When we are, you will wait for my command. When it comes, you will attack. You will become the fullest expression of your rage, and the walls of the enemy will crumble before you."

"Doom!" someone shouted. "Doom!"

The people took up the cry. *Doom! Doom! Doom!*

Behind his rags, Doom smiled. He looked down at Valeria. Emotions warred on her face, as intense as the battle of the energies outside.

Doom looked away. Seeing her conflict only intensified his own. He was as confused in her presence as he was grateful to be there. Too much had happened in this universe to be easily processed, and the memories of all the other universes pressed in on him with the clamor of horror.

Doom forced himself back to the present and to the

chanting of his followers. "We march!" he thundered, and they obeyed.

On this terrace and the one below, the long columns of refugees headed out the sternward doors of the mansions. They moved across the lawns, surrounded by the barriers that flared and rippled, a terrible curtain, the coming together of aurora borealis and forest fire.

Doom had modified the barrier for the final approach to the castle. Though the corridor dazzled with its lightning strobes, it was no longer opaque. Doom could see the castle now, looming in the near distance on its hill, and he could see the nature of the Red Skull's response to the threat. On the terraces above and below the barriers, the troops of Wolkenland had gathered. They kept a safe distance and fired continuously at the walls of energy.

Until now, the refugees had not seen the enemy trying to get at them, and Doom felt their apprehension as they walked in the open. They hunched and winced at the attacks. Doom marched ahead of them, head high, unimpressed by the display. The refugees took their cue from him and walked with greater confidence.

"Why do they keep shooting?" Valeria asked.

"Even though it's futile?" said Doom. "Intimidation."

"Have they been doing this all along?"

"They have." He'd checked each mansion's outer perimeter sensors during the advance. The number of troops had grown steadily throughout the day.

"But how could we be intimidated if we couldn't even see them?"

"They could not be certain you didn't," Doom said.

"Though ultimately, that is of little concern to the purpose of the display. The intimidation is self-directed. The troops *feel* that they are intimidating, and that they are actively engaged in the struggle. They have not approached the barriers, and so have been safe from harm. The Red Skull keeps them busy in this way, ready at hand for when he really can use them against us, and they see each other in combat. This is the more subtle, and more important, intimidation. It is aimed at the Skull's soldiers, not at us. It keeps them in line. It prevents desertion and mutiny."

"Ready, you said, for when he can use them against us. Will that moment come?"

Doom smiled to himself. "He thinks it will, and very soon."

"Will we be ready for that?"

"Oh yes," said Doom. "I am counting on that moment. It will be then that the Red Skull frees me and assures his defeat."

The faster they moved, the more pressure the Skull would feel, the more reckless he would be, and the less he would think through the consequences of his actions. Doom urged the refugees on faster, and they responded. Doom did not think the enemy soldiers could hear the chanting over the roar of weapons and energy eruptions. But they would see that a lone figure strode ahead of the masses, leading the assault. They would see that, and report it to the Red Skull, and that would trouble him. *Doubt yourself, Skull. Doubt your triumph. Second-guess yourself until you do what I know you will. Because you cannot help yourself.*

When he thought about the psychological warfare he waged on the Skull, and the effect it would have, Doom felt something that could never be called pity, but was deep understanding. How often had he second-guessed himself into defeat? He knew the humiliation, the helpless rage, and the desperate self-loathing that attended the event. Yes, he understood all too well what the Red Skull would experience. But he did not feel pity. He looked forward to the suffering. He planned to see it work its damage on his enemy. He would see the torments of his past become the Skull's present.

Doom's army crossed into the next properties and broke into the mansions. They were empty. It seemed the evacuation of the starboard residential quarter was complete, or at least as complete as it would be. Doom had assumed that once the attack had begun in earnest, the Skull would order the residents out of the contested region. Still, he had not been surprised to find someone in the last house. There had been other holdouts earlier, the most arrogant Lords of the One Percent refusing to believe that a threat could be aimed their way. Now that the advance had almost reached its goal, though, he imagined the remaining houses would all be empty. Even the most deluded of the wealthy would see destruction closing in on them.

Doom worked quickly, and then the corridor to the final mansions opened up. He allowed no rest period this time. Whatever form of retaliation the Skull had planned to stop the prisoners from reaching the castle, he would use it soon. Doom was certain the energy barrier would hold off even the worst attack for a while, but not forever. He had to make his next move quickly.

The shape of the Red Skull's vengeance revealed itself

as Doom approached the mansion. Ominous shapes rose above the castle's outer wall. Huge cannons moved into place. Their barrels were wider than the largest on any battleship. The rear portion of the barrels were thick masses that pulsed red and blue with the fearsome energies within. Their articulated carriages angled them until all five pointed at the mansion.

Those threats are real. Do not tarry.

As Doom disabled the locks on the main doors, the troops that lined the terraces ceased shooting and fled.

"Here we go," someone in the waiting crowd said, voice quavering.

Doom threw the door open. He looked back over his shoulder. "Yes," he said. "Here we go. You may come inside and cower if you like. I would recommend you wait outside, where you will have the best view."

"Of what?" someone else asked.

"Of the power of Doom." He gestured at the energy fields. "This is as nothing."

Without waiting for a response, he entered the mansion. Valeria came with him.

The main control panel in almost all the houses he had raided had been in a lushly appointed office, no matter the architectural style of the mansion. But not here. The panel sat on a table in the living room with a floor-to-ceiling glass wall that looked sternward. The configuration pleased Doom, an unlooked-for gift from fate. He would face the Skull's assault as he met it.

Soldiers streamed from the terraces to the hillside leading up to the castle gates. The black walls towered fifty feet high, and the brooding skull of the castle's main keep glowered behind it, the brow just visible from Doom's position. Doom looked at the embodied narcissism of the castle's architecture, amused by the insecurity it revealed.

The army formed ranks, leaving a wide expanse between the base of the castle mount and the terraces. Doom watched the troops through the flashing of the barrier.

"So many of them," Valeria said.

"They are unimportant," Doom told her. He tapped the panel and began his work.

"We still have to get through them."

Doom grunted. "Do they look like an army to you?"

"They do. An army of hate."

"I'll grant them that, but no more. Look at the gap they have left. Look how they huddle close to the gates. Is that the position of troops preparing to crush a force of untrained, partially armed former slaves?"

"No," Valeria admitted.

"They do not expect to have to fight," said Doom. "They believe they are an audience, gathering for the spectacle of the uprising's end."

His fingers flew over the controls. The ends of the cannon barrels glowed red. "A spectacle that begins now," he said.

The cannons fired. Scarlet beams, coruscating with fury, slammed into the energy fields. The lightning turned to flashing blood, and thunder screamed. Tremors shook the earth and the house. Cracks snaked down the height of the glass wall.

Hold fast, Doom commanded the barrier. *Our task is almost done.*

He focused on the controls to the exclusion of all else. The clash of world-shattering energies receded to the deep background. Valeria clutched his upper arm. Her touch registered more strongly than the eruptions, but even that he pushed to the far corner of his awareness.

He completed the circuit he had been building since the first house. He linked all the mansions together, fusing all their access to Wolkenland's power source. Then he pulled in the energy barrier. From the long double-snake it had been, running the entire length of the terrace, it became a compact ring around the two mansions that held the refugees. Its neon blood color became brighter and brighter as the cannons vented the Skull's fury on it. Doom calibrated the nature of the barrier from moment to moment, adjusting to the flow of energy. The barrier no longer repelled attacks. It absorbed them, taking the beams of the cannons, wrapping them around the mansions into a growing vortex of power.

Doom had not known the precise nature of the Skull's attack, but he had been certain it would involve using the power that lay at the heart of Wolkenland, the same power the mansions used. He was turning the island's energy against itself. The Skull's understanding of what that meant had to be crude, or he would never have made the attempt. The Skull must have imagined that the cannons drew on more of the power, and so could eventually overwhelm anything created by the access of the mansions. If Doom had left the barriers as they were, the Skull would have been right.

Doom changed the equation. Power swirled around the mansions, building up to a cataclysm barely held in check. The world outside the trembling walls became a shriek of light bent on destroying itself. Doom held the storm tight, held it until he felt its chains on the verge of shattering.

"Now," he said to the Red Skull. "I know you are watching. Behold the hand of Doom." He unchained the storm and sent it back to its origins.

The explosion sounded like the death of the world. Vicious light consumed land and sky. The shock wave shattered windows across the island. The wall before Doom blew outward, sucked away by the rush of force toward the castle. Valeria fell to her knees, hands covering her eyes, mouth open in an unheard cry.

Doom caught her arm and lifted her up. She pressed herself against him, and he held her, and for the length of the storm vengeance and gratitude lived together in his heart.

The storm spent its fury. Echoes of god-thunder rolled away in crackling booms over Wolkenland. The light of the wounded morning returned and revealed the extent of Doom's hammer blow.

The cannons were gone, vaporized. Nothing lived on the hill outside the gates. Blackened, carbonized shapes covered the slope where an army had been. For an expanse running hundreds of yards port and starboard, the outer wall had crumbled, and the gates lay open, melted and curled like foil.

Doom smiled at the sight of Wolkenland breaking from his blows. "Fall before me," he said. *As in the end, everything must.*

Doom's followers witnessed what he had done and knew their moment had come. They rushed forward, no longer afraid. They became their anger, and they charged out from the mansion grounds, across the empty land, and up the hill to the castle.

Wolkenland shook with a new thunder, the roar of their voices raised in ecstatic chant.

DOOM! DOOM! DOOM! DOOM!

TWENTY-ONE

DOOM! DOOM! DOOM! DOOM!

Shock and disbelief numbed the Red Skull. His mind screamed, but his body held him motionless in the panopticon's throne. He couldn't feel his fingers. His legs had turned into useless lead. The images and sounds from the outer wall of the castle held him fast. The screens were a gorgon's eyes, the sounds the hissing of her serpent hair. Reality had collapsed into the absurdity of a dream, and he would wake up, he had to wake up, he couldn't be awake.

No, no, no, no, no.

DOOM! DOOM! DOOM! DOOM!

The panopticon had turned on him. He didn't want to see what it had to show him. It insisted on showing him everything, taunting him with the spectacle of devastation, of the shattered wall and gates, of more than half the troops still on Wolkenland gone in a stroke, and the furious, triumphant charge of the people who should be in chains, suffering for their impurity and inferiority forever. It mocked him, too, with constantly updated figures of the casualties in Doomstadt. Those numbers barely registered. The mounting disaster on the ground beneath Wolkenland was a triviality compared to the invasion of the castle, and even the fact of the invasion became insignificant when compared to the chant.

DOOM! DOOM! DOOM! DOOM!

How dare they say that name? How could they know it? Didn't they know he held Doom? Why were they lying?

He sat and stared and shivered, and refused, with all his might and all his hate, to believe. But the slaves poured in through the walls, and they chanted that name, and reality did not correct itself, and he could not wake up.

The Skull shivered, blood running cold and flesh crawling. The shiver became a tremble. Clammy sweat ran down his forehead beneath his mask and stung his eyes. Shock became terror, and terror became panic. The adrenaline that had shot through his system when Caleb Mueller had woken him last night (a thousand years ago) was nothing compared to the burst that hit him now, finally jolting him out of his seat.

A single image triggered the adrenaline, the image of a lone figure leading the mob. Tall, powerful, commanding. Masked.

No, no, no, no, no. NO!

DOOM! DOOM! DOOM! DOOM!

Now he could move. The Red Skull lurched up out of the throne. He ran, a cry of rage and fear choking him with the need to escape his throat. The journey to the control chamber blurred. His vision narrowed to a tunnel. He had no sense of the space around him, no sense of the world. He had only the need to see, to know, to understand what terrible impossibility had happened.

He reached the control chamber, and his roar of confusion when he saw that yes, Doom was in the portal, yes, he was still being tortured, terrified the technicians present. They bolted from the chamber, leaving the Skull alone with the paradox.

He ran back and forth between checking the monitors and staring at the column of the Power Cosmic. Doom was there. He *was there*. He wasn't in the courtyard, heading for the inner walls.

Then who was that?

Hauptmann had been right. He'd been right to be afraid. He'd been right to doubt. The Skull had dismissed him, and now…

Who but Doom could have used Wolkenland's power like that? Who but Doom could have laid waste to the Skull's forces?

But Doom was here!

Wasn't he?

A new possibility occurred to the Skull. What if Doom had tricked him all along and left him foolishly deluded by the illusion of Doom's presence?

The man in the courtyard wore no armor. Doom's armor *was* here. Its physical presence couldn't be doubted. But if Doom had knowingly left it behind, the better to lull the Red Skull into an ignorant sense of security…

The idea chilled the Red Skull all over again. It implied a Doom so confident of his plan that he thought nothing of sacrificing his most powerful weapon, using it as nothing more than a distraction. And events were proving him right.

No, it couldn't be that simple. The armor had to be serving another, greater purpose. It had done a fine job of mimicking Doom's presence. How it simulated his spiritual pain, the

Skull had no idea. All very impressive, but still fundamentally nothing but a distraction. It had to be doing something else.

The Skull grunted as if punched in the chest. He lunged for the controls, the scale of his mistake looming over him like a toppling mountain.

He had never trapped Doom at all. He had let Doom place his armor at the heart of Wolkenland and siphon off its power like a vampire. That was how Doom had destroyed the cannons. The armor had turned the Skull's island into Doom's tool.

"Get it out, get it out, get it out," he muttered to himself. He punched in a desperate override and shut down all the security locks expressly designed to prevent anyone else from engaging in this action. He blessed the foresight that had made him build in an option he had never believed he would need. What madness would lead him to free Doom?

This madness. The impossible happening. All his other precautions rendered useless because he had not trapped Doom at all. Doom had trapped him.

"Get it out, get it out. Out, out, *OUT!*"

The last lock opened, and the Skull deactivated the trap. He pulled the Power Cosmic back down to its heart beneath the control chamber, away from the armor that was leeching away at his dream. Now the power would belong to him again, untainted by Doom's machinations.

The hall flashed emerald, and the air where the column had been imploded. A sudden gale hurled the Skull forward, and then back, hard, against the banks of controls.

The armor had vanished, gone, the Skull thought, into whatever universe had been open for that fraction of a second.

The Red Skull collapsed in the nearest chair, panting hard. Disaster averted. He became aware of the alarms sounding throughout the castle, and he heaved another sigh of relief. His forces stationed in the castle would be rushing to confront the prisoners. He had taken Doom's power, and if the troops didn't crush the uprising immediately, he had the means to do it himself.

Calmer, he turned back to the screens. A number had gone blank, no longer having any readings coming from the false prisoner. *It's gone*, he thought. *It's really gone.*

And then he thought, *What if it isn't?*

What if the vortex of universes had not swallowed it? What if it had somehow returned to its owner?

The Skull called up the surveillance feeds of the courtyard.

He began to scream.

Halfway to the inner wall, reality shifted around Doom. He had a fraction of a second of intuitive warning, the sense of something massive rushing at him, and he knew the Red Skull had made the error he had been awaiting.

The air shimmered. Light bent. Doom perceived the inner wall as if through a fish-eye lens, and then the reunification hit him, as brutal as the cruelty of universes. The agony of the portal seized him. For microseconds and for millennia, he tumbled through the infinite realities again, the collective of all potentials riffling through his being and beings, taking the incomplete halves and forcing them back together. He went through birth and death a million times, the difference between them extinguished, and he revisited every atrocity the Skull had made him experience, the path of his existence retracing itself, the chain of beings whipping back out of the possibilities until only the one for this universe remained. Worlds burned, failures shrieked, Valeria died, Hell's magic lantern display torturing him anew.

Millennia and microseconds later, it ended. The change had come for him mid-step. He completed the step with the sound of titanium striking paving stone. The rags of his enslavement no longer existed. His mask, his true mask, his true face, was in place again. He looked out at the world through its eyes. He looked at the world as its rightful ruler once more. He wore his gauntlets that had devastated armies. His cloak billowed around him, blown by the wind of the vanishing realities. And an older power ran through his veins once more, his birthright passed down from his mother.

Sorcery and science had returned to their master.

Around him, his followers slowed in their march, staring in awe. He had been one of their number and apart from them. He had been a figure abused, like them, clad in torn, filthy clothes, like them. He had been in the darkness and misery. Like them. But they had never seen his face. He had been the one apart, the one of ferocity, the one who broke the chains and led them out of the darkness.

That was what he had been an instant before. And now he was what they had been chanting. Now they saw the true Doom, appearing like a revealed god.

Sirens wailed from the castle ramparts. The gates of the inner wall opened, disgorging soldiers and heavy armor. Behind a motorized gun, Iron-Hand Hauptmann marched behind Franz Cadavus in his Murder Chair. The Exiles and the troops arrived with none of the arrogance that had been their hallmark before. Doom sensed their fear in the air. Though armed, they came to the fight because they had to, not because they wished to, or any longer had confidence in their victory. They had seen what had happened to the rest of the army. The terror of a similar fate would be haunting them.

So it should, Doom thought. And he would not disappoint them.

Before the guns could be brought to bear, before the deployment had even completed, Doom turned the intensified molecule projector on the foe. Right hand extended, palm out, he unleashed a sustained stream of synthetic molecules in a wide sweep. They expanded on contact with air, and over the expanse of the courtyard that separated the two forces, they had time to grow and accelerate. They turned into rocks, and then boulders. They hurtled at the Wolkenland forces, shattered mountain rocketing across the space. They crushed infantry and smashed through armor and cannon barrels. Artillery exploded, plasma eruptions consuming the troops caught in the blast radius. The ranks collapsed at once, screaming survivors trying to force their way back through to the inner courtyard.

Doom fired the hail of boulders until the gates fell. He ignited his jet packs and flew up over the wall. He strafed the turmoil below with concussive blasts and meteoric impacts from the molecule projector.

Troops scurried like panicked ants. Cadavus lay beside his shattered chair, reaching out for help from Hauptmann. Iron-Hand had run to the door of the keep and was hammering against it to be let in.

As the refugees entered the inner courtyard, Doom stopped

using the projector. His followers swarmed over the boulder-
and crater-strewn ground, overwhelming soldiers who no
longer had the will or ability to fight back.

Doom surveyed the battlefield, saw complete victory taking
shape, and didn't trust it. He had trusted his conquest in the
control chamber. He would not make that mistake again.
He flew closer to Hauptmann, and saw a man consumed by
terrified despair as he smashed his fist uselessly against the
door. His fear was too great. Doom had only contempt for the
vicious worm in uniform, but the one thing he would grant
Hauptmann was that he didn't turn to cowardice without a
good motive. Iron-Hand could surrender and hope for the
best.

Hauptmann hit the door so hard that his iron gauntlet
shattered.

Doom hovered lower so he could hear what the man was
shouting.

"Let me in! Let me in! Don't do it! Please wait! Don't do it!"

Doom jerked back up. He flew around the courtyard,
scanning for the trap that terrified Hauptmann.

The alarms stopped.

"DOOM!" The Red Skull's voice boomed out of every
speaker in the castle. *"Are you searching for your death? Here.
Let me show you."*

The castle shook, and new barriers thrust up from the ground
in front of the keep, and from within the inner courtyard wall.
The speed of the emergence launched Hauptmann into the
air. He arced backward and landed in a heap not far from his
abandoned fellow Exile.

Forged of featureless black metal, the walls shot up a

hundred feet in moments, guillotine blades rising instead of falling. They sealed the inner courtyard off from the keep and the outer grounds. The struggle between refugees and Wolkenland troops faltered. Both groups stared at the walls in apprehensive confusion.

Doom flew to the wall around the keep. He tried to scan it, but its density frustrated him. The beings that had first created its material had not been human. They had built something of near-adamantine solidity that also seemed to flow, its nature shifting from moment to moment. He cursed. Braced for a trap, he had still fallen into one.

"*The only thing more final than a blitzkrieg,*" the Red Skull said, "*is scorched earth.*"

Specks of white light, distant as stars, appeared in the depths of the walls. They swirled in complex patterns, grew brighter, and extended lines to each other, like the formation of an alien circuit.

"*You can fly, Doom. You can fly above the walls. Maybe you will survive. But she will die, like she always has. Even if you try to carry her away, she will die. I do not lie.*"

"I believe you," Doom hissed. That sounded like the kind of promise the Skull liked to keep. Doom glanced down. He saw Valeria. She had climbed atop one of the boulders and was looking at him. Waiting for him to save or abandon them all.

He would not run. He never had, and he never would. Doom had fought gods, and the Skull was no god. Doom would not let him win. And he would not let this universe kill Valeria.

"*After she dies, Latveria will die. I will erase it from the globe. I swear this to you, Doom. I make my most solemn vow.*"

"I believe you," Doom said again.

The lights raced faster. The circuit pattern spread around the entire expanse of both walls. He tried to scan the circuit instead of the wall matter, but they were both the same. He couldn't find a way through the strange metal, no way to track the source of its power and cut it off. Options vanished before him, and he felt the touch of fear. Not of death, but of loss. The fear of what the Skull's victory would mean.

"You can save them all, Doom. Spare her and your country from destruction. Submit and they live. That's all. Submit. A simple thing. Admit the truth of racial hierarchy and bow before your superior. Submit, and Valeria and Latveria will live. You have my word."

"I don't believe you," Doom snarled.

He placed his palm against the metal. He had no more tests to run, and no more time.

The circuit covered the wall. It began to pulse, brighter with each cycle, the heartbeat of annihilation.

In the courtyard, refugees and soldiers cried out to be saved.

Valeria stood still, her face turned up to Doom.

He looked at her one more time. *You will not die.*

Then he confronted the wall as its dark heart flared.

PART III

The sun glow'd fiery red!
The furious terrors flew around!
On golden chariots raging, with red wheels dropping with
blood;
The Lions lash their wrathful tails!
The Tigers couch upon the prey & suck the ruddy tide:
And Enitharmon groans & cries in anguish and dismay.

Then Los arose; his head he rear'd in snaky thunders clad,
And with a cry that shook all nature to the utmost pole,
Call'd all his sons to the strife of blood.

WILLIAM BLAKE, "EUROPE A PROPHECY,"
PLATE 15, LINES 3-11

TWENTY-TWO

The tide turned in Doomstadt to the sights and sounds of nightmare. Through the night soldiers screamed and died in the sky. Corpses rained onto the city streets. When, shortly before dawn, the waves of paratroopers stopped coming, the screams shifted to the streets.

Horror stalked Doomstadt, but the nightmare came for the city's enemies.

Verlak left the apartment and followed the screams. More of Doomstadt's defenders did the same, sensing the change in fortune. They came to witness their foes' nightmare, and to add their own portion to the terror. Verlak hooked up with the remnants of civilian militias who had lost their military leaders. In ones and twos, other guards joined the group. The Latverian forces had been spread across the city as the fighting had grown worse and worse. They had become isolated by a war of attrition they could not have hoped to win.

Now a tide of death had come for the Wolkenlanders. By the time the last of the paratroopers had thudded to the earth, most of the will to conquest had bled away from the Red Skull's soldiers. They still fought. They fought to hold their positions, to survive, and to flee.

The nature of the urban battles changed. Verlak gathered as large a group as she could. They no longer had to be everywhere. They just had to be strong. With no more reinforcements to contend with, their focus shifted to scouring the foe from Doomstadt.

Verlak led her growing contingent down the major arteries, moving fast and hitting hard against the enemy's positions. The Wolkenlanders were themselves spread out now, isolated, their numbers dwindling. They knew the screams came from their comrades, and they were frightened.

"Has Doom returned?" one of the guards asked her.

"Not yet," she said.

"Then why are the fascists dying?"

"That is the doing of Dr Orloff," Verlak said proudly.

They drew closer to the screams. The target kept moving. Shrieks would rip through the early morning air from buildings a few blocks ahead. By the time Verlak arrived at the point, the area had fallen silent, corpses hanging out of windows. Then the death cries would come from another region. She was catching up, though.

Finally, in New Town, on the wide Doom's Law Boulevard, she saw Elsa. Verlak's wife walked by herself down the center of the road, a matte black silhouette in her armor and helmet, her head turning side to side. Now and then she would pause, reach out in the direction she faced, and summon screams. Some of the shrieks came from buildings on the boulevard. Others from locations several blocks away.

Verlak remembered what Elsa had told her about the experience of wearing the helmet, how she saw the world when she hunted the urvullak. Elsa saw through buildings. Physical objects were the ghosts of themselves, no obstacles to her vision when she hunted her prey.

My love. My hunter. My Blade.

Heart pounding with joy, with pride, and with triumph, Verlak broke into a sprint.

Elsa slowed at the sound of running boots coming up behind her. She looked back over her shoulder. Verlak heard gasps of fear from the guards and civilians. They slowed down, dropping behind her. Someone shouted "No!" when Elsa raised a hand. But then she just waved at them.

Verlak caught up with her, and the others, finding their courage, approached more slowly.

"Can you see me, Ellie?" Verlak said. She touched Elsa's shoulder, careful not to impair the movement of her arms and her lethal gauntlets.

The helmet turned to Verlak. The effect of being observed by the featureless helmet was uncanny, even knowing it concealed the face of her wife.

"I see you, Kari," said Elsa. Her voice came out flat, inflection absent, seeming to come from a great distance. She was darkness speaking. Her identity as the hunter had taken over. Verlak's Ellie had stepped aside, withdrawn to let the predator do her necessary work.

The helmet jerked suddenly, Elsa's attention drawn to something beyond Verlak's shoulder. Her arm snapped out, and her hand clawed at air. Some distance to Verlak's rear, wails rose to the blue of the morning sky.

A shiver ran down Verlak's spine. The uncanny lived, too, in Elsa's every movement as she responded to a different world from the one Verlak perceived. With dancer precision and praying mantis grace, she harvested the souls of the damned, as she traveled a realm between life and death.

"I am glad you're here." That voice, so cold and alien. Yet it was Elsa's voice. She existed, there, inside the hunter.

"What is she?" one of the civilians asked with a quaver.

"She is Doom's servant, like us all," Verlak answered, her tone hard.

Elsa carried on down Doom's Law, oblivious to the conversation. She conducted death as she walked.

Verlak hurried to keep close. "We will stay with you," she said.

"Thank you," Elsa said.

Verlak wasn't sure Elsa had really understood. No matter. She ordered that an escort cordon be formed. Elsa wore armor, but that didn't make her invulnerable. She had to be protected. In the absence of Doom, she was Latveria's greatest weapon against the invaders.

And she is my life.

They traveled down Doom's Law, and then up Heroic Andrew Boulevard. Verlak scanned doorways, windows, and rooftops for snipers. She never saw any. Elsa had killed the enemies nearby and was going after the ones farther away, the ones who never saw her, though they always felt her at the last.

Verlak had lost her earpiece in the destruction of the ambush position. She had one of the guards give her one, and she issued new orders. Doomstadt would soon be reclaimed.

Redeployment had become possible, with reinforcements rushing to the other centers under attack. Elsa would get to them in due course, but the guard would not rely on her to do everything for them. The balance of power had shifted. Latverians could take back their country.

"I can't give you prisoners," the hunter said at one point.

"No need," said Verlak, unsure if Elsa could hear. There would be no mercy for invaders. Nor would there be any point extending it. The Skull would not permit his defeated troops to live.

At length, Elsa circled back to Old Town. She gestured less frequently. There were fewer screams to gather. And finally, near the castle gates, she stopped.

"Is it done?" Verlak asked.

Elsa nodded.

"Leave us," Verlak told the escort. "Go and rest. Then be ready to fight again, and bring the war to an end."

Guards and civilians crossed the moat bridge. Verlak and Elsa followed them slowly. Elsa removed the helmet, and she stopped where she was. Verlak held her shoulders, watching her face, haggard with exhaustion. Her eyes moved rapidly back and forth, then she blinked, and clicked back into the living world. Her gaze focused on Verlak, and a moment later she threw her arms around the captain of the guard. Verlak held her tight and felt Elsa's body go limp against her.

"It's OK," Verlak whispered. "It's OK."

"This was different," said Elsa. "Not like with the urvullak. They were already dead. They were…"

"Monsters?" Verlak finished. "These soldiers were monsters just as much as the urvullak. In some ways worse. You know what would have happened if they'd won. The things they would have done."

"I do," said Elsa. "That's just it. They were monsters, but human ones. So I felt this rage. So much rage."

"You used it well, Ellie. You saved us. You're Doomstadt's heroine."

"As long as you're safe, my Kari," Elsa whispered.

"What about you?" Verlak asked. Elsa had been in her hunter's fugue for a long time. So much would take a toll. She was proud of what Elsa had done. But she wanted her Ellie back, too. "Are you all right?"

"I will be." She gave Verlak a stronger hug. "Yes, I will be. I have you."

Elsa straightened. Their arms around each other's waists, they smiled at each other, then up into the morning sky, bright with new promise.

The sky vanished. Morning blinked into night. Starless night covered Doomstadt, blotting out the sun.

For a few moments, darkness reigned absolute. Screams filled the air again, the screams of the people in the castle courtyards and in the streets beyond, reacting to the sudden night with terror.

Then Verlak's eyes adjusted, and she saw the dull glow from huge exhaust portals.

"Wolkenland," she said, awed in spite of herself. She and Elsa held each other and stared, helpless and small, at fifty miles of floating rock, a god's fist poised to crush Doomstadt to dust.

In the instant of the flare, Doom fought the wall as he had the portal. He met alien science with ancient sorcery. He lashed out less with a spell than with the undiluted force of his psychic self. His being merged with the shifting metal. He became part of it, his mind entwined with the vortex of its molecules. He experienced the wall in its constituent mysteries, and as a whole.

The impenetrable matter was not its fundamental self. The metal acted as background, canvas and host for the circuit, and as Doom traveled the circuit, he realized its true immensity. It reached, continuous, unbroken, to the other wall, and beyond both, deep into Wolkenland, and outward, ever outward, beyond Earth, a structure ethereal yet indestructible, captured by inhuman architects yet free, as vague and omnipresent as the background radiation of the universe, and as sharply defined as a dagger to the heart of creation.

It had been stirred to anger. It would lash out with that anger, terrible to behold, and everything, organic and inorganic, between the two walls would cease to exist.

Doom sensed all this in the moment outside of time as he became part of the greater being in the wall. While he perceived but did not act, the sands of the hourglass were suspended. When he acted, they would fall again.

Doom could not stop the circuit's anger. It had come, and would not dissipate. It could only be expressed.

So he became the irritant. As the circuit completed and unleashed the rage, he scraped its being with the awareness of his own. The circuit had no sentience in the human understanding of the word, though it had anger and volition. It reacted to Doom's provocation. The rage reached for him.

You can fly, Doom, the Red Skull had said. *You can fly above
the walls.*

Yes, he could.

Maybe you will survive.

He would.

Doom withdrew his sorcerous self from the wall. He saw
through physical eyes again, and he was already shooting for
the sky, jet packs on full, before he had entirely pulled back
into his body. His will had reached out from the wall, defying
the strictures of time, to begin the action before even the most
infinitesimal moment had passed. He flew, and he redirected
every resource of his armor into the force field.

The flare from the wall, the flare that had half begun when
he merged with it, completed its shriek of rage. A shriek
redirected even as it came into being. Instead of wiping out
the inner courtyard, it exploded upward, a volcano erupting,
in the direction of the irritant.

Energy pure and utterly destructive, the breath of a cosmic
dragon, engulfed Doom. He lost control of his flight. The
nova explosion carried him high, and he summoned every last
portion of the armor's power to preserve the force field. He
roared spells of protection, weaving their wards into the field.
The blast felt like the judgment that ended worlds.

If he had been lesser, he might have believed that to be
true, and wavered in that despairing belief. He knew it to be
wrong, though. The Red Skull would not use tools that could
annihilate Wolkenland if he employed them. Doom endured,
and he endured because he must, but even more because he
could.

He tumbled up through light and heat murderous as the

interior of the sun. Pain, razor-slicing and laser-burning, reached through the force field.

Doom endured.

And then the fury passed, the blast reaching upward and traveling on. It would destroy any satellite unlucky enough to cross its path. It would travel, never diminishing in force, until it reached its true heart, at the center of the galaxy if not further. Only then would it be spent.

But the anger had moved beyond Doom.

Momentum carried him upward a short while longer, and in the wake of rage, Doom felt so limp, he could have slept on the rising cushion of air. Then the air no longer supported him, and he plunged earthward.

He let himself fall. He had several seconds to rest and recharge. All the time in the world compared to the moment before the blast. He took a steadying breath, cleared his head. His armor's reserves had already replenished themselves by that much more. He used them where he needed them the most at this moment. A retro-fire of his jet packs in the last portion of his descent slowed him down. He came down with impressive speed to the untrained eye, and the paving of the courtyard cracked on impact. He barely felt it. Power flowing back into him, he turned to the greeting that awaited him.

The Red Skull's attempt had extinguished what little remained of his army's morale. Doom did not doubt that yet more troops waited inside the keep. They might still be loyal, but if any of them knew what had almost happened outside, he wondered how committed they would remain to the Skull's cause. They would know that uniformity of belief did not give them any protection. They might turn against him, and that would mean their instant deaths. They might still be driven enough by hatred to fight, but Doom didn't think they would present a significant threat.

As for the troops in the courtyard, they had given up. They huddled next to the keep, sheep cowering beside a barn that would not open. The refugees had disarmed them, and they shouted Doom's name with renewed, ecstatic rapture. He had saved them again. From their perspective, they had seen him defeat the end of the world.

He looked upon their reverence, and it was good.

DOOM! DOOM! DOOM! DOOM!

He had landed not far from Valeria, and she came toward him, smiling.

When had he last seen her do that?

In the deep past of Victor, long before Doom.

She held out her hands to him.

He couldn't help himself. He took them in his.

"Do you see what you've done?" Valeria asked.

"Of course I do."

"Do you really? Do you understand the hope you've given these people? You've saved them in more ways than I think any of us can count."

"I did what was necessary," he said, wary of both her and himself. She was seeing meanings here that she should not. He knew her. She would be thinking in terms of liberty and choice. She might be thinking to make him draw a lesson from what he saw here, and become something other than Doom.

"Please don't turn away from the possibilities you've created here."

There. She'd said it.

Valeria held his hands tighter, and he didn't have the strength to pull away.

"Possibilities," he muttered. The word came out with less skepticism than he'd intended.

"After everything you've been through on this island, Victor, don't pretend you don't see how things can change."

"By *things* you mean me."

By way of answer, she squeezed his hands. He couldn't feel the pressure through his gauntlets, but he saw the muscles of her hands flex, and then he felt the pressure against his heart.

It would be easy to agree with her, easy to fall for the temptation of the moment.

A moment is all this is.

He didn't have to disagree with her, though. He didn't have to reject the moment. "We'll talk later," he said, putting aside what he did not have the strength either to reject or consider. "The struggle is not done." He looked toward the keep. "The Red Skull still hides from his reckoning."

And there was the matter of Latveria.

For the first time since he had become whole again, he had the chance to try to reestablish communication with Verlak. Despite the power of the camouflage shields of Wolkenland, the Skull had not cut off communication with the outside world. At least, he hadn't before the uprising. He had seen in the mansions that Wolkenland's clients maintained full contact with their companies and other interests.

It took him only a few moments to reach Verlak.

"*Lord Doom!*" his captain exclaimed. "*Is the Red Skull dead?*" Desperate hope in her words, which shook, in spite of her discipline, with relief in hearing his voice.

"The enemy lives yet. He is at bay, but not defeated. What is the status of your battle?"

"*The enemy in Doomstadt is dead. The troops in our other cities will be, too, soon…*"

"Good. So Dr Orloff found the key to the death implants." She had again confirmed his judgment about her. The hunter he had woken within had served him well.

"*She did, yes, but Lord Doom, Wolkenland is visible. It has caused massed panic.*"

Doom grunted. "Control the panic," he ordered. "You will hear from me again soon enough."

"*Yes, Lord D–*" Communications shut down, cutting Verlak off. The Skull must have sealed the island off completely.

But not hidden it.

The tactic troubled Doom.

"What is it?" Valeria asked.

"Wolkenland is visible," he told her. "The Skull has dropped at least some of the shields." *And raised others. He doesn't want any word escaping Wolkenland. No warning getting out.*

Warning of what?

"Maybe he didn't have a choice. Could the trap he tried to use have drained some of the island's power?"

Doom shook his head. "The energy sources that fuel Wolkenland are not the sort that can be drained, at least not by something minor like that."

"*Minor?*" Valeria gasped.

"Compared to the full potential here, yes. That was a piece of what made Wolkenland, but merely a small one."

"Then why drop the shields?"

"Because he feels that he does not need them any longer."

That disturbed him. It suggested the Skull had become reckless, and felt he had nothing to lose in shedding Wolkenland's disguise of respectability.

Now he will be even more dangerous.

Doom had rested long enough. He had to finish the matter now, before the Skull tried something worse.

Then hundreds of voices rattled at once. The Skull's soldiers clutched their heads, screams caught in their throats. Their eyes rolled back, blank, and they fell, all of them dead in an instant.

Only Hauptmann and Cadavus remained. They huddled, crouched and defeated, next to the keep. They stared at the fallen soldiers with numb resignation. They did not have the death implants. That didn't mean they were much better off.

"The Red Skull has cast off those who failed him," said Doom. Perhaps the only principle that he and the Skull could agree on.

"Does that mean he knows he's done?" Valeria asked, hopeful.

"Burning his minions before we can, you mean? Building a pyre for all instead of surrendering? I don't think so." Doom walked toward the keep. After the energy blast, the wall that had risen to surround the inner courtyard had disintegrated. The wall enclosing the keep remained. If anything, it seemed stronger. Still featureless, its inner sparks had gone, leaving a profound black. And now the air around the keep vibrated. A faint sound, like a distant, inhuman whistle, filled the morning, turning the brilliance of the sun brittle. A new shield had come into being.

"The all-consuming pyre would not be out of character for

the Red Skull," said Doom. "If he truly believed he were lost. But I do not think he has ever believed that, and he doesn't now. Wolkenland still flies. He has sealed himself in his keep. Making the island visible is an act of terrorism. It is part of his next offensive."

"What is he going to do?"

"I wish I knew." The ease with which he confessed his uncertainty startled him. He would never have admitted it so easily to anyone else. To speak to Valeria like this, to be open about how he felt, was a gift he had not realized he sought. The gift tempered his frustration at his ignorance of where the danger lay.

He reached the barrier. He barely had to examine it to see he could not breach it with any means he had at his disposal here. He turned to Hauptmann and lifted him up by the collar. He gave Iron-Hand a rag-doll shake to concentrate Hauptmann's mind. "What is he planning?" he demanded.

"I don't know," said Hauptmann, sounding so completely broken that Doom believed him.

Doom tightened his grip. Hauptmann struggled for breath. "Think hard," Doom said. Just because Hauptmann told the truth, that didn't mean there wasn't something in the back of his mind that he had forgotten or didn't understand. So Doom gave him incentive to connect the dots.

Hauptmann's face turned purple. "*Götterdämmerung*," he gasped.

Doom eased the pressure on Iron-Hand's throat. "What do you mean?"

"I don't know. Something he mentioned once or twice. *Götterdämmerung*."

"The world is full of megalomaniacs who think they're the ones to bring that about," Doom snarled. The word had been bandied about by every sad clown with a goose-step and a Wagner fetish. The worry that the Red Skull actually could bring about the twilight of the gods fueled his anger. "Your life depends on your answers, Hauptmann. I'll ask again what the Red Skull plans."

He gave Hauptmann another shake, but then eased his grip a little bit longer. Iron-Hand's brow creased with concentration. The man understood that Doom hadn't threatened to kill him. Doom had reminded him that he was as likely to be a victim of the Skull's apocalypse as everyone else.

"There was a probe," he said. "It brought something back. I don't know what. The Skull wouldn't tell me. But he wouldn't start the attack on Latveria until the probe returned."

"Returned?" said Doom. "Returned from where?"

"Jupiter."

Doom dropped Hauptmann. *Jupiter.* He thought furiously but couldn't come up with anything in Jovian space that would serve the Skull's purposes. But something had to. Something forgotten by everyone except the Skull.

Doom stared into the unknown. Premonition chilled his blood.

Whatever the Skull planned, he was safe behind the shield. Doom could not stop him.

I have to. He turned back to the wall. He needed inspiration, the solution he had not yet seen.

Instead of a solution, he received the Skull's mockery.

"*I warned you.*" The voice of a grating, petulant god. "*All you had to do was submit. Now Latveria dies.*"

Over the rounded peak of the keep, the barrier parted for a moment, and a missile roared out. Sunlight gleamed on the silver body for a moment. It arced down almost immediately and vanished from sight.

"*The end of Latveria has a name, Doom. Its name is Sserpo.*"

TWENTY-THREE

Sserpo.

"No," Doom whispered. He stared at the vanished missile's contrail. The Skull couldn't be that reckless. Didn't he realize what he had done, and what the full consequences would be?

Yes, the Skull was that reckless. No doubt he understood exactly what he had done, and he had pushed the button because he didn't care about the consequences. Perhaps he actively desired them.

"What is Sserpo?" Valeria asked. She looked as if she did not really want to know the answer. Even Hauptmann and Cadavus looked up at Doom with the curiosity of terror. "Is it a bomb?"

"No," said Doom. "It's much worse."

When the wall went up and the shield activated, the Red Skull paced around the circular space of the panopticon. He knew what he was going to do, but he went through the process of second thought. There would be no going back once he stepped onto this path. As the night and the dawn had turned against him, the decision had loomed closer and closer.

Now the moment had come.

He didn't have to do it, not really. He was safe behind the shield. Doom could not get at him. He still had operational control of Wolkenland. All he had to do was leave Latverian airspace. Keep going until the island hovered over international waters. He would be untouchable again.

But that wasn't true.

Doom had trampled every one of his certainties, and everything had gone wrong. He had been sure he had Doom trapped in an inescapable Hell. The conquest of Latveria had been a sure thing, too. But Doom had escaped, and his troops had been defeated.

Fleeing would solve nothing. Doom would stay on the island, and if he didn't, he would pursue the Skull wherever Wolkenland went, and find a way through the shield. Doom had already triumphed over much greater impossibilities.

He's coming after you. And he won't settle for humiliating you this time.

But he could take everything away from Doom first. He could utterly destroy Latveria, and much else besides.

But what about Wolkenland's international standing?

He had worked hard to secure its recognition. That had been a useful cover, a way of gathering the influential and the wealthy who remained still protective of their public images. If he had conquered Latveria without ever revealing Wolkenland, he would have had two nations under his thumb, and his power base would have been unchallengeable. Now he would be throwing all of that away. As for his clients…

The Skull snorted. He had already done irreparable damage to the island's diplomatic position. Dropping the camouflage shields had taken care of that. He ran a bitterly amused eye over the lowest row of the panopticon's screens. News services around the world reported on the island's sudden reappearance over Latveria. They didn't have anything but satellite images to show yet, but more would come. Doom would see to that. Before the day had passed, the world would see the footage of the war damage. Already, commentators shouted about implications and omens. If Wolkenland could appear anywhere by stealth, how could it be trusted? Wolkenland was a terrorist state and must be treated as such.

The Red Skull shrugged and turned away from those screens. All very boring, all so predictable. The condemnation would have come sooner or later. He had expected to be ruling Latveria by that point. Had he brought that about, he would have had the whip hand. He would have had the dual technological might of two nations. He would have dictated terms. Wolkenland triumphant over Doom's kingdom would have granted it something at least as valuable as its most powerful shields – the aura of invincibility.

But Wolkenland had been defeated, and he had chosen to make it visible. Yes, the darkness cast over Doomstadt and the regions beyond was an effective psychological weapon against the Latverians. But really, *really*, what had he been thinking? Why had he done that?

To force my own hand.

That was the truth of it, wasn't it?

When the probe had returned from Jupiter, he had told

himself that the Sserpo option was a final contingency, the one he would never have to reach for.

Except the possibility had excited him. It had thrilled him when he had first conceived it, and had lain awake at night, imagining the final cataclysm. When the probe had left for Jupiter, he had not really believed it would return with the prize. He had not really believed in the project becoming a reality.

He had held shattering power in his hands before. The situation was different this time. Once he started this attack, it would move rapidly beyond his control. Under almost any other circumstance, he would hate the idea. And in the initial stages of the project, he had demanded complete control over what would happen. But Thorne had shown him the impossibility of that demand.

"We can put in guidance implants, sure," she had said. "And they'll work fine at first, when it doesn't really matter. But once things really get going, they won't. It's the problem of scale. The implants can't grow."

The Skull had come to like the thought of unleashing something beyond all control. He had entertained himself with visions of what could happen. And it would be easy to remove Wolkenland from harm's way. He would want to watch for as long as he could, though.

He stopped pacing. He *would* watch. He was going to do this. And he would do it not just for the sheer ecstasy of cataclysm. He would do it because Doom would have to react to the new threat, and then the Skull would reclaim Wolkenland. He had lost many of his soldiers, but the island had resources of strength as yet untapped. Its residents had been traumatized by Doom's advance. They would fight for their island and their privilege. At least they would when they saw how to do so. It was time for them to join the crusade.

The Red Skull took one more look at the screens around him. The defeats on Wolkenland, and the international condemnation, would cease to matter in a few minutes. He would erase the new humiliations Doom had dealt hm.

He would erase everything.

The Skull grinned eagerly. Then he left the panopticon, and made for the highest level of the castle, and Greta Thorne's laboratory.

When he arrived, he felt a shiver of joy as he took in the space. *Laboratory* was too weak a word, though it pleased Thorne to use it. Hundreds of yards wide, it formed a shallow dome, the crown of the castle's skull. At the center, the missile waited for its passenger and his word of command.

Since he had last visited, many of the huge generators that created and shaped containment fields had been withdrawn to the edges of the hall, signs that Thorne had succeeded in reproducing the more compact stasis field they needed. She had had to create a massive energy envelope around the capsule brought back by the probe. In order to control the specimen inside, they needed to be able to turn their own field on and off at will. That meant shutting down the one that had held the being for so many years, and doing so in a way that did not unleash the danger prematurely, and doom Wolkenland to destruction.

The new capsule stood beside the missile. Inside a clear cylinder that pulsed with alien energies now under human guidance, Sserpo floated in a nutrient bath. The Skull placed a hand on the cylinder. The beast did not move. It could have been a statue. The reptilian had orange, armored hide. Bipedal, it had thick toes and fingers, a short tail, and a gargoyle's face. It was only a few feet long. A trivial thing.

Thorne worked on the other side of the cylinder from the Skull. Tablet in hand, she shifted her attention between it, Sserpo, and the laptop on the wheeled table in front of her. She had barely glanced at the Skull when he entered the lab.

"Is it ready?" the Red Skull asked.

It took Thorne a few minutes to respond, and when she did, it was as if she hadn't heard his question. Perhaps she hadn't. Once she disappeared inside her head, even the Skull found it almost impossible pry her out.

"It really is remarkable," Thorne said. "Because nothing about it makes sense. How can this be an aquatic reptile? It's built for the land. I mean, yes, there's webbing between the toes and fingers, but those are arms, not forelegs. And a bipedal lizard? Ridiculous. And we've never encountered any others of this species. How can that be?" She shook her head. "Pure nonsense. As is its growth. How did that happen? Where did all the extra mass come from? Where did it go when the process was reversed?" She clapped her hands in delight. "Such an absurdity. It's been a privilege to work on it."

"But is it ready?" the Skull asked.

Thorne finally listened. "Oh yes," she said. "Any time you like."

"Launch it."

Thorne cocked her head. Eyes gleaming, she said, "I *have* continued to experiment with control implants. I'm afraid nothing works."

"I understand."

"I want to be sure you do. Once Sserpo is freed, we have no say in what the animal does."

"I understand," the Skull snapped. "*Launch it.*"

"As you will," Thorne said, with no reluctance at all. The shine in her eyes became brilliant.

She had been waiting for this moment from the start, the Red Skull thought. This was the ultimate line to cross. The loss of control excited her even more than it did the Skull. The irrevocable beckoned, and she answered its call with ecstatic joy.

Thorne tapped her tablet's screen. A single tap. She must have had the command present before her all the time, an icon of perpetual anticipation. She licked her lips.

Articulated arms descended from ceiling recesses to take the cylinder and load it into the missile's nose cone.

"Is there a parachute?" the Skull asked.

"No need," said Thorne. "Not with the stasis field. It will deactivate ten seconds after impact."

"How quickly will Sserpo grow?"

"I couldn't get an accurate estimate. But quickly, of that I'm sure. Very quickly."

A silo, sunken into the floor, held the lower half of the missile. Already, steam rose from below, as pre-launch mechanisms engaged. The peak of the dome pulled back, letting sunlight into the hall. The air quivered in the grip of the shield. That small portion of the keep's protection would open at the moment of launch. Just a brief window of vulnerability. Doom did not know what the Skull planned. He would not be waiting just out of sight to seize that moment.

The Red Skull reassured himself by moving to one of the lab terminals and calling up the inner courtyard surveillance lens. Doom was there, throttling the pathetic Hauptmann.

Good. He would have the luxury of taunting Doom. It would be satisfying to tell him how his country was going to die.

"Sserpo," Doom said to Valeria, "almost ended the world several decades ago."

"How can I not have heard the name before?" Valeria asked.

Doom grunted. "How many times has the world almost ended since then?" he responded. "Especially in recent years. Each apocalypse supersedes the previous one in the collective memory. And the threat of this one, mercifully, did not last long."

The Sserpo terror had been before his time. It had not directly affected King Vladimir's Latveria. The terrors of that regime had been all-consuming for people like Doom and Valeria. The world had almost ended, and then it hadn't, and they had not known it at the time. Doom had studied the event later, but only in passing. That danger had long been over when he seized power. There had been no reason to think about Jupiter, and what might be orbiting it. He had completely forgotten there was anything there.

"Sserpo," Doom continued, "was a reptile, of species unknown." He had to act, had to stop the threat, but the missile had been launched, and he would not be able to prevent the initial stages of the danger. He needed to organize his thoughts, to see his way clear. Speaking to Valeria helped. Part of him had trouble believing the Red Skull really had committed to this act. "Somehow, it came into contact with something that made it grow."

"Was this the result of an experiment?"

"If so, no one ever came forward to make demands during the rampage, or to take responsibility afterward. The cause of Sserpo's growth has never been discovered. The speed and scale of the beast's expansion defied all physical laws."

"How big did it get?"

"It could reach halfway across a continent," said Doom. The footage he had seen beggared belief, even in this age of gods and monsters. "It stood thousands of miles in height. At the point of greatest crisis, its mass was about to destabilize the Earth's axis."

Valeria shook her head. "That's …"

"Ridiculous," said Doom. "Such a thing could not be. No, it could not. Yet it happened. Perhaps that is why Sserpo has faded from the collective memory. It is easier for the mind to forget than to attempt to encompass the sublime." Even he found that true. He had filed the knowledge of Sserpo away like an abstraction, as if the historical reality were, in fact, a thought experiment and nothing more, a best-ignored blip in the functioning of the universe.

Even now, the abstraction resisted conception as a concrete threat. How could he imagine all of Latveria flattened by a single footstep?

"How was Sserpo stopped?" said Valeria.

Doom gave a mirthless chuckle. "A Jovian civilization removed it from Earth. By means of an interplanetary sky-hook. They then reduced Sserpo to its original stasis and placed it in orbit around Jupiter."

"A sky-hook…" Valeria repeated, eyes wide with disbelief.

"We cannot look to the Jovians for aid this time. This civilization has, of course, never been heard from again."

Valeria shook her head, rejecting the surreal.

"A tear in the fabric of probability. A slumbering god's nightmare manifested on Earth. A global hallucination. These have all been advanced as explanations. In the end, forgetfulness seems to have been our species' instinctive reaction to Sserpo. But the Red Skull remembered. Or his dreams of destruction led him to the memory. He confirmed the reality of Sserpo and brought the nightmare back."

And had launched it into Latveria.

He had to think clearly. He could not let his rage goad him into a mistake.

"If it grows like it did before," said Valeria, "it will end everything."

"Yes," said Doom. *I know.* And he broke past his wrath at the threat to Latveria. It was the Red Skull who had given in to his emotions. Whether Sserpo destroyed Latveria and the world or not, he had shown his hand and abandoned all chance of a victory beyond the pyrrhic.

"You have to stop it!"

"Yes," Doom said again. In speaking, he had begun to formulate a possible plan of attack. For all he knew, it was as deluded a strategy as the world's forgetfulness had turned out to be. It was all he had as a way forward, though.

What he had not been able to find was a way to be in two places at once, and he cursed the Red Skull yet again.

He looked down at Valeria. "I must leave you," he said, spelling out the first of the consequences.

"I know," she said.

After all he had fought through on Wolkenland, was this how this universe would choose to kill Valeria through him? By sending him away and leaving her at the mercy of the Red Skull? The traumas of the prison portal pressed hard on him, and Valeria's million deaths flickered before his mind's eye.

He had no illusions. The Red Skull had not spent all his strength. He would counter-attack as soon as Doom left.

Valeria reached up and touched the side of Doom's mask. "You have to go," she said. "If you don't, all of us are lost either way."

He nodded. He turned away before he could say anything else that would worsen the pain of the inevitable.

He did pause, though, after taking a few steps away from Valeria. He looked back at the refugees. They gazed at him, a mosaic of hope, fear, and determination. "I go now to save the planet from a madman's dream." And to once again show the world why it needed Doom in command, now and forever. He gave his followers one more order. "Hold Wolkenland until I return."

He flew off, following the dissipating contrail. The renewed chanting of his name went with him.

The missile slammed into forest land fifty miles north of Doomstadt. Tracking stations monitored its descent, though anti-ballistic defenses had no time to react. In Castle Doom's security center, Kariana Verlak, exhausted and coasting on fumes of adrenaline, saw its flight, and had an eternity of seconds to anticipate a nuclear blast. So had every officer present.

Silence fell in the center, the quiet of inner farewells. Elsa had come with her to the center, and though she, too, could barely stand, she was there to see where she would have to go next to swing her scythe again. Verlak took her hand, and she held on tight, grateful at least that they were together for the end.

When annihilation did not come, and long-range sensors registered a relatively minor explosion in the forest, miles from the nearest settlement, Verlak joined everyone else in a gasp of relief.

"A dud!" one of the officers shouted. "They launched a dud!"

"Can we really be that lucky?" Elsa whispered.

No, Verlak thought.

A moment later, another officer called out, "There's something moving at the blast site."

"*What* is moving?" Verlak demanded, even as her gut told her that she really did not want to know.

"I don't know, captain." The man frowned. "We're getting some biological readings. But they don't make sense. It's getting bigger. Very fast."

Verlak exchanged a look with Elsa. The other cities would have to wait. "I want armed drone flights there five minutes ago, if not sooner."

"Yes, captain."

"All squadrons, redeploy from current flight missions. This is the new target. Whatever is there, I want it destroyed before it reaches any settlements."

I want it destroyed. She already guessed that she might as well be blowing candles out on a cake for all the chance she had of her wishes being fulfilled.

"It's really growing fast," the monitoring officer said, sounding frightened.

The beast awoke, and it hungered.

It stood up, stomped through the flames that surrounded it, and into the trees. When it reached out for its first branch of foliage, it was already fifteen feet high. Its hunger becoming fiercer, it snatched more branches, and then an entire tree. With every step, it saw the ground recede, and the forest became smaller, offering less of the illusion of nourishment. It hit four hundred feet and scooped up the rest of the woods in its fists.

As it passed its first thousand feet, Sserpo roared in frustration. Nothing it ate ended its hunger. The urge to consume burned through it, and so did the instinct to lash out at a world that offered no satisfaction. A mile high, it left the forest. Its feet left craters as it walked. The earth groaned beneath its tread. Tremors radiated outward from its march, becoming more intense as Sserpo grew from colossus to deity. Five miles high, it clawed at the clouds that floated by its torso, and it roared again. It made its voice heard across Latveria and beyond.

Minutes after it had emerged from its stasis chamber, ten miles tall, Sserpo destroyed the village of Doomfluss without even being aware of it. Sserpo moved in a widening spiral from its point of emergence, and cataclysm walked with it.

In the towns and cities of Latveria, the citizens who had fought with rabid tenacity against the invaders shuddered in fear as the rage of a dragon sounded over the land, and the ground beneath their feet trembled harder and harder with the awful rhythm of destruction's steps.

Marvel Untold

When Doom closed in on Sserpo, ahead of the drones and aircraft sent by Verlak, the reptile towered more than thirty miles high, its head in the upper stratosphere. The monster could be seen from Wolkenland.

Raging with the hunger it could not satisfy, Sserpo leaned down and slammed its fists against the ground, sending earth tremors felt across half of Europe, triggering new eruptions of Etna, Vesuvius and Santorini.

Doom rocketed up to a head that looked like a planet come to ravenous life. Sserpo sensed him in all his insignificance and snarled a challenge.

TWENTY-FOUR

The peace that Grigori Zargo had known since the end of the battle with the urvullak frayed gradually for some time, so gradually that he didn't realize it at first, and put the bad dreams and restless sleep down to the squirming of memories.

He had come to Mount Sivàr after the Devourer had been destroyed, and the urvullak defeated. He made his home on the peak, in the cave that had been the hermitage for the witch Maria von Helm. The mountain, a lone peak east of Doomstadt, isolated from the rest of its chain, had been grieving the loss of the witch. It accepted him readily as its new companion. Zargo left the mountain rarely, going down only to replenish supplies. He spent his days in meditation with the Earth.

Once, not that long ago by the measure of the calendar, but an age past by the reckoning of his identity, a retreat would have meant prayer. That was when he had still been a priest. He sometimes felt the pang of melancholy for the loss of his former identity. Doom had stripped that self from him, that comforting disguise, when he had commanded Zargo to use his geomantic skills. Doom had pushed him, harder and harder, through one crisis after another, until Zargo finally accepted that the sorcery of stone was his true calling.

Miraculously, when Zargo had left the cities behind and withdrawn to Mount Sivàr, Doom had not dragged him back. He had let Zargo be. In the mountain, Zargo made peace with the truth of his being, and he felt the Earth forgive him for the violence he had subjected it to when he had made it swallow an entire village of the undead.

Time passed, and Zargo learned to sleep through the night once more. He no longer woke up screaming, and no longer tossed and turned, wracked by the guilt of his discarded faith.

He found peace, and then it began to leave him again. The old nightmares and guilt did not come back. He didn't know what woke him, and what troubled him. He tried to put the disturbances down to a passing, unconscious trouble. But something grated at his meditations and communion with stone, too. The gnawing sense of wrongness in Latveria grew, but he could not find the source of the problem. He sent his consciousness through the mountain, into its roots, and streaming along the ley lines of Latveria. The bedrock of the nation quivered, harmony plucked out of tune, but the source of the trouble remained beyond his perception.

Then, this morning, the earth wailed.

Zargo jerked awake, gasping for air, hands clawing at his chest. The mount rang like a tuning fork. And through the sorcerous ether and into his mind came the voice he had hoped he would not hear again.

Zargo, Doom called. *Look to the north and west. Latveria is at war, and so are you.*

Zargo had a moment to mourn his illusion of peace. Months had passed without Doom seeking him out. He knew Doom had been here, when he had lured Helm out and into his scheme to free his mother from Hell. Zargo knew that this could never be a true refuge from Doom. But Doom had not summoned him, had not contacted him at all, and the idea that the mountain really was Zargo's place of retreat had been too powerful to dismiss as a dream.

But Doom called him now, as Zargo knew he always would.

He had the moment to mourn, but he did not have another to achieve resignation. A roar to dwarf mountains shattered the morning air, and Mount Sivàr shook hard enough to split the roof of the cave. Zargo rushed outside, almost losing his footing as the floor shifted back and forth with the rhythm of the tremors. Out in the air, he held on to the mountain, that which had been so stable and now wanted to melt into air. He looked where Doom's voice had commanded, and he staggered again.

To the west, a land mass hovered over Doomstadt. The strange distress he had felt in the Earth for the last while now made awful sense. Gravity had been disrupted by the unnatural, and the stones cried out. Somehow the floating island had been invisible to him until now.

North of the island, Zargo saw a monster the orange shade of Precambrian granite. It was distant from Zargo and yet far too close, because it shrank all distance. It was so huge, his mind had trouble processing the message of his eyes. Mount Sivàr would not even reach the creature's knees. When the thing walked, the earth shook.

"Tremendum," Zargo whispered in horror.

All his life, and especially during his years as a priest, Zargo had sought a glimpse of the numinous. Now true sublimity confronted him, and he saw how foolish his quest had been. There was no joy to be had in the numinous. Only awe and terror resided there, monstrous and destructive.

Zargo sent the smallest sliver of his consciousness through his hand, into the mountain, and down into the wider land, and the pain in stone and continent was the howling shriek of a torture victim. Zargo recoiled, pulling his being away from the torment, but the damage to his soul had already been done, and he felt each tread of the horror as another wound.

Through the ether, into his mind, Doom spoke again. *Can you slow Sserpo? The beast is heading toward Doomstadt.*

Bracing himself, Zargo reconnected with the mountain. *I'll try*, he thought, sending the words down geomantic streams. He had never tried to communicate in this way. He trusted in the interconnection of the occult realms to bring his message to Doom. Then, fighting not to be overwhelmed by the Earth's pain, he reached out down the lines of force to where Sserpo walked.

It felt like moving against a riptide. The earth rippled like a splashed pond beneath the beast, waves of agony crashing against Zargo's psychic self, threatening to carry him off in the foaming crash of pain. Zargo kept reaching out, sweat coursing down his physical body. He took hold of the earth at Sserpo's feet and commanded it to rise. Rock shifted from moment to moment between solid and molten, and it rose up around the monster's legs, the seismic shocks huge, Zargo inflicting still more torment on the land as two huge volcanic cones formed and held the creature.

Sserpo took another step, and the cones exploded, billions of tons of rock turned into gargantuan shrapnel that flew for tens of miles, falling back to earth in a meteor hail. The monster did not even notice the failed restraint. Zargo's psychic being whiplashed out of the earth, and he fell back gasping against the thrumming mountain face.

I can't, I can't, I can't.

Doom's voice resounded in his skull again. *The island, Wolkenland. Can you take control of it?*

Zargo turned with relief to that effort. Wolkenland floated serene, arrogant, untouched by the damage inflicted by Sserpo. He reached out again.

And found nothing.

A solid wall of nothing blocked him from Wolkenland and denied him a grip on the island's stone. His consciousness slid around the mass as if it did not exist, though a heavy, negative presence weighed on his awareness. Zargo probed for a crack in the shield. He found none. It was smooth as glass.

It's shielded from me, he thought.

Doom's answer came quickly. Zargo flinched at the frustration that made the thought sharp and hard as a spear tip, but mercifully, the anger was not directed at him. *Stay ready*, Doom said. *The moment will come.*

The strain in Doom's thoughts made Zargo's blood run cold.

"What *is* that?" Daniella Pittman exclaimed. She sounded funny, as if the question had come out instead of a scream too big to escape.

Lance Diffring was standing at the aft-facing window of Hayden Wynne's top floor sunroom. He had been staring at the keep, and its smooth black shield, wondering what was going to happen to Wolkenland, and most particularly to him.

Diffring had not been able to take part in the evacuation. When he had recovered consciousness, he had been trapped in his home by Doom's energy barriers. As soon as those had vanished, he had fled the house and run, hell for leather, for the port side. He had found an abandoned hovercar in the promenade and taken it the rest of the way to Wynne's mansion on the aft end of the topmost terrace. The evacuated starboard billionaires had been taken in by their colleagues, some to assigned locations, others finding refuge with people they knew well, and might even call friends. Diffring had been on friendly terms with Wynne, an investor, for about ten years. He had brought Wynne in on the Wolkenland project in the first place. Wynne took him in when Diffring arrived at the door, but was frostier than usual. Diffring didn't think that fair. It wasn't *his* fault things had gone so badly wrong.

Diffring had looked around, for at least a few minutes, to see if he could find Addyson. No sign of her. Perhaps she had never returned from the mines. Perhaps she was dead. Diffring wondered if he might feel some loss at some point because of that. He shrugged. Something to think about another time.

There were ten of them in the sunroom. Wynne and his wife Florence, and a handful of other evacuees, Pittman among them. She had founded three different social media networks, each enjoying a brief moment in the sun before the next It App replaced them, and each time she had shown an uncanny sense for when to sell up, taking in a massive fortune just before the bloom faded from the rose, leaving the new owners with yesterday's fashion. When Diffring first wandered up to the sunroom and saw her there, the look on her face was that of a prodigy acutely conscious of the sudden loss of their gift. She had not had the instinct to jump ship from Wolkenland before things went wrong. Diffring had spent the last while wishing he had had that chance.

"*What is that?*" Pittman repeated, tone sharper, urgency rising to the threshold of panic. Diffring and the others joined her at the forward window, and Diffring had his first view of the god that the Red Skull had brought to Earth.

Exclamations of wonder and fear surrounded Diffring. He couldn't say anything at first. When he did, his tongue felt clumsy in his mouth, and all he could manage was a banality. "Sserpo," he said. "The Red Skull told Doom." The Skull's taunts had played across Wolkenland.

"Thanks, that's really helpful," said Wynne. His voice cracked high, showing his sarcasm for the bravado it was.

"Is it coming for us?" Pittman asked.

"How far is it?" Aden Kramer, an oil baron, babbled. "Is it close? I can't tell. Is it getting closer? Is it? Is it?"

"It's getting bigger," Diffring said. As they watched, the monster's head, which had been visible just above Wolkenland's horizon, pushed higher and higher, through the clouds. The body filled more and more of the view. Diffring kept thinking of it as a god. Only a god could be so huge.

The panic of the others calmed his own fear a bit. Being the voice of calming authority had been his job on Wolkenland. It felt good to step back into that role, after the terror of encountering Doom. Sserpo inspired infinitely more awe, but it wasn't in the same room as Diffring. He didn't know if the distance between the island and the monster was shrinking. The existence of any kind of distance gave him comfort, and he grasped it.

"What is happening, what is happening, what is happening?" Kramer sobbed.

"Be quiet," Pittman snapped, using irritation to dampen her terror.

"What's happening is that the Skull has turned the tables on Doom," Diffring said, pleased at how confident he sounded. "There's nothing for us to worry about." He came very close to convincing himself. A bit more effort, and he would do so.

Wynne tore his eyes away from Sserpo long enough to stare at Diffring in disbelief. "How can you say that?"

"Because it's common sense," Diffring said. "The Skull isn't going to put himself in danger. Ten-to-one he has Sserpo under remote control."

"And if he doesn't?" Pittman said.

"Then so what? Wolkenland isn't anchored in place. We just leave." Diffring made a show of strolling to the middle of the room and sitting down on the couch. He crossed his legs and rested an arm across the back, the picture of relaxation. He tried to keep from looking out the bow window. He only managed to keep to that resolution some of the time. Immensity kept tugging at his gaze.

"But how big is it going to get?" Florence Wynne asked, sounding very worried.

"As big as it has to be," Diffring said. "We're on a flying island, people! What makes you think the Red Skull doesn't have a single big animal under control?"

With a visible effort, Wynne turned around and set his back to the window. He glared at Diffring. "I'll tell you what makes me think that. The last twenty-four hours, for one. You're telling me that's what things under control look like? You're telling me you're in my house because everything is just fine, A-OK Daddy-O?"

Diffring made a placating gesture with his hands. *Let's be calm. Let's all be calm.* "Sure, things went wrong. This is them being righted."

Wynne shook his head. Florence clung tightly to him. They both trembled. "I should never have listened to you," Wynne said. "I should never have set foot on this damned island."

Here we go with the blame again. Diffring clamped down on the retorts that came to mind. Pretty rich for Wynne to play the injured innocent. Sure, Diffring had told him about Wolkenland. But Wynne could have backed out at any time. He had been one of the early, enthusiastic backers. He and Diffring had a history that predated Wolkenland by years. They had been ideological fellow travelers for a long time, and Wynne had often been the real firebrand of the two. He had stuck his neck out in public in a way that Diffring never had.

In fact, Diffring had had to do what he could to downplay Wynne's presence on Wolkenland for the world's press. If anybody wanted to run with an "Island of the Fascist Billionaires" angle, Wynne would have made that easy for them. Wynne had rarely missed a day at the viewing gallery in the mines. He was a true believer in everything Wolkenland stood for. Everyone in this house was. None of the willingly blind here. They had all given the Red Skull the stiff-armed salute whenever they had the chance, and they would all have built Wolkenland themselves if that had been possible. Wynne pulling the "I should never have listened to you" strategy sounded like a coward using out his Get Out of the Hague Free card.

"You can say what you like," Diffring said calmly. It helped him to keep his eyes on the gilt coffee table when he spoke. Blot out the ever-more-looming sight of Sserpo, and the utterly sealed off keep. "I have confidence in the Red Skull. He knows what he's doing."

He hasn't abandoned us.

The thought, even in the form of denial, made him feel queasy. *If the Skull decided to jump ship…*

He hasn't. He hasn't. Don't even think that.

He plastered a smile on his face, grinned through the nausea.

"There's nothing keeping you here, you know," he went on. "You have your hovercar. Take off if you're scared."

"And go where?" Wynne asked. "They don't have enough range to even get out of Latverian airspace."

"No one is abandoning Wolkenland."

The Red Skull's voice snarled out of hidden speakers in the walls. Wynne blanched. Diffring's grin became genuine. So the Skull had been listening all along. Good. Let him know who his true allies were.

"I speak to all the residents of Wolkenland," the Skull said. If learning that the voice was not addressing him personally set Wynne's mind at ease, he showed no sign of it. Eyes wide, breathing coming in pants, he looked frozen to the spot. Florence had let go of him and taken a step away, as if he were contagious.

"Sserpo is of no concern to you."

Diffring cocked a *told you* finger at Wynne.

"*The beast is the end of Doom and Latveria. Your concern is the reclaiming of Wolkenland.*"

Diffring's smile faltered. What did the Skull mean? He wasn't talking about conscripting the residents into the fight, was he? Diffring was no fighter. He left that to the professionals. Wolkenland's army had taken huge hits, and Diffring didn't know how many troops were left. But there had to be enough to take care of the uprising, weren't there? Now that Doom had flown off to fight Sserpo. Right?

Right?

"*Will you let a rabble composed of inferior races take what is yours? Will you let them occupy a single square foot of Wolkenland? I think not.*"

"No!" Wynne shouted with frantic fervor.

Diffring bit back laughter. Then he felt uneasy again. What exactly was the Skull getting at? Of course the slaves had to be expelled from the courtyard of the castle. Of course they had to be punished. He didn't think he'd ever get their stench out of his home. But what was he supposed to do about it?

"Do you feel something?" Pittman asked.

Diffring did, now that she mentioned it. A deep, steady vibration through the house. He shot a worried look at Sserpo, still larger, and closer now. The monster's footsteps. No, he realized, thankful. The vibration was uninterrupted. It built up. It sounded like an engine rumbling into life.

"*You are not soldiers,*" the Red Skull said. "*But you are warriors. You are warriors in the cause of Wolkenland. You are warriors in the cause of true hierarchies. Now is your time of glory. Now you will show your true strength.*"

The vibration became even louder.

"Look outside your front windows. Look into the grounds of your estate, and you will know that victory has always been assured."

Diffring rose and joined the others at the starboard window. The vibration grew louder yet, making his teeth rattle. The conical hedges of Wynne's topiary shook violently, and then moved apart. Diffring blinked, confused at first, then saw that the center of the grounds had split in two. The halves moved apart with a grinding rumble. Sod, shrubs, and trees fell into the gap. The landscaping had been done over metal doors, each more than a hundred yards long.

As they parted, a platform rose from the interior of Wolkenland. It carried a row of dark, squat vehicles. They were about ten feet wide and fifteen feet long, with thick, stubby cannons mounted on their roofs. They looked enough like tanks that Diffring expected to see treads on them. Instead, their skirts sat flush with the ground.

Diffring looked beyond Wynne's grounds and saw that the same kind of vehicles had risen in the other properties.

He pictured what even one of those tanks could do to escaped slaves on foot, and he suddenly felt very good about being a warrior.

"Are we going to drive those?" Pittman asked softly, torn between apprehension and anticipation.

"Oh, I hope so!" said Diffring.

"Behold the instruments of your vengeance," said the Skull. "These have long been prepared for your use, should the need ever arise. I have foreseen every possible contingency. Wolkenland needs you now. Their controls are as simple as your hovercars.

Even simpler, as you do not have to fly. You drive, and you fire. The cannon will destroy whatever is in front of you."

"I can do that," said Diffring. He could. Nothing to it.

"Before your advance, the rebellious slaves can do nothing. You will come upon them with the anger of gods. Go now, and take back Wolkenland."

Yes, Diffring thought. *YES.* This was more like it. He needn't have worried. The shield around the keep didn't mean anything bad. Just protection for the castle when the residents started blasting the slaves to ash. Nothing wrong at all, everything under control.

In the corner of his eye, Sserpo moved and grew, the booming of its steps a greater thunder than Diffring had ever imagined.

All good. All good. Everything under control.

He took part in the rush downstairs. Everyone was in a hurry now to be the first out the door, the first into one of the tanks, the only worry now that there might not be enough vehicles for everyone.

But there were.

Diffring ran to the nearest one. *Let me at them. I want those slaves in my sights.* A side door on the right-hand side slid open as he approached. He ducked inside and found a seat in the middle of the space, in front of a windscreen that was clear as glass but rang like metal when he rapped a knuckle against it. In front of the seat was a steering wheel with triggers on the left and right. When he took the wheel, his index fingers fit naturally around the triggers. As his hands contacted the wheel, a low blue light bathed the interior, the tank hummed, and it rose a few feet off the ground. Diffring pushed forward on the wheel, and the tank moved.

He cackled with delight. Within moments, he felt as if he'd been driving heavy armor all his life. He fell into a line behind two other tanks as they skimmed over the grounds toward the estate's gate. Aden Kramer was just ahead of him. Diffring bumped into the back of Kramer's tank twice between the estate and the bottom of the access trail.

"Idiot," he fumed. Had Kramer never driven a car? Why was he going so slowly?

Diffring wanted to reach the castle. He wanted to show the slaves the meaning of punishment. They had tried to break out of their rightful place. And they had attacked him in his own home.

He giggled again. He couldn't get to battle fast enough. The Red Skull had called them warriors, and he was right. Diffring's earlier trepidation had evaporated.

His fingers itched to pull the triggers. He almost blasted Kramer out of the way. His breath came faster. He felt light-headed at the prospect of massacre.

"Wolkenland!" he shouted. "Wolkenland!"

He drove up the slope toward the castle's shattered outer wall. Sserpo was behind him, out of sight and out of mind. A screen on the simple black dashboard showed the position of Diffring's tank in relation to the others. He barely glanced at it, except to thrill at the sheer number of death machines making for the castle.

"Wolkenland!" Diffring kept shouting "Wolkenland!" He bounced up and down in the seat.

Up ahead, in the lead, Pittman's tank closed in on the gap in the wall. She fired. A searing green beam burst from the cannon.

Diffring screamed with joy.

The Billionaires' Crusade had begun.

TWENTY-FIVE

Back in the panopticon, the Red Skull watched events roll toward victory. It was not the one he had conceived at the start. He would not have chosen it. But it did not displease him.

Many square miles of Latveria had been flattened by Sserpo. The scars would remain forever, and the beast had not even arrived at Doomstadt yet. Soon, though, very soon. Only a handful of steps would bring the monster into the city. The Skull had already issued the orders to reposition Wolkenland, clearing the way for Sserpo, and for the people of the city to see what would shortly annihilate them all.

The Skull would never sit in the throne room of Castle Doom. But neither would anyone else. If Latveria had never been his to rule, it would be his to destroy. That would satisfy him.

Now Doom had closed with Sserpo, rushing to his preordained defeat. Doom could have nuclear missiles built into his armor. They wouldn't make a difference. No weapon of his could stop the monster.

The Skull thought of the fevered gleam in Thorne's eyes. She fully expected Sserpo to destroy the world, and so, the tap of her finger on the screen became the single greatest act of willful perversity in human history. She rejoiced in that knowledge. Her life's work was now fulfilled.

The Red Skull had thought some more about what must come as he watched Sserpo grow, and the consequences draw closer. He still felt the thrill of chaos. But the prospect of extinction did not excite him. He would happily burn everything down, but he wanted to be there to see the fire.

Did he think Sserpo would destroy everything?

It might. It very well might.

But just as likely, some coalition or other of superbeings would find a way to neutralize the monster. Launch it back into space at the very least. So many apocalypses averted in recent years. None of that would help Latveria. Its history would be over in a matter of minutes. But the Red Skull could not imagine the universe without him in it, so the world would somehow survive. And if it did, authorities would come calling on Wolkenland.

Or they would try. All he had to do was put the concealment shield up again and vanish. More opportunities for conquest would come with time. Wolkenland would be much more ready for them if it functioned with a restored unity. He had lost face with the damage Doom and his ragged army had inflicted. He needed to correct that. And he needed to head off even the possibility of future dissent.

His eyes turned from the island's perspective of Sserpo to the drone surveillance of the Billionaires' Crusade. With Doom gone, he could have sent flights of drones down on the slaves.

This, though, was much better. The massacre would be faster, more brutal, more satisfying. And it would tie the residents to the Skull forever. He would own them completely. He would have the footage of their crimes. Already he had recordings of live footage from inside the tanks. Lance Diffring's bouncing and excited screams of "Wolkenland!" made for very fine cinema. These people would shortly be, in the eyes of the rest of the world, war criminals.

The Skull found the idea ridiculous. They were simply restoring the proper order of things. But truth did not matter to the weak of the world. And their perception did matter to the residents of Wolkenland. They feared being ensnared by the legalities of the societies they despised. So, if a wrong look or errant whisper displeased the Skull, he would throw that person to the wolves. They could never turn against him now. He would be some time rebuilding his ruined army. But he had assured himself absolute control over the people of Wolkenland.

Another victory, another true one.

And the truest of them all, the best of them all, was what he had done to Doom. It didn't matter if Doom survived his clash with Sserpo. Everything that mattered to him would be destroyed. Everyone who mattered to him would be dead.

"I hope you do survive," the Skull said. He looked back at the image of Sserpo, wishing he could see a speck and know it to be Doom. "I tortured you with the losses in all those universes. Now I'm going to torture you with the loss in this one."

The monster's hand, huge as a mountain chain, came at Doom. As soon as he saw the movement, he changed course, vectoring out of the path of the hand's descent.

He had time to see the danger coming. The hand began the swat with miles and miles to go. But the fingers alone were thousands of feet long. Sserpo's immensity distorted perception in the same way it distorted gravity. And the hand grew still larger in the length of time the gesture took. Doom barely managed to get out of range, and the passage of the hand stirred up gale winds, even in the thinning atmosphere.

Doom kept climbing. Despite how minuscule he was to the monster, Sserpo had seen him, and considered him a threat worth attacking. *Good.* He changed the angle of his ascent again, and the gargantuan eyes followed him.

Then there is hope.

Sserpo roared. Doom's armor reacted with a noise-canceling shield that saved his hearing. The sound wave knocked him off course, and he tumbled, cursing, out of control, for several seconds. When he recovered, both of Sserpo's hands came at him, a clap that would annihilate a city. *I am no insect and will not die as one.* He shot up again, pouring extra power into the jet packs, fighting for an edge of more speed, a sudden burst that would throw off the monster's aim.

He escaped again, but the vortex caused by the clap seized him, and the second shock wave tested the limits of his force field. Raging, refusing to be caught now that he had his goal in sight, he fought free of the maelstrom and arrowed at Sserpo's head.

Missiles arrived there first. The explosions were barely visible, pinprick blooms on the impregnable armored hide. Unharmed but enraged, Sserpo jerked forward, miles out of Doom's angle of approach. Its roar blew up the drones.

"*Lord Doom,*" came a voice on the military network of his

communicator. "*We have you on radar. We are almost with you. How can we assist your attack?*"

Doom blinked and called up a display before his mask lenses. Multiple fighter squadrons were closing in on Sserpo. He had tried to contact Verlak as he flew away from Wolkenland, but still couldn't get through. Now their separate efforts against the monster risked colliding.

"No," he said, as he flew toward Sserpo's head again. "Withdraw immediately. You can do nothing against Sserpo. Are you in contact with Captain Verlak?"

"*No, my lord. We have been unable to reach her since flying out from under Wolkenland.*"

So the communication blackout extended straight down from the island, isolating Doomstadt. Very well. Doom could work around that. "All but one of you make for Wolkenland," he ordered. "Keep out of range of its defenses and wait for my command. One of you return to Doomstadt and report to Captain Verlak. Have her send up a flight of heavy transports to be ready for the evacuation order."

The commands he gave were for the best possible outcome. Saying them aloud felt like dicing with fate, an invitation to the worst.

If I fail against Sserpo…

I will not.

The fighters banked away, just as they came into view. Sserpo caught sight of the evading attackers. Bellowing in frustration, Sserpo dropped to all fours. From sixty miles up, Doom saw the land ripple like a pond from the impact. Huge dust clouds had risen, punched up by Sserpo's march. They were spreading, blocking sunlight, the beginning of a localized volcanic winter. Sserpo scraped up a huge tract of land and devoured it. Farms, villages, roads, a forest vanished in an instant, leaving behind a sudden canyon of parallel furrows, ten miles long and a mile deep.

Sserpo stood up again, quickly, and violent storms burst into being in the wake of its movement. Doom had hovered, helpless to stop the destruction. He stayed close to where he judged the monster's head would next rise. He saw only one possible way to stop the rampage. None of his weapons would harm Sserpo, or even be noticed by the beast. All Doom had left was his will.

In two more strides, Sserpo would trample Doomstadt. No chances except this one possibility, and no more time, only this moment, this now, this ephemeral and already dying moment.

Doom flew in front of Sserpo's face, coming in from the side. Sullen eyes, each a mile wide, glared at Doom, the gaze of the infinite focused on the infinitesimal.

A miracle of a kind.

Doom attempted to work a second one.

He knew, to his anger, of many individuals on Earth alone whose psionic powers were stronger than his own. But he had trained himself until he had honed the abilities he did have to a razor's edge. The hypnotism he practiced did not depend on spoken suggestion, or even on the subject's level of comprehension. A basic sentience and eye contact were enough. If Doom's psionic strength, in and of itself, was minor, a much greater strength backed up the hypnotism. The strength of his will knew no bounds.

Doom had hypnotized non-human beings before. He had

never imagined trying to do so with a creature of this scale. He had never imagined a creature on this scale.

And growing. Always growing.

He looked at the eyes, so vast they filled the world, two reptilian, gleaming, black suns. He confronted anger and hunger that would, in a very little time, crush the planet. He projected his will into them. Sserpo grunted, then jerked as if in surprise. *You feel me,* Doom thought. *Soon you will obey me.* Sserpo blinked once, and then its eyes remained open, locked into a struggle for control with Doom. He sensed the pressure of the animal's instincts, looming over his mind like a thousand-foot tsunami. He ignored it. If he acknowledged it, the wave would strike him and drown his mind.

Only his will mattered, the will that had overcome the grip of Hell, the will that would yet remake the world in Doom's image. A titan's will, a god's will, a will so great it was the absolute in a universe of the relative. Sserpo's tsunami of instinct ran up against a far greater cliff wall. The thousand feet broke against the thousand miles, became foam, and withdrew, a defeated wavelet.

Stop. Doom commanded.

Sserpo stopped. It continued to grow, destruction spreading as the mountains of its feet expanded, toed claws digging new furrows, new canyons, without a single step being taken.

Doom hovered for a moment, carefully taking his bearings, making sure he could have full consciousness of the world without losing his grip on Sserpo's mind. He held his emotions in check. He had not won yet. Exultation could too easily lead to distraction.

The reptile remained obediently motionless.

Before another second went by, Doom angled south and down, back toward Wolkenland. He shot toward the island, jet packs straining. It had moved since he left, drifting south and west, exposing Doomstadt to the tread of Sserpo.

This way, Doom's will told the monster. He could feel its mind as if he gripped it in his fist. Docile now, unable to resist, his thoughts its own.

Sserpo took its first step under Doom's command. It moved aside from Doomstadt, where the curve of its spiral path had been bringing it. It followed him, and it made for Wolkenland.

It would not take Doom long to reach the island. No more than a few minutes. But the minutes now seemed like an age, and Wolkenland a continent away. How long had passed since he had flown away?

Too long. Long enough for the horrors of the other universes to arrive in this one.

That was the lesson of the portal torment. He would be too late, always too late. He would only arrive on time when he was Valeria's murderer. When she died at the hands of others, he would be helpless to stop the fall of the blade. Every single step he took, every effort no matter how great, to prevent her death only ensured it would happen.

A multiverse of tragedy, locked in.

Another absolute, after all.

But no, *no*, he would not permit it. He was Doom, and he would force *this* universe to obey his will. He flew faster, racing fate.

She could already be dead. The Skull could have had her killed as soon as I left.

No, she would not be. He would not allow that defeat. He had saved Doomstadt. He would save Valeria, too.

Take Wolkenland, he commanded Sserpo.

The Earthcrusher god leaned forward, reaching across the miles to seize hold of the fleeing island.

Rita Chen, acting as lookout in the outer wall's breach, saw the tanks emerge into the mansion grounds along the terraces. She ran back to the inner courtyard, shouting the warning. She and the other refugees looked at Valeria. She had been the voice of hope in the mines, their intercessor with Doom, and they instinctively turned to her for leadership now.

Her mind blanked. Valeria stared at the rifles her companions held. Even if any of them had proper training with the weapons, what use would they be against tanks? None, she knew.

We can't fight this new force.

Her heart beat faster. Her thoughts spun, rats in a maze, colliding uselessly with no solution.

We can't fight.

Panic bubbled up in her chest, and despair lurked in the darkness behind it.

Stop it, she told herself. She had survived the reign of Vladimir, the days of oppression and the nights of waiting for the hammering at the door. She refused the panic, and when she beat it back, she saw what she had to do.

We don't have to fight. We just have to survive.

It was the Red Skull who was running out of time. Doom would stop Sserpo, and then he would be back, and the Skull would fall. All Valeria and the others had to do was make the Skull run out of time. Survive just a bit longer.

The wall that had risen to enclose the inner courtyard had vanished when Doom had redirected the energy blast. But the original wall still stood, built from such mundane materials as granite and concrete. The only gap was the smashed gate. Unless the Red Skull's clients used their weapons to punch more holes through the wall, they would all have to come through the bottleneck of the entrance. They had no training either. They would, she hoped, take the path of least resistance. They would see a way in and take it.

"Do the tanks fly?" she asked Chen, praying for a negative.

"Not exactly," Chen said. "It looks like they hover a couple of feet off the ground."

Valeria looked around the courtyard, its surface broken up by craters and piles of boulders. Obstacles, she thought, hope rising. Each boulder a tiny portion of embodied time.

"Look around!" she called out to the other refugees. "This area is a disaster for vehicles. They won't be able to maneuver well unless they take the time to shoot rocks, too." She pointed to the keep, surrounded by the perfect cylinder of the perfect barrier. "We take shelter around the curve of the castle's shield. They'll have to go around it to get to us."

"That won't take long," said Chen.

"We'll make it long enough," Valeria told her. She ran to the left, and she waved for the others to get moving. They didn't need the encouragement. They could all hear the hum of the tank engines drawing closer.

"Split up!" Chen shouted, and Valeria saw the inspiration she had seized. "We'll go around both sides. Shoot at them as they come in the gate."

"What good are these against tanks?" someone asked.

"We don't know," Valeria said, "and neither do they! None of those people have ever been in combat either!"

Though they seemed eager enough to play in a war they thought they could not lose, eager to wipe out the people whose suffering had entertained them in the mines.

Monsters, she thought.

Chen clapped her shoulder, and she took off in the opposite direction. Valeria ran past Hauptmann and Cadavus. They hadn't moved, still demoralized heaps on the ground, a few feet from the vibrating black shield. They glared at Valeria.

"You're all going to die," Cadavus hissed.

"According to you, we should be dead already," she said, and left them behind.

The refugees streamed past the keep. As soon as the gate disappeared around the curve, Valeria stopped. She had picked up a rifle after Doom left, and she eased her way back a few yards, until she could just see the gate. Many others followed her example, until she waved them back. "Just a few of us," she said. "We have to stay under cover. As soon as we're not doing any good, we're joining the rest of you."

Joining them to be trapped by two phalanxes of tanks, once the Wolkenlanders made their way around the keep. She knew how this would have to end, if Doom did not return. They all did.

He will return. She believed it because she had to. The same belief inhabited the faces around her.

Valeria raised the rifle, pointed it at the gate, and waited.

Her experience of time became strange. With each successive moment of the present, she was alive, uninjured. All was well. At the same time, she could see the end of the present coming up. Was this how a prisoner awaiting execution felt? she wondered. Or passengers on the *Titanic* right up until the moment they felt the touch of icy water?

All well, until it wasn't. Life continuing, until it didn't.

A cannon fired. Energy screamed. A violent green flare lit up the space beyond the gate.

What were they shooting at? Valeria wondered. There was no one in the outer courtyard.

More blasts sounded. A lethal beam shot over the inner wall, shooting up at the sky and taking off a chunk of the ramparts.

Valeria shook her head. They were children, she realized. Children with monstrous toys. They were playing, exulting in the new kind of power they had been given. They had only ever seen other human beings as potential rivals or allies of convenience if they were rich, and as data points to be used or resented if they were poor. They believed in the poison the Red Skull represented, but even that belief was also a game. And now they were coming with the big toys to crush the smaller ones.

The first of the tanks appeared at the inner courtyard entrance. A wide windshield nestled underneath the cannon. The interior of the tank was illuminated, revealing the grinning, excited face of the woman at the controls.

Valeria fired at the same time as the other refugees. A dozen beams struck the windshield. The tank swerved so violently, Valeria thought the shots had punched through the windshield. They hadn't, but the driver had raised her hands in alarm and sent her vehicle out of control. It careened into a large boulder, smashed the rock and bounced back, spinning around until it faced the wall. The cannon went off, punching a hole through the wall and setting off another explosion on the other side.

Valeria shot at the next tank through the gate, and kept firing. The concentrated fire of the refugees dazzled and terrified the drivers. Tanks collided, reversed, accelerated, and stopped dead. They bunched up at the entrance, fired at random, within and without the inner courtyard. A tank that had come through the hole in the wall took a direct hit. It exploded, its cannon lifted up on a pillar of crimson and green flame.

Then the blasts became more organized and consistent. The tanks in the outer courtyard trained their guns on the inner wall and worked to bring it down. Stone and concrete disintegrated, and entire sections collapsed.

A line of tanks appeared before Valeria.

"Run!" she shouted. She and the others sprinted back, following the curve of the shield. Behind her, the world turned into a volcanic eruption of green devastation.

All well, until it wasn't. Life continuing, until it didn't.

TWENTY-SIX

Idiots, Diffring thought. So many idiots. The Red Skull handed out tanks like candy, and this was how people treated them. They didn't know what they were doing. Clowns with cannons.

Pittman had shot at nothing when she crossed the gate to the outer courtyard. That set off everyone else's over-eagerness. Trigger-happy idiots fired cannons at still more nothing, and idiot drivers got in each other's way, and then the bottleneck happened, and then the slaves actually fought, and then everything went wrong for several minutes.

Diffring yelled at people who could not hear him because they were yelling at him. The traffic on the tank's radio was a shrieking blast of outraged voices shouting over each other. Diffring swore as tanks banged into his and he hit others in front of him. Stop and go, jerk and halt, and he couldn't get to the fight, couldn't start dishing out the punishment.

But then things sorted themselves out. After the yelling, after the chaos, after the friendly fire mishaps, Diffring found himself in an organized line of tanks, bringing down the inner courtyard wall, and a minute later, he had a clear way forward.

Too bad Wynne wouldn't see what came next. Diffring felt sorry for what happened. Wynne's fault, though. He careened out of nowhere, right in front of Diffring when he punched the fire button. The fog of war, that was the term, wasn't it? These things happened. Good to know his cannon worked though. Wynne's tank had gone up, boom, zeppelin-time.

No more accidents now. Just the iron line, bringing the pain. Down went the wall, and the tanks surged forward.

Diffring's yells were happy ones again. He jittered with excitement behind the wheel. He couldn't see any slaves yet. They'd run like rabbits. "No more fight in you now, is there?" he shouted. No one to shoot at, but he fired anyway, and so did everyone else. The courtyard became an inferno of blinding green. The tanks split up into two groups to move around the keep. The lines were tight, and there was more armor coming up behind. Only the front lines would be able to fire.

Too bad for the others, Diffring thought with a grin. They would lose out on the big fun. They wouldn't get to deliver the lesson. Be part of the wipe-out.

Any second now, and he would see his cannon fire rip through the people who had humiliated him.

Any second…

The sky turned a burnt orange. He looked up, puzzled.

Sserpo's hand reached down.

Diffring screamed.

The world jerked and tilted. The wheel flew out of his hands. The tank flipped and rolled. He bounced around the interior, a pinball of flesh. Metal pounded his bones and bled him. Pain burst in his skull. The tank stopped moving and it was upside down. He lay on the ceiling, and he didn't know if anything was broken, if everything was broken, and he couldn't stop screaming.

Sserpo grabbed Wolkenland at the bow end. The edges of the island crumbled in the monster's grip. Huge chunks of rock rained down to the land below. The beast began to lift its prize, mouth open to devour.

Stop. Doom told Sserpo. *Do not raise the island.* Much higher, and the air would become too thin.

Strike the shield, he ordered.

In the panopticon, the Red Skull rose out of his throne when he saw Sserpo stretch out an arm after Wolkenland. The monster had suddenly advanced with purpose, too quickly for the engines to fire up to full speed and evade. The terrible hand took hold, and the island's violent shudder hurled the Skull to the floor.

He scrambled back to the throne and frantically stabbed at the viewing controls, looking for answers and solutions. There had to be a way out. The situation could not have turned against him so completely.

One of the screens picked up the image of Doom streaking through the sky toward Wolkenland. Sserpo, with a step, had arrived first. The monster held the island, started to bring it up, then stopped.

Why?

The monster looked as if it were waiting for something.

What?

A command, the Skull realized. The thing that all of Thorne's research had failed to produce for the Skull, control over Sserpo's actions, Doom had achieved in a matter of minutes.

The Skull howled, frustration and rage beyond the scope of words tearing out of his throat.

Sserpo held Wolkenland with its left hand. With its right, it made a fist.

"No!" the Red Skull shrieked. "Stop!"

The fist came down like an asteroid on the keep's shield.

Sserpo's fist struck the creation of inhuman science. The power that fueled the keep's shield was inexhaustible. That did not make it infinite in strength. As Doom reached the boundary of the island and flew toward the keep, the shield of matter and energy shattered.

Black lightning erupted around the ten-mile-wide fist. Pieces of the shield flew out across Wolkenland, some crashing to the ground, others disintegrating into miniature hurricane vortices. The death of the shield left the keep exposed, vulnerable, and wounded. The domed roof had fallen in, and the crumbled walls showed wide breaches. The castle had become something more than a ruin, and something less than a fortress.

Remain still, Doom told Sserpo.

The colossus stopped moving, but it kept growing. If Doom left things too long, Wolkenland would disintegrate in Sserpo's grip, a fragile toy crushed by an unthinking child.

Doom shot over the island's airspace to the castle's inner courtyard. The final seconds before he saw the situation on the ground dragged by with a special torture. Then he arrived, and he beheld what the Red Skull had engineered in his absence.

Tanks everywhere in the courtyard, heavy armor like a carpet of rats. He had seen some of the same tanks sitting outside mansions on the terraces. Not all of the Wolkenlanders had taken part in the war, then. Plenty had, and they were here, almost crawling over each other to get at the refugees. A few of the tanks had turtled. Others had collided and blocked the movement of the others. But the main force of the columns was moments way from coming around the wall of the keep and trapping the refugees between lines of guns.

Doom came in like a comet of rage over the tanks. He strafed the portside attackers, combining concussive blasts and strikes from his magnetic polarity controller. The metal in the tanks revolted against itself. They tore themselves apart as if being ripped open by the claws of a huge predator. Their power sources destabilized and exploded, triggering a chain reaction of annihilation.

Doom circled around the back of the keep, flying low over the refugees. He caught glimpses of faces awed and terrified by Sserpo, and of faces rejoicing in his return.

And he saw Valeria. Alive.

He had defied the tides of history in the Multiverse this far. He would to the end.

"Get down and stay down!" Doom ordered his followers. They obeyed, dropping to the ground. With no cover to be had, the best they could do was keep their heads down out of the line of fire.

Doom landed in front of the starboard mass of tanks. He didn't attack right away. He gave them a target and let himself enjoy the moment before the satisfaction of unleashed wrath. The drivers saw him coming, and they fired. The energy beams, lethal to flesh and mundane construction, flashed and dissipated when they struck his force field.

Doom hit back, striking them as brutally as they had tried to strike the refugees. A wall of explosions rose up before him, tanks shredding themselves and their occupants, fireballs rolling back over the line, triggering more. Doom marched through flame and wreckage. He was destruction, and he was vengeance, and he took the Billionaires' Crusade apart like so much tissue. More shots flashed wild against his force field, and tanks tried to slam into him. Doom gestured, imperious, power blazing from his gauntlets, and the vehicles exploded.

Some of the drivers had left their tanks, whether by choice or by necessity. A few of them ran. Doom ignored them. He would deal with them in due course. Others, maddened by the frenzy of war, no longer capable of even the minimal rational thought required for self-preservation, tried to stand their ground and shoot him with beam rifles left behind by the fallen soldiers. He gazed at them with contempt. His force field barely reacted to the shots. He picked up the burning hulk of a tank and threw it. The wreck bounced across the ground and rolled over the Wolkenlanders.

Doom turned back to take on the remaining tanks portside. As he did, a lone shot zapped against his shield. Doom turned around. Lance Diffring, the public face of Wolkenland, shook his rifle with anger and stamped with frustration.

"*STOP! RUINING! EVERYTHING!*" Diffring wailed. He aimed the rifle and shot three more times.

"Are you quite done?" said Doom. "I think you are." He smacked Fascism's public relations man with a concussive bolt that sent him flying into the bonfire of tanks.

Then he destroyed the last of the Red Skull's army. He scoured them from Wolkenland's earth.

The hammer blow of Sserpo's fist shook the castle to its foundations. The screens in the panopticon exploded, showering the Red Skull with broken glass. The ceiling cracked and sagged downward, on the verge of full collapse. Pieces of stonework fell in an ominous rain. The cracks spread down the walls, opening wider. Sparks and flames flickered and danced across the splits in the walls. The panopticon went dark. Only dim red emergency lights running around the perimeter remained to show the Red Skull the way out of his domain.

Anger and fear fought for dominance in his heart as he ran for the door. It tried to open at his approach but slid only a few inches aside before its power died.

The ceiling cracked and groaned, shifting as it prepared itself for death.

Snarling, cursing Doom and fate, the Skull grabbed the edges of the door and pulled. Stuck fast, the door refused to move.

The groaning grew louder.

You haven't killed me yet, Doom. And you never will. The Skull stepped back, pulled some micro-explosives from his belt, and placed them around the corners of the door. He stepped back, the rockfall coming down harder, larger pieces bruising his shoulders.

The blast hurled the door out into the hall beyond. The Skull sprinted through the doorway, chased by the groan that became a roar. The ceiling collapsed behind him, burying the panopticon beneath tons of rubble and sending out choking clouds of dust into the hall.

My castle. My beautiful castle.

Everything was falling apart, all the magnificence of Wolkenland gone. Doom had ruined his masterpiece.

Coughing, eyes stinging, the Skull made his way to the nearest stairwell. He couldn't trust the elevators. The whole castle felt as if it had been knocked out of true. The walls leaned, shunning right angles. The floor, uneven, sloped up and down. It thrummed with the echoes of collapses taking place elsewhere in the keep.

The stairs were worse, the air harsh with both dust and smoke. The Skull took them two at a time, bracing himself for the walls to close in on him at any moment.

Other walls were already crushing him. Doom had turned the Skull's *Götterdämmerung* against him. The Skull did not appreciate the irony of the gesture. He raged at the injustice of the reversal. Instead of Latveria and the world, only Wolkenland was about to be crushed out of existence. It gave the Skull no comfort to think that Doom had not yet reversed Sserpo's growth. That would happen. Of course it would.

The Skull had lost Wolkenland. The island's last hour had come, its dream dead before it had even truly been born. Very well, then, let it die. The Skull had one last move against Doom. He had never thought he would need it. He had explored the possibility only because he had to find out *everything* Wolkenland could do, even if the action was its last.

The island had not blown up. So its power core must still be intact. The Skull held on to that.

And Thorne. He needed her to be alive. If she had still been in the lab when Sserpo had attacked...

But perhaps she had not been. The launch of Sserpo's missile had removed the main reason for her to be there.

And no one believed in the blaze of glory like Thorne.

The Skull arrived at the control chamber. The technicians in the room were terrified, but they had not abandoned their posts. The hall was the most heavily reinforced in the castle. If it died, so did all of Wolkenland. The floor here was still level, the walls straight, the lights on. Even the sounds of ongoing damage were muffled to near inaudibility. In here, the Skull could almost make himself believe that nothing had happened. The pale faces of the technicians told him otherwise. They had felt Sserpo's blow. And they kept looking at the screens that showed the thing that held the island.

"Where is Thorne?" the Skull demanded. "Has she been in contact?"

"She hasn't," the tech nearest to the Skull said. The man swallowed, gulping at his own nerve to be the bearer of bad news. "We don't know where she is."

"*Find her,*" the Skull snapped. He paced around the hall while techs searched surveillance footage and put out the calls. Many of the posts they tried to contact didn't answer. The Skull felt the castle contracting around him. How much still worked beyond this room?

It didn't matter. Sserpo had the island. All was lost. Only one thing mattered, the one more thing the Skull could do. The one more thing that he could use against Doom.

But he needed Thorne.

And then she arrived. No one saw her coming. They were all looking elsewhere. Useless drones. But she came, on her own. She limped into the power hall, clutching her left arm, her hair matted with blood, her face streaming red. When she saw the Skull, she rushed over to him, new energy in her movements.

"Not what we expected, is it?" she said, and laughed. "Not what we expected at all."

If anyone else had said that, with such mad joy in their eyes, the Skull would have put a bullet between those eyes. But he needed Thorne. At least for the moment.

"The exoskeleton," he said. "I want it."

Thorne smiled, at once a child at Christmas, and a child about to pull the wings off a fly. She clapped with glee. "Of course!" she said. "Of course!" She limped toward a sealed vault, ten feet high, against a wall.

The Skull followed her. "You perfected it then?"

She laughed, long and loud. "Not at all! Not even remotely! The problems are as intractable as they were at the start. It's the Power Cosmic, and the mix of all the other energies we're using. Much too wild. It takes all the capabilities of this chamber to harness it for the island's needs."

She paused to listen to a series of explosions. "Outside, do you think?" She wiped blood from her face and carried on without waiting for an answer. "What we've done here is really a miracle. Have I thanked you enough for the opportunity? We're turning a portion of the power against itself in order to tame it. Remarkable. Paradox harnessed by technology!"

"I know all that. But what about the exoskeleton?"

"Don't you see?" Thorne asked. "It can't possibly perform the same task. Not unless it remained physically connected to this chamber, and even then, I doubt that would be enough."

Despair, black and choking, rose to surround the Red Skull. "You're telling me the suit is a failure. That it doesn't work at all."

"Did I say that?" Thorne sounded genuinely surprised and puzzled. "Did I mean that? By no means! How disappointing that would be. What a waste of time and effort and potential." She placed her palm against a panel on the side of the vault. The front split vertically, and the two halves opened up. A platform rolled out, carrying the exoskeleton.

"It isn't perfect," said Thorne. "That's what I meant. Of course it works." She smiled, teeth bright against her mask of blood.

The black-and-red exoskeleton glinted in the light of the hall, the shine of lurking power. The chest looked a solid mass, with a hulking power pack emerging like an immense tumor from the shoulders. The arms and legs would cover the back of the Skull's limbs. The feet were foot-thick platforms, and the gauntlets were the hands of a giant. It waited for the Skull to climb into its embrace and give it purpose.

Thorne bowed and gestured for him to step onto the platform.

Her enthusiasm gave him pause. "It works, but it's imperfect, you say."

"That's right." The smile wider yet, her excitement mounting.

"What exactly do you mean by that?"

"The exoskeleton taps directly into the power sources of Wolkenland and deploys them."

What he had told her he wanted the suit to do. "But?" he asked.

"Problems with control."

"With the controls?"

"With *control*." She frowned, displeased with her machine, and then the prospect of what it might do made her brighten again. "You'll have only limited say in how much power is unleashed and in what way."

"Limited," the Skull repeated. What did the fool think he wanted to do with this? Perform surgery? "I am not looking for precision."

"In that case, you'll be very pleased!" Thorne's excitement returned in full force. "It should flow in the general direction you desire. And there will be so much of it, the general direction should be more than enough." She winked. "At least, it would be for me."

It would be for him, too. "Activate it," he said, and jumped onto the platform.

Thorne touched a button on the platform. The red portions of the exoskeleton glowed. The black hummed. The chest case opened for the Red Skull. He backed into the suit, and the chest closed. It pressed hard against him, and it took a moment for his breathing to adjust to the pressure. He slid his hands into the gauntlets. A heavy vibration ran from them and resonated through his body. He felt like a stallion barely being restrained before the start of the race.

Thorne climbed up and closed the clasps around his ankles, shins, thighs, arms, and forehead.

With his head bound, the Skull felt a spasm of worry, as if the exoskeleton were wearing him and not the other way around. Thorne could be planning to kill him, the incomplete suit a death trap.

But no, he knew better. Her loyalty was beyond question. She had always spoken the absolute truth to him and dedicated her genius entirely to how he chose to release it on the world.

He tried to flex his fingers. The gauntlet stayed rigid. He couldn't lower his arms. "I can't move," he said.

"Of course you can't," Thorne said, cheerfully casual as she crouched to complete fastening him into the suit. "It's in standby mode." She stood up and examined him. "There." She nodded, pleased. "Perfect. Are you ready?"

"I already told you to activate it."

She laughed, delighted. "That you did!"

Thorne reached for a button on the Skull's left shoulder.

"Is that how I turn it off?" he asked.

She paused, looking deeply puzzled. "Would you want to?"

No. He didn't think he would. "Do it," he said.

She pushed the button. The suit came to life with the electronic squall of monstrous birth. Circuits closed, and the machine reached out to the power of Wolkenland. The power answered. It surged through the exoskeleton like electricity through an incandescent bulb.

The Red Skull and Thorne screamed. He screamed from an ecstasy so extreme it turned to agony and back again to pleasure. Galaxies exploded behind his eyes. He jerked his head back, mouth wide, tendons straining.

He had held the Cosmic Cube. He had controlled its power. It had been his so fully that its loss had been the severing of a limb. Now, now, he felt as if he had *become* the Cosmic Cube.

Power filled him and demanded expression. He could tear universes open. He could make reality dance.

Thorne screamed for a purity of pain. The Skull regained control of his body, and he looked into her face. She could not let go of the suit. The circuit had closed and taken her with it. The smallest sliver of the power traveled up from the suit and through her body. Her body burned itself up from the inside out as if she had swallowed a star. She screamed, and she laughed with delight every bit as pure as the pain.

She was laughing until she died. Her burned corpse clung to the exoskeleton a moment longer. Her skull, visible through flaking, carbonized flesh, seemed to be laughing still.

The Red Skull flexed his arms, and the corpse collapsed in pieces at his feet, another tool he no longer had a use for. His head pounded with surplus power. He had to let it out.

Around the hall, the technicians had left their posts. They huddled together, uncertain, their discipline and fear so intermixed that they did not flee. They stayed and hoped to be given orders.

He didn't need them any longer. He was Wolkenland now. Time for the island to fall away.

He slashed at the air, and a blazing aurora of violet and silver formed around him. It pulsed once, like a cat preparing to spring, and then the Skull slashed at the air again, driven by the need to release the power. The aurora mirrored his movements, then arced out, as if thrown by his gesture. It lashed out from his gauntlets, a curving lightning, the creation-rending shriek of matter as it fell into a black hole. The whiplash of the arc struck the technicians. They, the consoles, and the wall behind them vanished in a blaze of devouring energy.

"Yes!" the Skull shouted. "*Yes!*" He had become the soul of the island, one with its power.

The Red Skull spread his arms, and great serpents of power blew apart the center of the keep. The ceiling collapsed above him, but he just waved his hand, and the explosive arc took out the rubble, leaving only sky above him.

"DOOM!" the Red Skull roared. One with the power, a walking explosion, he slashed the keep out of existence and sought the death of his enemy.

TWENTY-SEVEN

The keep exploded and vanished in the same instant. Whipping arcs of undisciplined power erupted from inside, the arms of a hurricane. They struck out across the space a short distance above Doom's head. They annihilated what remained of the inner courtyard's wall.

The Red Skull brayed Doom's name.

The refugees hugged the ground, mere chance their only protection. Valeria glanced up, and Doom met her gaze. In the split second of that connection, he had time to wonder if at some level she sensed the intensity of the universe's determination to kill her.

A split second of musing only, and the Red Skull had not even finished bellowing for Doom. He had appeared now, wearing a large exoskeleton, surrounded by the coiling, snapping arms of power. He stood on what had been the floor of the power hall, and had become the flat peak of a plateau of ruin. From deep in the floor, the glow of the island's heart surged, and it flowed directly into the exoskeleton, like an umbilical cord of energy.

Now you think you can face me, Doom thought. Good. Let us make an end of it.

"*I'm here!*" Doom amplified his voice, making it thunder, making it a challenge to the Red Skull. He flew up, passing directly in front of the Skull, drawing his gaze, and then shot up faster, on a diagonal taking him sternward, away from the castle mount.

"*Flee, coward!*" the Red Skull crowed. He rose into the air, carried by the convulsing power, the link to the cosmic center of Wolkenland extending, the cord of lightning unbreakable. He flew in erratic, jagged bursts.

He had limited control, Doom realized. That was both good and bad. The wildness of the Skull's strikes might give Doom an opportunity. They might also hit him through unavoidable chance. He didn't care to test his force field against Wolkenland's power. He had already suffered enough in its grasp.

Doom put as much distance between himself and the Skull as he could, drawing the Skull on, away from the ruins of the keep, and giving himself the chance to find a strategy of attack. The Red Skull read his flight as cowardice, as he would, and that was useful, too. Any error could compound itself.

The Skull railed on and on, his voice carried along his lightning flashes. He was barely coherent, flying on the ecstasy of the power trip, as exhilarated as Doom had been agonized in the portal. He had enjoyed the feeling of pursuit, but now he attacked in earnest. The arcs whipped out in infinite violence at Doom. They extended without limit, slashing and blazing so brightly the morning became night in contrast. Doom dodged the initial strikes. The arcs struck the ground and still kept going, their lengths rising and falling, like electrified serpents. They devastated the promenade. Monumental statues flew into pieces, and the terrain flew upward, geysers of rock. The far end of the arcs came up under the council hall. They severed the port and starboard walls, which fell to either side. The roof collapsed, and a domino fall of pillars rolled out of the rubble.

The Red Skull gestured like a manic conductor. The arcs jerked and lashed in response, exploding back and forth at random across the width of the promenade, cutting in terraces and turning the mansions to flaming rubble.

Doom jerked back and forth in the air, his own movements random to throw off the Skull's aim, but the randomness of the arcing tested him badly. He had to concentrate on too many things, on not being hit, on seeking an approach to the Skull, on maintaining Sserpo's hypnosis, and now on the state of Wolkenland, which the Skull had forgotten.

He dove suddenly, the surface shattering as the twin power whips roared through where he had been a moment before. He climbed again as fast as he could, seeking space to maneuver.

Too much to think about at once, but he had had to split his attention even more. He tried contacting Castle Doom's security center again, and this time he got through. "Are Wolkenland's shields down?" he asked.

Verlak answered. "*They are. And we've lost the energy signature from the engines. The power on the island seems to be out of control.*"

It certainly was. No engines. Wolkenland did not fall only because Sserpo held it.

Zargo! he called across the ether. *Take Wolkenland. Take it now. Do not let it fall!*

The energy arcs snapped hard on both sides, vicious chance trapping him between them. They glanced against his force field. The explosive collision of energies fed back into his armor and lit up his nervous system. His body froze, and then twitched in shocked reaction. He dropped, and the Skull roared in triumph.

Through all the pain, through the loss of control of his body, he held on to consciousness. His will refused even a microsecond of loss of focus. He held on to Sserpo's mind, and the beast held the island.

Doom forced his body to respond again twenty feet from the ground, and he shot up once more.

Enough of this. He had given Zargo his orders, and the former priest had never disobeyed. He would be holding Wolkenland aloft now, too. He knew better than to fail.

So enough. Time to end things.

"*You can't escape, Doom!*" the Skull yelled. He jerked his head left and right, as if blinded by his own power.

"*I do not need escape,*" Doom responded, amplified voice clashing with the thunderclaps of the arcs. He flew straight at the Skull. "*Doom does not flee. He lures his foes to their destruction.*"

The moment of doubt hit the Skull. He paused in his erratic flight.

Take him, Doom commanded Sserpo.

The monster's free hand closed around the Skull, a planet swallowing the fascist. Doom had to jerk back to avoid being consumed by the hand, too. The movement of fingers miles long stirred up gale-force winds across the island, ripping the roofs off mansions, tossing hovercars like leaves.

Sserpo tightened its fist as it pulled back.

And then the monster screamed. Stung by a hornet stab of the Power Cosmic, Sserpo's hand twitched open. Doom grunted, the monster's pain rocketing through his mind, and the shock jolted Sserpo out of its hypnotized state. Its Krakatoa roar echoed across all of Europe, and it lashed out at Wolkenland. Before Doom could seize its will once more, it released the stern of the island and brought its wounded fist down on the bow end. A third of Wolkenland disintegrated. The mines and the region around them, meteor-struck, exploded into dust. The middle of the island heaved up and split. A chasm opened up from port to starboard, and Wolkenland broke in two.

The shattered land began a slow descent, but it did not plummet. Zargo had taken hold, and Doom breathed a sigh of relief as he reached up into the furious eyes of the monster and reclaimed its mind. He dared not have the monster grab the pieces of the island. It was so colossal now, its body still in pain, that an involuntary muscle twitch would destroy everything.

Zargo would not be able to keep Wolkenland aloft, but at least he was controlling the descent. Doom shut the concern from his mind and went after the Skull.

He had survived Sserpo's grasp, but tumbled, stunned, a seed on the wind, miles above Wolkenland. The energy arcs spiraled and slashed with no direction. Doom rose to meet him.

One chance, now. One chance to use the weapon that might defeat what the Skull had become.

Doom's head still throbbed from the aftereffects of the blast that had sideswiped him.

My turn.

As he closed in, the Red Skull recovered. He saw Doom converging on him, and he screamed in rage. He reached out as if he meant to strangle Doom. The arcs came at Doom in sudden straight lines, the Skull's howling anger so great it gave him a better measure of control for a moment. They shot at Doom and through the broken crust of Wolkenland.

Doom used the Skull's wrath. He altered his flight just enough, jerking up and out of the way of the blasts.

The distance between them closed before the Skull could strike out again.

The aurora still surrounded the Skull. Doom poured all the power he could spare into his force field and braced himself for the pain. The Skull spread his arms wide to embrace his foe with death. Lightning flashed from his eyes.

The flash and the clash came, but Doom was ready. The field broke the wave of power and saved him from annihilation. He held on to the control of his limbs with the determination of a god. He slammed through the convulsing agony.

And struck the Red Skull with his neural disruptor.

He hurtled down, using gravity for greater speed. Above, the Skull shrieked as he lost control of all his impulses. The currents reversed and the energy arced, suddenly called back to its origin.

The power of Wolkenland turned on its master and itself.

A quasar flashed over the island, and vanished. Explosion and then implosion, eerily silent, the sound of annihilation swallowed by the self-devouring maelstrom. Colossal winds seized Doom and tossed him. He rode out the turbulence and righted himself. Then he turned back to look for the Skull.

A faint violent glow pulsed weakly where he had been. It vanished, too.

"'Nothing beside remains,'" Doom muttered. He felt only tempered satisfaction. The Skull had not suffered long enough.

Now he could expand his focus again. He realized that the island's descent had accelerated. The ground was still miles away, but time had found another way to slip away toward catastrophe. Zargo's ragged thoughts reached him, redolent of erosion and fragmenting stone.

Can't much longer... too heavy... slipping...

"Captain Verlak," Doom called. "Send in the transports for immediate evacuation. Wolkenland's defenses are neutralized."

As he flew back to the castle grounds, he spotted tanks in some of the estate grounds. Many had been destroyed by the Red Skull's power chaos, but their presence had significance. Not all the residents had obeyed the Skull then, and joined the Billionaires' Crusade. The willfully ignorant had elected to remain so to the bitter end.

There might be survivors yet huddled in their mansions, Doom thought.

Prisoners to be evacuated.

He arrived at the castle grounds as the first transports approached. Large as ocean liners, capable of hovering motionless even a few feet off the ground, Doom had designed and used them to transport his forces on missions of conquest outside of Latveria. Now their ramps descended to accept refugees fleeing yet another nightmare.

Doom saw Valeria at once. A wave of relief washed over him, one so great it might have been joy. She had moved away from the others and stood instead of crouching and holding on to the trembling ground.

Doom came down in front of her. "This universe has spared you," he said.

She nodded as if she knew exactly what he meant.

In Zargo's grip, Wolkenland slid and stuttered down through the air toward its end. It moved north of Doomstadt, the two halves of the island roughly parallel. Huge ruin, majestic corpse, it made its last journey like a raft approaching a waterfall. It drifted closer and closer to the ground, its shadow vast and crushing. Those over whom it passed looked up with fear and awe, but much of the fear and awe they felt was inspired by Doom, because they saw that this miracle, this flying island, had died, and they knew their ruler had killed it.

Zargo held Wolkenland aloft until it reached the most uninhabited portion of Latveria, in the regions of the Carpathians depopulated by the plague of the urvullak, where shadows were deeper than night, and legends coiled in forgotten crevasses. There, Wolkenland, empty of life and of power, came to earth. It broke apart against the mountains, it toppled peaks, and in the scattering of its enormous bones, it remade the shape of the range.

The voice of its dying faded, and the dream of the Red Skull ended.

EPILOGUE

In every cry of every Man.
In every Infants cry of fear,
In every voice: in every ban,
The mind-forg'd manacles I hear

WILLIAM BLAKE, "LONDON," 5-9

Doom used his miniaturization technology on Sserpo. The neutralization of the monster took priority over all other considerations. He could not keep the creature docile indefinitely. He had to sleep. Even if Sserpo did not move from its spot, it would eventually destroy Latveria, and then the world, simply by existing. Already, it had grown past the atmosphere's mesopause, and its head rested in the thermosphere. It should not have been able to breathe.

Then again, Doom reminded himself, the first time it had trampled the Earth, it had grown even larger, and had thrived with its head in the vacuum of space.

So much about Sserpo defied any explanation. At least for the moment. And for the moment, what mattered was a solution to the problem, not its cause.

A few hours after the fall of Wolkenland, the reducing ray cannon rumbled out on heavy treads from Castle Doom to where Sserpo stood, a single step from crushing Doomstadt. When Doom turned the ray on Sserpo, it initially seemed capable only of arresting the growth, not reversing it. Free of the most extreme urgencies of battle, Doom had the luxury of contemplating, and admiring, the force that made Sserpo what it was, a force so powerful that it could resist, even temporarily, the ray. Doom increased the intensity of the ray, and finally, grudgingly it seemed, Sserpo began to shrink.

It took twice as long to bring Sserpo down to its original size of a few feet as it had for the monster to grow, the reducing ray having to fight the countervailing power every step of the way. Doom had the sense of placing a coiled spring into the mobile stasis chamber next to the reducing ray cannon.

Elsa Orloff had traveled out with the cannon. Now she put a hand on the clear cylinder of the stasis chamber. She had watched the entire procedure, eyes wide with fascination. "What will you do with the creature?" she asked. "Return it to space?"

"And leave it for the next unthinking fool to chance upon, and use it to unleash a new cataclysm?" Doom grunted. "I think not. And I have no intention of giving up the opportunity to study such a specimen. Consider the problems it poses."

"How does it grow?" Orloff asked. "Where does the extra mass come from, and where does it go? It wants to eat, but doesn't need to. Like it breathes, but doesn't need to. How?"

"You see then, doctor. You have already explored one side of the infinite. Now another has appeared before us." He watched as the stasis unit, mounted on caterpillar treads, moved off toward the castle. Another prize of immeasurable power was his. As it should be.

In the great courtyard of Castle Doom, the thousand refugees gathered, gazing up at Doom as he addressed them from a tower balcony. On a rampart overlooking the east side of the courtyard, Verlak watched them watch him. Elsa stood beside her, their shoulders touching.

"You have proven yourselves worthy of citizenship of Latveria," Doom said. "You are free to stay, or to leave. Should you stay, know all who make this nation their home must always show themselves worthy of that honor. The true test of the Latverian is obedience to Doom. You were deluded when you entered Wolkenland. You shall have no illusions about the terms of Latverian service. For it is service."

"Do you think they'll stay?" Elsa asked.

"Some, I think. Maybe a bit more than should."

"What makes you say that?"

"Not all of them understand what he's saying." She doubted they grasped what fealty meant in Latveria. She wouldn't enjoy arresting any of them down the line, after all they had suffered. But if their actions made it necessary, she would.

Elsa raised an eyebrow. "I would have said he's making himself very clear."

"Doesn't matter," said Verlak. "Many people think they're listening when they aren't. They just hear what they want to hear. He rescued them from slavery. That's all they'll retain. They'll believe they're home based on gratitude alone."

"You don't think they should be grateful?" Elsa sounded surprised.

"Of course I do," Verlak said with feeling. "You know I do. They should be grateful." Her eyes narrowed. "If they weren't, I'd shoot them myself. But do they really understand what it means to be grateful to Doom? I do." She felt it and lived it every day. Her duty and her gratitude were one and the same. "You know what it means," she said, and smiled with love and pride at the thought of her wife's accomplishments. "But do they?"

Elsa looked thoughtful, gazing into the far distance now, where Verlak knew she saw things that lived in nightmares. *I'm right here*, she thought. *I'm right beside you. I always will be.* She said nothing, because she didn't have to, and she knew Elsa needed quiet at this moment.

"I think some understand," Elsa said at last. "Maybe some," she said. "A few," she corrected. "You're right, Kari. Gratitude to Doom means walking the path he sets for you. And remaining grateful even when it gets dark."

Verlak covered her hand with hers. Now it was time for her to speak, and to provide comfort if Elsa needed it. "And how goes your journey?"

Elsa looked at her, and she was fully present again. "I've been to places I never imagined. I've done things I couldn't have dreamed even a few years ago. Things that I wouldn't *want* to have dreamed. And you know what?"

"What?" Verlak asked, worried.

Elsa leaned her head on Verlak's shoulder. "I wouldn't want to be anywhere else, be with anyone else, or do anything else. I was meant to be a hunter. I know that now. Doom showed me the path that belongs to me."

Well-being warmed Verlak's chest. Tears of love and joy welled. She put her arm around Elsa's shoulder and squeezed.

"Latveria's grateful to you," she said. She nodded in Doom's direction. "He is, too."

"And do you know what Doom's gratitude means?" Elsa asked.

"I do." When the sun god of Latveria turned his rays upon her, she knew the world was good. And that was just the most superficial import of Doom's gratitude. "I think you do, too."

"Yes."

Verlak smiled. "Why don't you tell me what it means?"

"It means he'll open new and stranger paths for me to walk."

"And how does that make you feel?"

"Grateful. Again."

Verlak laughed in the perfection of the day. She gave Elsa another squeeze. "I'll be right there behind you," she said.

Elsa kissed her cheek. "I'm counting on it."

Doom finished his address. An atmosphere of anxiety hovered over the refugees. Good, Verlak thought. They had heard him. Perhaps they understood. That would make her job easier later if they had.

The refugees filed out of the courtyard, ushered to the exit by guards. A second, smaller audience, a captive one, in chains, was ushered in for Doom's next address.

Verlak and Elsa leaned forward on the parapet. Verlak had been curious to see how the refugees would respond to the options fate offered to them. She had a vested interest in seeing how this crowd reacted to what awaited them. Until now, the enemy had not received a full and just punishment. Death, even the terrifying one Elsa had brought, was too quick a mercy for what had been done to Latveria. And these were the people in whose cause the soldiers had fought.

Doom looked down on the imprisoned billionaires for a long moment, letting them feel the weight of his gaze. Verlak did not envy them.

A cold wind blew through the courtyard. It made Doom's cape billow around him. Dark clouds had arrived in the late afternoon, a suitable omen.

"You are war criminals," Doom said. His voice, low and icy, a warning and a threat.

At least a few of the prisoners did not heed either.

"You have no authority to make that claim!" one protested.

"You have no authority over us at all!" another said. "We have rights! We're citizens–"

"Of Wolkenland?" Doom interrupted. "Your nation no longer exists. You are citizens of nowhere."

A worried pause. Then someone laid claim to American citizenship, and another demanded to speak to the Russian ambassador, and a clamor of frantic repatriation rose from the courtyard.

You miserable worms, Verlak thought, *you still don't get it.* Hatred for the Wolkenlanders coursed through her veins like venom.

As if reading her thoughts, Elsa said, "Their bubble has burst, and they still don't realize it."

"They will, though," Verlak said.

"I'm counting on it," said Elsa, her tone low and dangerous.

Doom let the clamor of the worms build for another few seconds before he spoke.

"*Silence!*"

His voice cracked like thunder, demanding and receiving obedience.

"I am Doom. That is all the authority I need. Your protestations are meaningless. You invaded Latveria, and for that you will pay."

"We didn't know!"

Verlak had been waiting for that particular wail. Her jaw clenched in anger. Elsa's breath turned into a growl.

"You didn't know," Doom repeated, contempt dripping from the iron voice. "There are among you those who may well believe that, and who believe that exonerates them. Were you imprisoned on Wolkenland? Were you forced to take up residence on the island? It was useful to you to turn the other way. It suited you to pretend you could not see the marching soldiers, and that you did not know the publicly expressed beliefs of your fellow residents. If you truly did not know, you were the Red Skull's useful idiots, and that fact alone condemns you."

The wind blew harder. The prisoners huddled in on themselves in their misery. They did not clutch at one another for comfort. Instead, they kept far apart, as if fearing the contagion of guilt. They did all they could to stay away from Hauptmann and Cadavus, both on stretchers, but conscious and frightened.

"What are you going to do to us?"

The question all of them wondered, but none had dared to ask until now.

"Yes," Verlak whispered. "Let's hear it."

Elsa nodded.

"You will live," Doom said, and his tone turned the words into a threat. "Your fortunes, your businesses and your industries are forfeit. Reparations for war crimes."

"Good," said Verlak. "Good."

"He took their souls," Elsa said.

"You are condemned to hard labor in perpetuity," said Doom.

Verlak nodded in appreciation. "Their bodies, too," she said.

Doom leaned down to look at the insects groveling below him. "We have mines in Latveria, too," he said.

Doom waited alone in the throne room for Valeria to arrive. He sat on his elevated throne of granite and iron, the great, golden "D" of his emblem inlaid in the back above his head. He had his arms on the rests, fingers curling over the ends. He sat thus when he rendered judgment and passed sentence. As he was about to do now.

On himself.

The massive bronze doors to the chamber opened, admitting Valeria. They closed behind her with a solemn boom. She walked through the echoing space of the throne room, dwarfed by the gothic vaults where gloom gathered and meditated. She stopped at the dais and looked up at Doom.

"You heard me speak?" he asked.

"Every word."

"You approve?"

She didn't answer right away. "Of the punishments, yes," she said.

"But not of everything," he said. With dread, he saw that the conversation was proceeding exactly as he had planned.

She didn't answer right away. When she did, she surprised him by changing the subject, as if she couldn't yet face what both of them had to. "Is he really gone?" she asked. "Is the Red Skull dead?"

"He is gone," said Doom. "That does not mean he is dead. He has returned from what seemed certain and complete destruction before. It is as if as long as the ideology he embodies survives, then so does he. No, I do not believe he is dead." Then he forced the issue. "You did not approve of everything you heard."

"The way you spoke to the refugees," Valeria said. "That was… That was…"

"Yes?" he said, making her say it. He spoke with no warmth. He did not rise and come down to her level, and he did not gesture for her to join him. He confronted the pain and began the process of cauterization.

In truth, he had passed judgment before she had entered. His sentence had already begun.

"You didn't sound like that on Wolkenland," Valeria said. "You spoke today as if they could be punished, too."

"I am not responsible for what you think you heard."

"What I *know* I heard." She put a foot on the dais, as if she meant to come up to him. To touch his arm again.

To hold his hand.

He did not move, and she stepped back. "Victor…" she pleaded.

"No," he said. "I am Doom."

"You don't have to be. You proved that on Wolkenland. There's a way back for you."

"There is only forward," he said. "I am what I must be, and the world must be mine, or it will die. I proved *that* on Wolkenland."

Valeria backed away, face a mask of sorrow. "I'm sorry I hoped."

"Your hopes do not concern me," he said.

"I don't understand what's happened."

He could tell her. He could tell her that if she kept her hold on his heart, that he would kill her. He could tell her that he had experienced his murder of her a thousand times over, in a thousand different ways. But if he told her, she might say *No, not this time, not here, you proved that, too.*

And he might weaken and believe her.

He might weaken, too, in other ways. She had not imagined what she saw in him on Wolkenland. In her presence, he might forget the path that was his to walk. He might forget that he was Doom, and seek to be Victor again.

And who would rule the world as it must be ruled then?

His destiny, and her survival, demanded that he tear her from his heart. He must strike hard, and take the wound, scar his heart to match his face.

"It is not for you to understand," he said. Every word drove the dagger deeper into his chest. The pain on her face turned the blade incandescent. He knew the uses of cruelty, but he had never turned them so forcefully on himself. "There is a shuttlecraft waiting to take you to the destination of your choice. I do not want to know where that is. Now go."

She hesitated. Her eyes pleaded, clinging to a last hope, still offering the promise of the other path.

"*Go!*" he said, before he could weaken.

She left him.

Doom remained in the chamber, gazing at the empty space where she had been.

He stayed there long after he knew she would not return, waiting for the molten agony to harden into a scar harder than basalt.

Because it would harden, become as hard as he was, and forever must be.

Hard as the rule that would, in the end, extend from this throne, and cover the Earth.

ACKNOWLEDGMENTS

What a wonderful journey my travels with Doctor Doom have been. It's with decided melancholy that I bid goodbye to him, Verlak and Orloff for now, but I do so in the hopes that this is not my last farewell.

My huge and grateful thanks to everyone who made this journey possible. As ever, thank you to the teams past and present at Aconyte Books, including Marc Gascoigne, Nick Tyler, Anjuli Smith, Ashley Stephens, Jack Doddy, and Ness Jack. Special thanks, once again, to Lottie Llewelyn-Wells for her superb editorial guidance. She has an unerring eye not just for what a book wants to be, for what it *needs* to be.

Thank you to Marvel Comics for letting me have so much fun, and so much freedom, with a character so very, very dear to my heart, and to Sarah Singer, Claire Rushbrook and Caitlin O'Connell for their wonderful editorial feedback.

Thank you to Fabio Listrani for yet another glorious cover, and for giving this entire trilogy a look that has been my inspiration as I wrote.

Thank you, as ever, for the mutual support and writing sprints to Michael Kaan, Derek M Koch and Stephen D Sullivan.

And again, always again, *joyfully* again, thank you to my wife, Margaux Watt, and to my stepchildren, Kelan and Veronica, for all their love and support.

I would also like to acknowledge some of the inspirations informing the trilogy as a whole, and in particular *The Tyrant Skies* and *Reign of the Devourer*. First up are two particular comic stories. The two-part tale of the Red Skull's takeover of Latveria first appeared in the stories "The Invaders!" and "A Land Enslaved!" from *Astonishing Tales* (1970) #4 and #5, and later reprinted in *Super-Villain Team-Up* (1975) #15, which is where my young self encountered it. This story, written by Larry Lieber and illustrated by Wally Wood, George Tuska and Mike Esposito, has haunted my imagination for over 40 years. *The Harrowing of Doom* refers to the events in it, and it forms the background for *The Tyrant Skies*. The other crucial story is, of course, Jack Kirby, Larry Lieber, and Stan Lee's tale "Sserpo! The Creature who Crushed the Earth," found in *Amazing Adventures* (1961) #6. And with regards to Valeria, one of the stories that played a role in shaping *The Tyrant Skies* is "Under Her Skin," written by Mark Waid, with art by Mike Wieringo and Karl Kesel, in *Fantastic Four* #67.

It should come as no surprise that Stephen King's *Salem's Lot* gave me the seed of the idea that became *Reign of the Devourer*.

Doctor Elsa Orloff owes her last name and some of her ancestral details to two other Doctors Orloff – one was played by Bela Lugosi in *Dark Eyes of London*, and the other by

Howard Vernon in Jess Franco's *The Awful Dr Orlof* (yes, just one "f" in that title, but a second would be added for all the other, myriad manifestations the character would take on in Franco's subsequent filmography).

Other films have informed different elements of the books. The laboratory of *Bride of Frankenstein* influenced my vision of Doom's lab in *The Harrowing of Doom*, and there are numerous other nods to the classics of Universal and Hammer in *Reign of the Devourer*. And I owe the premise of checking for brainwaves in corpses to Lucio Fulci's gruesomely poetic nightmare of a film, *The Beyond*.

Finally, my heartfelt thanks to you, gentle reader. I hope you have enjoyed the journey as much as I have.

WINNIPEG, 2022

ABOUT THE AUTHOR

DAVID ANNANDALE is a lecturer at a Canadian university on subjects ranging from English literature to horror films and video games. He is the author of many novels in the *New York Times*-bestselling *Horus Heresy* and *Warhammer 40,000* universe, and a co-host of the Hugo Award-nominated podcast Skiffy and Fanty.

davidannandale.com
twitter.com/david_annandale

MIGHTY HEROES
NOTORIOUS VILLAINS

EPIC SUPER POWERS
AMAZING AVENTURES

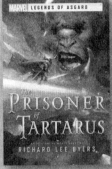

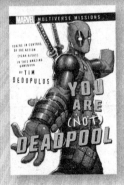